Praise for *American Drifter*

"Fast-paced action . . . Although these authors come from different backgrounds, Graham has definitely brought her intelligence and flair to the book, allowing Mr. Murray's hand at writing to become a true success right out of the proverbial gate."
—*Suspense Magazine*

"This novel, which serves as actor Murray's debut as an author, is a great entry point for him. The characters are deep and richly written, with both their flaws and merits put out in full display. The attention to detail and description of events, places, and anything else that surrounds the characters is magnificent, and the reader is swept up in the atmosphere that pervades Rio's Carnaval. The story itself is one [that] is intriguing overall, with crime, passion, and romance. . . . This is a fantastic novel that is absolutely worth a read."
—*RT Book Reviews*

AMERICAN DRIFTER

HEATHER GRAHAM
AND
CHAD MICHAEL MURRAY

A TOM DOHERTY ASSOCIATES BOOK • NEW YORK

This is a work of fiction. All of the characters, organizations, and events portrayed in this novel are either products of the authors' imaginations or are used fictitiously.

AMERICAN DRIFTER

Copyright © 2017 by Heather Graham and Chad Michael Murray

All rights reserved.

A Forge Book
Published by Tom Doherty Associates
175 Fifth Avenue
New York, NY 10010

www.tor-forge.com

Forge® is a registered trademark of Macmillan Publishing Group, LLC.

ISBN 978-0-7653-7488-2

Our books may be purchased in bulk for promotional, educational, or business use. Please contact your local bookseller or the Macmillan Corporate and Premium Sales Department at 1-800-221-7945, extension 5442, or by email at MacmillanSpecialMarkets@macmillan.com.

First Edition: November 2017
First Mass Market Edition: November 2018

Printed in the United States of America

0 9 8 7 6 5 4 3 2 1

To my wife, Sarah, you are, without a doubt, the definition of grace. Without you I'd be nothing more than a caveman. For my two children G and A, Dada loves you more than you'll ever know. You inspire me with each breath, moment, and memory. Finally, thank you to Heather for guiding me through this adventure. Your thoughtfulness, teachings, and honest approach to all that life encompasses will never be forgotten.

P.S. GO BUFFALO!

AMERICAN DRIFTER

PROLOGUE

Maybe he was a crazy man.

The old woman watched him watch the fountain, staring as if entranced, entirely unaware of the busy flow of humanity moving through the crowded streets of Rio de Janeiro.

Dressed in khakis and a T-shirt, he carried a backpack, as did so many of the *americanos* who came to travel the rain forests and small towns of Brazil. Their American dollars could still buy much; they could drink and play easily in the cities surrounded and secreted by the jungle-like growth of the countryside.

This one seemed to be different; there was something about him. He was shaggy like the others; his hair was too long and his face was scraggly with an untrimmed beard. Beneath that untrimmed beard, though, was a beautiful face, well formed, and eyes that were a gentle blue, nice against the tawny gold color of his hair.

Something about him touched her. He didn't come to the fountain to pop open a beer, inhale it and toss down the can. He didn't light up a cigarillo or pull out a bag of marijuana—as some did here, heedless of the foot traffic. He stared at the fountain with awe and appreciation, as if it were an oasis in the desert.

The fountain . . . yes, it was special. Tio Amato had built it years ago, but had now forgotten it, other than to see that the water kept flowing and once a year it was cleaned. While fairly new in the old city, the fountain and the sculpted cherubs and elegant goddess statuary that surrounded its center hinted of Greek artisans, and the water flowed pure and free. In the center there was a giant obelisk. It seemed phallic, but then Tio Amato was a man much impressed with his own sex, so that did not matter. Or maybe it did; maybe to Tio Amato it was like the pride and youth and sex he thought he would keep forever. Maybe, in his mind, it was like the heat of Brazil and the beat that could stir so much of the country.

The water was a gift to the people, and the children of the neighborhood came there to play. They were young and innocent, free from the cares of money and hard work. They didn't care about class distinction; they didn't mind that they shared the fountain's waters with one another. Not unless their mommas or nannies pulled them away.

Yes, Tio Amato kept the fountain flowing; it was

his contribution to the neighborhood where he had been born, where his "enterprises" had made him rich, where his massive *casa* sat, and where he could reign as the king. But no matter why Tio Amato had built it, the fountain was good. It was a strange picture of wild beauty in the rush and hubbub of the city. It was bordered by a little patch of scraggly trees and a bench where she could sit and feel the breeze without the heat of the sun.

As she watched, she felt a kinship with the young man. She had seen many such a man in the city, many that looked like him, some speaking to themselves, others sitting with vacant eyes, cups before them. Sometimes they begged; sometimes they did not. They were weary and their eyes were dead while their bodies still lived.

For several moments, this man stared at the fountain with the same dead eyes. Then he dropped his backpack and began to shed his clothing. She thought that she should speak then, and tell him that she was there and that the rush hour of humanity that thronged the mornings of Rio was about, but she held silent.

Carnaval was coming to Rio de Janeiro; the city was insane with visitors of all nationalities, rich and poor, black and white, native and other—and yet, among them, she thought that there was something special about this man.

He hadn't come to Rio to *use* the city.

He had come to be a part of it.

He was ragged and dirty and possibly one of the craziest men here. Something in him had broken, she could see that. But he also made her think of something pure. His love for the fountain had a touch of the fantasy seen in a child's eyes. So she sat silently. Naked, he stepped into the fountain. He lifted the water and sent it high, sparking as it lit into the air. He laughed and began to move, dancing, as if offering up homage to a god on high.

She smiled. He was much more beautiful than any other man she had seen come to the fountain. She was glad that she hadn't spoken; for an old woman, it was a strange moment of joy to watch the movement of his supple young body. He played in the water, savored the feeling of it, and delighted as he frolicked there beneath the sun.

But soon, she noticed a certain car winding through one of the side streets to the square. She rose from her seat in the shade and moved forward. "*Senhor, Senhor,* come out now, you must come now. He is coming. Tio Amato is coming!" she said. She spoke English, but not well.

He paused and turned to look at her, frowning as if he couldn't comprehend her words.

"*Senhor, Senhor,* come out now; if it is Tio Amato he will hurt you, or see that you are hurt. If it is only his men . . . they will hurt you worse. They will force you out, they will be cruel. Please, come out."

She hurried toward him with her shawl, heedless that the precious piece of clothing might be ruined, and wrapped it around his shoulders. "Come . . . come."

He stepped out of the fountain, looking at her. She

wished that she were young and beautiful, but he smiled, and he seemed to like the many wrinkles that crisscrossed her face.

"Thank you, *senhora*; gracias." He carefully returned her shawl and reached for his clothing.

"This is the city. It is Tio Amato's neighborhood. The law here is different. The law is what the rich men say the law should be."

"But it's beautiful," he told her, reaching for his backpack and throwing it over his shoulder. "The fountain is beautiful. And you are beautiful. Thank you."

"I am old," she said, flushing as she straightened his shirt, as she would have done for one of her *niños*, her grandsons. "You must be careful. You should be back in your country. What are you doing here?"

"*Senhora*, I'm stronger than I look," he told her. "And I'm here because . . . I must be." A look of pain crossed his face, quickly replaced by a smile. "I have done my duty, and now I'm here."

She saw something in his eyes, and she felt as if his soul was damaged, though she didn't understand at all.

"I'm looking for something," he said.

"What is it?"

He shook his head. "I have to keep looking."

"You should go home," she warned.

"Maybe I am looking for what makes a home, *senhora*."

The car that she knew to belong to Tio Amato was wending its way through the busy morning foot and automobile traffic. The driver must have slammed his fist on the horn because a loud blast disrupted the heat of the day.

"Go, please," she said.

"I will see you again, *senhora*."

He turned and headed down a side street, joining the throng of humanity, as she made the sign of the cross over her chest, praying silently.

God keep him, she thought, for only God could watch over fools and crazy men.

And the lost.

CHAPTER 1

River Roulet knew the strange whistling sound—it was far too familiar.

The sound heralded the arrival of a bomb.

His body instantly flinched as his natural instincts for survival set in.

The bomb fell. The earth shuddered and exploded into a violent storm of debris. Men screamed and missiles seemed to hurl around the dusty desert land-scape.

The missiles were men—and body parts.

He felt himself breathe; he hadn't been hit. His hearing was numbed and he was blinded for several seconds and then the debris began to clear.

He saw them—the woman and child—standing atop a small rise in the dry and brittle landscape far beyond the bombing. They were there . . . a distant blur in the distance, as the mist of dust and dirt began to clear. He struggled to stand, to warn them there was danger, but they were gone, and when he looked around, he was alone in a sea of death.

He let out a hoarse cry.

And he woke himself up from the nightmare that plagued him far too often.

There was no desert around him; the air was rich, his surroundings verdant with the foliage that grew in profusion on the outskirts of the city of Rio de Janeiro.

For a moment, he lay shaking, trembling. He took a deep breath, fighting the confusion that made it seem as if the mist from the imagined explosion had crept into his mind when he first awakened from the dream. War was behind him; he had come to Brazil to explore what was beautiful and different in nature, far from the past and far from memories of the past. The battle was over; he had let go of everything except that which he could carry on his back.

There was no regimen to be followed, there wasn't anything he owed to anyone, and his days were now free; he'd vowed to forget the bombs and violence that had plagued the years gone by.

He'd had a glorious bath in the fountain—something he could manage because it *was* Brazil—and the morning stretched before him with a magnificent sun overhead, a touch of cool moisture in the air, and this new world to be explored.

For a moment, he felt a sharp pain in his head. The

dream awakened memories; memories he didn't want to have, memories he had come here to lose. They were there somewhere, he knew, at the back of his mind, but if he pressed his temple between his thumb and forefingers, the threat that they would erupt in full subsided.

The past seemed to tease. It would return in the nightmares, but if he awakened, if he pressed the nightmares back, nothing bloomed into truth in his mind. He'd come here to bury the horrors that had gripped him, to begin anew.

He forced himself to feel the ripple of the breeze and hear the lilting, tinkling sound of the nearby stream as water danced over pebbles and rocks.

The pain faded.

He'd slept under the canopy of the jacaranda trees; the earth had been soft enough and it had been good to sleep in the open, but tonight, he'd head to the hostel owned and managed by Beluga, the massive African-Brazilian he could count as one of his few real friends in the Rio de Janeiro area. Beluga's place was outside the city, surrounded by foliage and rich farmland. It was a beautiful place to sketch, and a pleasant place to stay.

He paused for a moment to take in the quiet. He loved Rio at any time of the year, and it was particularly hectic now that Carnaval grew near. The city felt supercharged. The horns blaring in the busy streets were enough to deafen. No matter—samba bands vied with them now at all hours of the day and night.

Being here right now, where the jungle retained a

tenacious hold, he could hear the sound of the leaves rustling as birds swept by. It was a nice change.

Just as Beluga's would be nice tonight.

River rose and stretched, shaking off the remnants of the dream. He paused for a minute and listened again to the sound of the jungle that encroached upon the city. As he looked up, a parrot took flight and soared over the trees; he wished he knew more about the birds and other creatures here, but he had time to learn. He had all the time in the world.

Rio de Janeiro was wonderful—one of the most wonderful cities on earth. On the one hand, it was massive, with a population of more than six million of the world's most diverse people—twelve million in the larger metropolitan area. While Portuguese was the primary language, people could be heard speaking any language known to man. They were black and white and every shade in between. River thought that was one of the things he loved most about Rio and Brazil—the diversity of people and the way that skin tones and backgrounds had become so multitudinous that only the very rich or incredibly snobby ever noticed any difference between white, brown, black, or red—or any color in between.

Two things were incredibly important in Brazil: samba and soccer. Not that there weren't world-class museums and theaters and concert halls. But the people loved their soccer teams and their music. Samba schools were everywhere. And, at any time, when music could be heard through an open doorway, people might be seen dancing in the streets—practicing their newest moves.

And the streets were constantly filled with that music beneath the ethereal shade of the mountains, the blue skies, and the deeper blue seas. The city was magic and River loved it, from the beaches of Ipanema to the jungle forests that encroached upon the city.

This was Rio. While acceptance of just about anything was the general rule, it was still a country where there were the very rich; there were the very poor. It was true that money could matter; that the rich could consider themselves a bit more elite. But when Carnaval neared, there were the very rich everywhere, and the very poor everywhere, and it seemed that then, it didn't matter so much. There were also the tourists—who did not know the *bairros,* or neighborhoods, of the city. There were big city buildings, skyscrapers that touched the clouds. And there were farmers on the outskirts still tilling their fields as if the land had never seen the arrival of big business. Rich tourists might go to many of the big balls, but even they knew that the Carnaval was really in the streets.

Carnaval had been celebrated in one way or another since the eighteenth century; first, it was taken from the Portuguese Festa de Entrada, or Shrovetide festivals—always a day to enjoy before the deep thought and abstinence of Lent. In later years, the Rio elite borrowed a page from the Venetian Carnavale and introduced elaborate balls. The majority of the people were not the elite—they had their own festival in the street and it was more fun, and soon, even those who were very rich wanted to play on the street, as well. The bands were magnificent: the samba was done on the walks and boulevards, and performers were everywhere.

There were so many wonders to be seen in Rio. But the greatest wonder of Rio was still to come, and one could feel the pulse of a city that was filled with natural beauty and joy. As in most cities, there were neighborhoods, and if you stayed, if you became part of the people, you knew the little fountains and the mysterious trails into the jungle and the special places where, in the midst of that twelve million people, you could be alone.

He was glad that he hadn't come just for Carnaval. He had come to explore. To know and understand the people.

Reaching into his pack, he drew out his map of Brazil. He loved to study the map and read the guidebooks on the country. It was huge and he intended to see a great deal of it, beyond Rio, at his leisure. Later, he'd talk to Beluga, and see what Beluga had to say about the wonders to be seen when he started traveling again. He set his finger on the map, circling Rio de Janeiro and São Paolo, thinking that he might travel to the Southwest. Or, perhaps, he'd head inland to see the wonders of Brasília, the planned city that now housed the federal capital. The country was massive; there were so many places he could go.

River gathered his belongings, shouldered his

knapsack, and headed toward the sound of water. The picture that met his eyes was beautiful and peaceful; wildflowers grew haphazardly next to water that glistened beneath the sun. The sound of children's laughter drifted from downstream, closer to the city. He splashed cold water on his face, dug in his bag for his toothbrush, and cleaned up.

He was hungry. There was an open-air market just down the hill and he could find all kinds of delicious things to eat there.

The walk, he thought, was as beautiful as all else. He knew that a lot of Americans considered Brazil an exotic place—but one to visit, not a place to stay. It was true that here the middle class was slim; people tended to be very rich or very poor. But it cost nothing to look at the wild profusion of foliage and trees, breathe in the air, and feel the warmth of the sun.

There was a noise up ahead.

Without thinking, River paused. He didn't know what made him refrain from moving forward, but some instinct kicked in.

Now a splash. On the road ahead where a little bridge crossed the river.

He moved off the path, climbing up the foliage- and tree-laden hill that rose next to the river to see what had given him chills. Carefully, he moved to a jagged crest and looked down.

There was a car on the bridge—a black car like the one that had approached the fountain the day before.

The trunk was open. River had the feeling that something had just been taken from it.

And thrown over the bridge.

Three men were out of the car, looking over the wall of the little cement bridge.

They were all big, muscled, and wearing almost identical blue jackets. All looked to be somewhere in their late thirties or forties, dark-haired, heavy-set.

Paid thugs?

From his vantage point, River could see the water—but not what had been thrown into it. The river was fast-moving, churning in little white waves and bursts.

It seemed the men were looking at something, or for something—and that they were satisfied by what they saw.

A fourth man rose from the backseat of the car; he was about six feet tall with dark wavy hair and a lean, muscled build, dressed in a suit that even at a distance appeared to be designer apparel. He looked strong, impressive, even; but when he turned slightly, River felt there was something in his face that kept him from being attractive when he should have been very handsome with his dark hair and well-honed physique. There was a twist to his mouth and a hardness in his eyes. It seemed like cruelty was stamped into his features.

Tio Amato? he wondered.

The drug lord who ruled much of the city?

He'd never met the man and looks could be deceiving, he knew.

The three thugs approached what appeared to be their leader and spoke in hushed tones that River couldn't begin to hear. Then they returned to the car, which promptly revved into gear and continued over the bridge.

Carefully, River shuffled back down the hillside and walked to the bridge, to the point where the men had looked over the water. He saw nothing. Nothing but water, white-tipped as it rushed over stones, beautiful beneath the sunlight.

He stepped back, still puzzled, still uneasy. His eyes flickered to where his hands had touched the concrete wall.

There was something there. Tiny droplets of liquid, in a burned crimson color.

Blood?

He didn't touch it, but he stared at it. He felt something curling inside him.

Was it blood? Could the man who considered himself lord of Rio kill—and dispose of bodies in such a manner?

He debated telling the police what he had seen. But he was an American. For all he knew, the police could be on Tio Amato's payroll as well. Furthermore, he wasn't sure what he could really say. *These men were on the bridge. I think there are blood spots there now?*

Had he seen the man kill anyone? Had he seen a body?

No, and no.

He stood still for a moment, debating.

Maybe someone as bad—or worse—had been killed.

No, that was rationalizing a lack of action.

But would he be believed by the authorities—or by anyone—if he tried to tell them what he had seen?

And even if he was believed, would it matter?

He had no proof. There was no one else here. He had no video. Nothing.

After a moment, he decided that he would tell Beluga what he had seen; Beluga had been born here and had never gone far. He'd know the lay of the land.

Beluga would know what to do.

CHAPTER 2

As River debated, a middle-aged woman with a few children at her side, carrying a straw bag of market purchases, walked by him on the bridge. He smiled at her. Somehow, she set his mind at ease.

Mouthwatering aromas filled the air; River had reached the market. Fresh-fruit vendors were the first he saw, and then stands where all kinds of meat sizzled on grills or skewers. He bought a mango first, pulled out his Swiss army knife to peel away the skin, and bit right into it, enjoying the sweet, succulent taste and fibrous texture. Brazil offered a wide variety of cultures and their cuisines—the natives had made good use of fish and the abundance of the land, while Africans brought as slaves had contributed with various spices and the Portuguese had brought in their love for meat and cheese.

At his next stop, he bought a bundle of *chouriço*, seasoned sausages, and at another stand, *salgadinhos*, delicious little cheese buns. Though River was capable of surviving on very little, he happened to be fairly flush at the moment. For some reason, he had good luck at the track. He knew how to pick a horse, even though he didn't know how he knew how to pick a horse. He just could, and it paid off. He could buy himself an expensive suit or designer jeans—he just didn't want to. He liked his appearance; it allowed him to get to know the country and the people. He preferred the countryside and the rainforest and the outskirts of the massive city to the concrete jungle and civilization. Rio was cosmopolitan, but, somehow, it also had a way of holding on to what was old and natural and good.

With plenty to eat, River wandered the market; a lot more than food was sold at the many stands placed haphazardly, as if by a child, on the clearing that bordered the city streets.

Even here, Carnaval was in the air. Music competed from a number of boom boxes and iPads with speakers. Samba competed with the American top forty and ballads and even the Brazilian national anthem, "*Hino Nacional Brasileiro.*" Children kicked soccer balls through the aisles; busy vendors either admonished them sharply or just shook their heads in dismay.

Tourists were abundant—they'd found the market.

Handsome men flirted with young women—and old. Flirting, River had learned, was complimentary here. He smiled as he saw a charming young man tease a middle-aged woman. She laughed, enjoying his words.

He passed a stand of leather goods and negotiated the price of a new belt, the vendor pretending he spoke no English and River pretending that he believed him and using his broken Portuguese. It was while he was trying on this new belt—with comments of approval from the vendor and his wife—that he heard the whining.

Along the same jagged aisle, busy with locals, tourists, and children, there was a stand where a man sold trinkets and jewelry. His display of goods was covered by a glass dome; obviously, he thought that his goods were precious. Maybe they were.

The goods didn't draw River's attention; the dog did.

He saw the creature that had made the pitiful noise; a large, bone-thin hound of some kind, with German shepherd thrown in. The man was busy extolling the virtues of a necklace to a customer. River bent down to pet the dog.

He was starved, but a beautiful creature, the best of genetics combined. He had massive brown eyes, a long shaggy coat that couldn't quite hide his bones and, in the midst of it, a beautiful shepherd-shaped face that might have graced the best of the AKC competitions. The dog seemed friendly, despite the fact that he was starved and had probably been abused.

River crouched low, close to the dog, and reached into his bag for one of the *chouriço* sticks he had purchased. The dog lapped it up eagerly, wagged his tail, and bathed River's face with a slew of sloppy kisses. River laughed, then started as the owner screamed at him.

He rose; the man was speaking so quickly that he couldn't follow his Portuguese.

"It's all right," River said in English. "I just gave him a *chouriço* . . . just a bit of food."

The man continued to rant at him.

Then he kicked the dog.

The creature yelped in pain.

River stared at the man, feeling his temper start to burn. He'd gone to war; he'd met the enemy in hand-to-hand combat and he had killed because he'd had no choice. He'd never purposely lifted his hand against another to do harm of his own accord.

He was ready to change that mantra. This guy deserved the vicious kick he'd given the dog.

With significant effort, River controlled the impulse to step forward with his fists flying. Hitting the man wouldn't help the dog—and he might wind up in a Brazilian jail.

But neither could he leave the abused animal.

In a flash, he pulled his Swiss army knife from his pocket and slit the piece of rawhide tying the dog to the stand. The owner lurched forward, but River grabbed the makeshift leash first and fled.

In seconds, he was flying through the crowded pathways that led through the market, the dog excitedly running at his side. People jumped out of his way as he ran, but still he almost plowed into a woman who sold brightly colored blouses in a kiosk near a jewelry stand.

He could hear the man screaming behind him. Cursing, raging about River being a thief, urging others to stop him.

But no one did. People made way for him.

He thought that the man would keep coming after him, but he stayed with his stand. His jewelry was more important to him than his beaten dog.

River kept running anyway, until he cleared the market, turning onto the dirt road that led to Beluga's hostel. There was a copse of trees there just before another bridge that crossed the river.

He ran with the dog until he reached it, then paused at last, breathless.

He looked at the dog. The dog looked at him and wagged his tail. It was a big tail.

"Well, I'm glad you're happy. Now I'm a thief!" River muttered, though he kept his voice light. His back against a tree, he sank to the ground, trying to catch his breath. The dog began to slather his face with his tongue again.

"Okay, okay! Let me get into the bag—I have more food. You poor thing; you are just a beautiful pile of bones."

He fed the dog slowly, afraid that after starving for so long, the dog would choke and vomit if he ate too fast. When the *chouriços* ran out, he went for the *salgadinhos* until those were gone too.

"What do I do with you?" River mused, petting the dog. "I guess you'd be a good-enough companion, huh? You need a name." He paused. "I'll call you Convict, since I may have just become one, if that bastard really cares about you. So, Convict, what do you think? Do you like that name?"

He didn't know if the dog understood him—especially since he was speaking English and the dog had probably learned any commands in Portuguese. But Convict barked happily, his fan of a tail flying again.

"We'll head to Beluga's. What do you say?"

Convict barked.

River removed the biting chain from around the dog's neck and walked a few paces experimentally.

To his relief, Convict kept pace, pausing now and then to inspect and sniff at a tree or a bush—and doing what dogs did.

After stopping at the stream for Convict to drink, the two of them started uphill, on the dirt-and-stone road that would take them to the hostel.

When at last the ground plateaued River spotted his destination on the outskirts of the clearing. It was composed of three buildings: Beluga's own little house; the barn—though there were no horses anymore; and what Beluga called the longshed—it housed up to twenty guests a night. Beluga's house was whitewashed, one story and two rooms, with planters that always seemed to offer flowers in a variety of colors at both windows. The longshed was whitewashed as well, with a funny little L-shaped add-on where Maria, Beluga's housekeeper, lived and worked. The kitchen was there too. Sometimes, the sounds of Maria making coffee in the morning were a bit loud in the shed—but that was all right. Travelers were supposed to be up, drinking that coffee, and on their way—or paying for a second night's stay.

The barn, where River sometimes slept, was to the right of the shed.

River always thought it touching that—as with Beluga's own little house—Beluga kept flower beds around the shed and the barn.

Beluga loved flowers. To see him smile when he touched one was something that made everyone else smile as well, those giant hands of his so delicate as he gave a rose petal a gentle brush.

Beluga worked the place himself, alone except for Maria, a tough but kind widow who had lost her husband and two of her children in a flood, but still lived with her faith intact. She had salt-and-pepper hair and had obviously been very beautiful in her youth, though time had brought wrinkles to her face and a thinness to her body.

Beluga's property sat on a little hillock with lots of land surrounding it, plenty of space for Maria to hang her laundry in the sun and for Beluga to keep a gathering of ragtag chairs where he could sit and puff on a cigar, sip his coffee or brandy.

As River approached, Convict in tow, he saw three backpackers ambling away and Maria coming out of the longshed with a bundle of laundry. Beluga was helping her with the work, hanging sheets on the line.

He looked up and frowned as River walked toward him. He was a massive, broad-shouldered man, six-four or -five and muscular.

"No dogs, you know that."

"I had to take him, Beluga. He was being beaten and starved."

Convict sat politely looking at Beluga and wagging his tail.

"I can see the starved part," Beluga said. "Still, he's a dog. No dogs. You keep him out here. Besides, I don't know if I have a bed for the night."

"I didn't know you started taking reservations," River countered.

Beluga rolled his eyes and went to hang another sheet.

"Want some help?" River offered.

Beluga shrugged. River shifted out of his pack and went to hang a sheet.

"So where did you get the dog?" Beluga asked.

"At the market. Come on, Beluga, look at him! He's a great dog. Obedient and affectionate. And not prissy—I wouldn't have come here with a prissy little dog, I would have known much better," River teased. "This is a manly dog. And I had to. The guy kicked him—because he was mad at me for being decent to the poor thing and feeding him. I really had no choice. Honestly—anyone half human really didn't have a choice."

Beluga kept working in silence. Then he paused when he went to pick up another sheet. "Probably old fat José. He's been through a few dogs. Thinks they'll protect his jewelry—half of it's fake—and then when they want to be fed, he beats them. Did you hurt José?"

River wasn't sure if Beluga was hopeful that he had hurt the man or just worried that he might have done so.

"No."

Beluga hung the sheet and went and sat down in one of the lawn chairs. Convict went to him, shyly, wagging his tail.

"You're a big boy, you stand tall!" Beluga said, patting the dog. Convict set his nose on Beluga's lap. "No, no, none of that. You're not staying here."

But he kept petting the dog. River grinned. It hadn't taken long; Beluga could say what he wanted, but he had already been befriended by the dog. But that was Beluga. He was truly a gentle bear of a man, not at all pretty—he had a really crooked nose and his eyes were too small. But River had seen him find a way to help people by pretending they'd paid enough or telling them that a three-for-one-night special was going on when he knew they were really broke.

Better not to say too much at the moment about the man, the market, or the dog.

River sat next to Beluga and pulled out his drawing pad. He didn't know why, but Beluga liked to watch him draw—he thought that River was good.

Every once in a while, River thought he was okay

himself, but he didn't draw to become a great artist. He drew scenes because he enjoyed drawing, and if he could capture the essence of something that was beautiful or that intrigued him, it was incredibly satisfying.

Once, he'd drawn Beluga, and the sketch was one of his favorites; he was really proud of it. The man's immense size—and his gentle nature—had somehow come through, along with the character lines in his face and the innate wisdom in his eyes.

Sometimes, Beluga told River that he'd take a few of the drawings in lieu of cash when he wanted a bed for the night.

River hadn't wanted any kind of a trade, though, for his likeness of the man. That had been his gift to Beluga.

Now, he had something to convey.

River began to sketch the scene at the bridge that morning. He made broad strokes to create the Brazilian scene, the sky, the jagged hilltops, and the mountains beyond. He drew in the foliage and then the bridge with the men standing on it, looking downward, and the man he assumed to be Tio Amato standing by the car, waiting. He could picture Tio Amato's face in his mind's eye, and the drawing became more detailed as he drew him in.

Beluga watched him.

"You saw that man—you didn't take anything from him, did you? That man—he is not like fat José."

"Yes, I saw him. No, I didn't take anything."

Beluga tapped the pad. "You don't mess with this man."

River turned to him, serious now. "Beluga, what should I do? I think that he killed somebody."

Beluga waved a hand in the air. "You think? You think? You leave him alone."

"Beluga, I saw him and his henchmen or thugs or whatever parked at the bridge. They had taken something from the trunk, I'm pretty sure, and they threw it over the bridge into the water. Then those guys," he stopped to point at the three men, "those guys stared into the water before coming back to this guy—Tio Amato?—and saying something. When I went on down to the bridge, there was nothing in the water but there was something on the wall. Blood, I'm pretty sure."

Beluga was dismissive. "You're pretty sure? What, you got some scientists who do those tests in your pockets or something? You know nothing." His voice grew intense. "River, you're a good guy." He patted his chest. "You got heart. You stay away from that man."

River was thoughtful a minute. "I can't just stay away. He killed someone. He stole a human life."

Beluga groaned. "Yes. I *know* he killed someone—several someones," the big man said, scratching Convict's head. "I stay away from Tio Amato. He lives in a big house on a little hill right in the city. It has high gates—and a swimming pool and a movie room and a dozen guards. He pretends he does good things, giving money to churches and schools. He gives to the churches so that the padres will let him in and ignore what they know in their hearts—that the money he has comes from selling drugs—bad drugs, heroin, opiates, street mixes with poison—to the young people. He gets them hooked, and they need more drugs. Then Tio Amato has more money and cars and planes—and he sells the drugs in other places. And when people get caught working for him, they know never to say his name because he reaches into the police stations with his money too, and those who would talk against him wind up in ditches—or thrown over bridges. I had friends . . . friends who were excited to work for him, excited for the money they would make. Friends who believed he was just a rich man who was misunderstood. Maybe they needed to believe that—the poor can be desperate. But these friends I've had over the years . . . some of them just disappeared one day and were never seen again. River, listen to me on this. You stay far away from him, my friend."

"You want me just to forget that I saw a body dumped? The body of a murdered man?"

"You don't know what you saw. If you try to report it—you're dead."

"Okay, Beluga, I was heading to the little bridge. I heard a splash. I crawled upward on the cliff and looked down and the men were staring over the bridge—and the car's trunk was open. What do you think?"

"I think you forget what you saw and mind your own business."

"Come on, there have to be honest police in Rio."

"There are—but which ones? The ones who are honest would do something—maybe—if they could. They never have anything that will allow them to search Tio Amato's house, to prove that he sells the worst drugs. That he kills at will. If they ever had proof—which you do not have—they could do something. Look, River, I like you. I want you to live, I want you to draw. Forget this—you're a foreigner. There's nothing you can do. There's definitely nothing you can do with what you have."

"It's not . . . right," River said.

Beluga was quiet for a minute. "Years ago, I managed a hostel in the city. It was a little place—no pretty land and trees like this, but travelers came and I enjoyed meeting them and seeing them come and go. I could tell them all about Rio de Janeiro, tell them when the best entertainment was going on, what to see, what to do—how to see the magnificent Christ the Redeemer statue at the most beautiful time of day, when the sun rose and the mist cleared."

River waited for him to go on. After a moment, Beluga shrugged and lifted his hands, stretching them outward in a helpless gesture. "River, Rio is different; Brazil is different. People are the same—we want to live and let live, have children, watch them grow, sleep, eat, and have sex with those we love. But there are the very rich and the very poor. I was born very poor; I grew up hauling and working for others. When I was little, I was shoved out of lines. When I grew up, I learned that the rich expect to be at the front of the line. I worked my way through school as a farmer; I grew up then to box and fight—for the pleasure of the rich. I got tired of fighting for the amusement of others, but I made some money doing it. I had a wife, and she died, and I didn't want another—but I still loved and needed people around me. I made enough to buy my own business. I'm still a big man," he said quietly. "A strong man. I felt I no longer had to prove it—or that I had learned about the rich and life. But I made a comment to a tourist, a young fellow, telling him to stay away from the house on the hill. He had come to Rio to party, and he was looking for something more than a drink. He didn't listen to me—but he must have mentioned my name before he disappeared. I was walking the city a few days later, asking if he had been seen. The next thing I know, five men attacked me in an alley. I hurt them; I can do that. But in the end, I was beaten to a pulp and broken in many places. I'm surprised I was not simply shot— and tossed over a bridge. I learned from that; I stay away from the city and from that man. Do you understand me?"

River listened gravely, thinking that he could not imagine Beluga in the ring; he was so gentle despite his size. He had known Beluga a long time, or so it seemed, or maybe he had just liked him so much that it seemed they had been friends forever. He hadn't really known much about the man's past.

He did understand Brazil. Money did matter; money had power.

But he couldn't accept that money could buy murder; as Beluga had said, the majority of the people were good; they wanted lives filled with enough to eat, good music, and love and happiness.

He also knew that no matter where you were in the world, there were those who were more than willing to hurt others—to kill, even—for their own gain.

"I understand, Beluga. But there must be a way."

"Not for you, not for me. Don't you see? It cannot be you. Maybe some government agent who is good and honest will figure out a way to bring him down. All that can happen between you and Tio Amato is that you are hurt and broken—and perhaps tossed in a river yourself. No!" Beluga's voice changed and he straightened to his full, impressive height. He obviously wanted to change the subject. He tapped on the paper. "Who is this?" he asked.

"Huh?"

"There—that man a bit in the distance."

River looked at the drawing. At the far side of the bridge—looking up at where he would have been himself—was another man.

He was in casual clothing: jeans, T-shirt, and a hoodie. He wore dark glasses and had sandy hair. Many of the Brazilians were light-skinned—people of German and other European descent were plentiful in the city—so he might have been Brazilian, and he might have been a foreigner.

River didn't remember sketching him on the paper—and he sure as hell didn't remember seeing him.

"I don't know," River said with a shrug. "Artistic license, I guess."

"There was no one else on the bridge?"

"No, I passed a woman and a few children as I traveled on in, but I don't remember seeing another man. I just conjured him out of my imagination."

Beluga considered him for a moment, brows furrowed. "Maybe it is you, watching him? I like this drawing. I will take it for your stay tonight."

"You just told me that there might not be room."

Beluga shrugged. "I'll find room for you—in the barn or on the back porch of my house. But, no dog."

Convict whined, setting his nose on Beluga's lap.

"You're a dog; you can stay outside," Beluga told him.

"I'm calling him Convict," River said.

"Advertise the fact that you're a thief!" Beluga shook his head.

River grinned.

"What you need, my friend, isn't a dog. It's a girl. A pretty girl. A Brazilian woman, someone with the sun racing hotly through her veins, who loves to dance. Beautiful and seductive. Yes, that's what you need. You should pick flowers to bring to a pretty girl and maybe find a guitar and serenade her."

"I can't steal a girl from the market, Beluga—that would just be wrong."

Beluga groaned. "Let's finish these sheets. Then make the beds up for tonight. After that you can sit and draw, and Maria will have some dinner ready. You fed this dog already?"

"I gave him my breakfast."

"We'll have to go slow, but maybe there's an old roast bone inside. That would be good; he could savor the taste and then we'll get him something else later. I'll have Maria stop at the market and find real dog food—you are not to go back there for a while!"

River nodded. "Thank you—and I'll thank Maria."

"You will do more than thank her. You will give her money for food—and for taking the trip," Beluga said, wagging a finger at him.

"Of course."

Beluga snorted and disappeared into his house. River smiled and leaned back, feeling the warmth of the sun and patting the dog.

A minute later, Beluga returned with a massive bone for Convict.

So much for going slowly. The bone was huge.

The dog seemed almost afraid to go to Beluga to take the bone, but Beluga spoke to him softly in Portuguese and, in a moment, Convict moved to him, his tail wagging low at first, and then higher as he accepted the bone and began to gnaw upon it.

The dog was not accustomed to kindness.

River studied Beluga as the giant man watched the dog, pleasure in his eyes as he saw how much the animal enjoyed it. *Beluga*, he thought, *is an amazing man*. He'd endured hardship and he knew pain. He had not become a cruel man because of it; he'd become a better man.

River marveled at how the dog's life had changed, now that he was here.

A man's life could change too, he thought.

Yes, he determined. His life had changed as well.

CHAPTER 3

River could feel the cool caress of an air conditioner against his skin and hear the hum of its motor.

Music played lightly in the background. It sounded like an old Fleetwood Mac CD.

The room where he dozed was in shadow. It was daytime, but the blinds had been drawn. Little streams of light seemed to peek through the blinds, bringing in a touch of golden warmth and a slight display of pastel colors; dust motes seemed magical in the little rays of light. From outside, he could hear children laughing as they played, a bouncing ball, and cars rolling by on a distant highway.

He felt a touch on his shoulder, as gentle as a balmy breeze. Smiling, he opened his eyes.

Her face was caught in shadow.

"I didn't mean to wake you," she whispered, her voice a brush of tenderness that stirred his heart.

He reached for her. "I should be awake; it's day."

"Yes," she teased, her fingers on his brow, sweeping back the lock of hair that fell across it. "It's daytime, but you need some rest."

Catching her by her shoulders, River drew her down to his side and rolled atop her, smiling. She was warm, living, vital, and he needed her so much. "It's daytime, and the shades are down and . . ."

His whisper faded. He still couldn't see her face; it was caught in a burst of light from outside the window.

Then he heard it; the whistle of a bomb. He cringed, trying to hold her close, bracing for the fallout that was sure to come. He held nothing; the gentleness, the cool whispers—gone.

He was alone on hard ground.

Pastel shades faded to the harshness of desert brown. He heard a scream of terror ripping through the air and suddenly, all was gone, and it seemed that he was caught in the stygian darkness of night . . .

River awoke in a flash, bolting to an upright position. He looked around, shaking off the remnants of the dream. The light in the room was shadowy and dim, but outside, the sun was just beginning to peek out. It was early morning—too early to be awake. He gritted his teeth and gave himself an irritated mental shake—and hoped he hadn't screamed aloud.

He was on a cot in the back hallway of Beluga's house; at his side, Convict whined softly. Beluga had given in on the dog and River had made him a bed out of one of his dirty shirts. There hadn't been room in the hostel but, true to his word, Beluga had seen to it that he had a place to sleep. And since Convict had followed River and Beluga about—behaving with incredible manners—as the two men had worked together repairing window frames during the afternoon, River and Convict were both Beluga's guests that night.

There were actually four cots in the back of Beluga's house—in what he called his Florida room, since the floor was tiled and the walls were lined with frosted-glass windows and a giant mural of downtown Miami.

River was usually alone back here. But as his eyes adjusted and his mind cleared, he saw that the farthest bed was occupied.

It was a young woman—a strikingly beautiful young woman with rich dark hair that fell around her shoulders in tousled waves. She leaned on an elbow, watching him, almond eyes narrowed in concern. She was so striking, such a vision of absolute and ethereal beauty. He hadn't expected to see someone like her, sleeping—or trying to sleep—in the same room.

He felt breathless.

She nodded and looked at him for another long moment. Then she turned around, cuddled her pillow, and adjusted her position on the cot, ready to go back to sleep. He flushed, sorry that he'd awakened her. At his side, Convict gave a little whine.

He set his hand on the dog's head. "Pretty girl, huh, bud?" he whispered to the dog.

He lay back down himself, eyes open, intrigued. He couldn't talk to her; she'd made it apparent that she wanted to go back to sleep.

Of course, there was the morning.

He wouldn't bombard her. He would just hope to meet her.

He didn't think that he'd sleep again, though. He lay awake, constantly aware that she was close, so close. He couldn't remember the last time he'd seen anyone who had intrigued him as she had.

Was she Brazilian? Or a traveler from a faraway nation? Was she on an adventure . . .

Or escaping from something—or someone?

He rolled to face the wall—and not her sleeping form.

He didn't think that he would sleep again.

But he did.

This time, there was no gentle trailer running before the onset of the nightmare. He was in a small, sand-covered desert town, moving carefully from house to house. It was a mission he hated; insurgents abounded in the mix of families just trying to survive. Most had abandoned the town, but he could turn a corner and find a cowering mother and child—or an enemy bearing an Uzi.

And the enemy could be a child—yes, a child carrying an Uzi.

And it was so very wrong. He knew, and he was afraid. He knew, and his heart seemed to bleed even as he feared, because children should be innocents; they shouldn't face war, they shouldn't face evil.

He felt the heat, the weight of his pack, and his military-issue rifle. The air tasted like grit. He dropped down, turning—praying that the noise behind him was one of his fellow soldiers. He heard gunfire, a spate of automatic gunfire. *Rat-tat-tat-tat-tat.* He searched for the source.

He breathed in smoky, acrid air and dirt. The dry dust of the country was everywhere, constantly, and now it was joined with the awful smell of burning and gunfire and . . .

Pancakes.

Yes . . . pancakes and bacon, delicious things cooking, and he wanted the dirt and the black powder and all the horror to go away.

But the war was the reality. The gunfire . . . raging again.

Rat-tat-tat-tat-tat-tat!

Muscles clenched, he dropped lower to the ground. He looked everywhere, all around him.

The enemy could be anywhere.

"River!"

He woke, instantly ready, digging into his pack for the military weapon he kept in his bag along with his clothing, money, and sketchpad.

"River! Whoa, it's Beluga!"

River froze, his fingers curled around the gun. He winced. Maybe he shouldn't carry the damned thing. The nightmares should have been receding; they weren't.

No, he was all right. In Brazil, he might need to defend himself, especially since he considered himself to be on an adventure—and he traveled roads less taken.

"Sorry, Beluga."

"Sorry!" Beluga roared. "You'd better be sorry!"

"I wouldn't have shot you, Beluga," River said. "Honestly—I know how to use a weapon. I'd have never shot you."

"How do you know what you would do?" Beluga demanded. He waved a hand in the air. "You were half asleep!"

"You're one of my best friends," River said quietly.

"And there's a sadness," Beluga said, shaking his head. "All right, then. You wouldn't have shot me."

"I'm sorry."

"I know you are. Now it's time to be up. Everyone is out and gone." Beluga was angry. River couldn't say that he blamed him.

"Everyone?" River asked.

"Everyone."

He'd blown it. He should have just stayed awake through the dawn. He would have met the beautiful young woman.

He wouldn't have had the nightmare—again.

River was startled by the depth of disappointment he felt. He glanced quickly to the cot at the far end of the room, near the back door. But, of course, Beluga was right—everyone was gone.

Including the beautiful young woman with the eloquent almond eyes and the stunning face.

"I'm getting up, Beluga. Who was the young woman you had here last night?"

"What young woman?" Beluga was clearly annoyed. "You want me to know about a particular young woman? The place was full; there were a dozen young women."

"But this one was special."

"All women are special. Now, you get up and out so that we can clean up this room in case we need it for tonight."

"Okay, okay!" River rose, gathering his belongings quickly. "Hey, I'm sorry. Really sorry, Beluga."

"I know," Beluga said, softening for a moment before shaking his head impatiently. "You should go do something for yourself today. Hey—meditate! Did you know—I meditate. Makes me a nicer man, yes? Take some time and sit on the beach, feel the breeze, feel the strength of the mountains behind you. You forget how much Rio has to offer. Carnaval is coming—watch the jugglers or the stick walkers—or the women in costumes and feathers or costumes that are feathers. No, I know what you'd love! You should go to the Christ the Redeemer statue and meditate there. Ride the cable car and see the strength and beauty of the mountains while you look down at the valley and the city. Yes, that's what you need to do—these dreams of yours are not good for you. Or me—when you brandish a gun."

"Beluga—"

"Yeah, yeah, you wouldn't have shot me. I should take it away from you!"

"If that's what you feel," River conceded.

His friend sighed. "No, I won't take it. With the way you live, you hold on to it—but don't wag it at me again, friend." He reached down and tossed River his backpack. "Theo came by; he said to tell you he was going to the track. Maria is going into town; she'll drop you there if you wish. It will be good for you to see Theo—but then you find somewhere that makes you happy and find yourself some peace. Me, I sit—I watch the mountains. They give me peace."

"May I at least use the bathroom?" River asked.

Beluga waved a massive hand at him impatiently. "Yes, yes. Then you meet Maria outside!"

"Yes, sir!"

"I will see you when I see you." He hesitated, looking at Convict.

"The dog can't go to the track," River said. "Hey, maybe I'll just—"

"Just go to the track and meet your friend. You spend too much time alone. I will watch out for the dog."

"Wait!" River said, digging into his backpack for money to hand to Beluga. Beluga looked at him, arching a brow.

"For Convict; I'm sure you told Maria to buy him dog food."

Beluga hesitated, then took the money. "The dog is all right. I don't mind buying him food."

"Yes, but I brought him here and you're watching him for me."

Beluga shrugged. "All right. I will take this. He's a big dog. We'll buy a lot of food."

"Beluga—"

"Get ready; Maria will go soon."

There was no sense asking Beluga about the young woman right now; he was in a mood and River didn't really blame him. Anyway, she was obviously gone. And he was glad—glad that she hadn't witnessed the way he had awakened from yet another nightmare.

Beluga turned and left, and River glanced at the empty cot at the rear of the room again. He didn't remember being so fascinated in a very long time.

Ten minutes later he headed out the front door. While he waited there for Maria, his eyes wandered to the steel rack of free local papers; they were there for the tourist trade to know what was going on and they contained editorials as well—all in English. He glanced at the top of the paper in the rack . . . and his heart stopped.

There she was!

There was an editorial in the paper. It began on page one with a small picture of the writer and continued onto the next page, placed among advertisements for a samba school and a Venetian-style ball and a picture of one of the parades that offered scantily clad women with great feather headdresses throwing kisses to the crowd.

He quickly picked up the paper, ignoring the pictures and ads.

The name under the picture was Natal—no surname, just the first name. The article was titled "The American Dream—is it truly freedom?"

So she was a writer!

There was going to be a way to find her.

He heard a *beep*. Maria was ready to drive him into town. She was in the driver's seat, watching, waiting for him.

"Sorry! I didn't mean to make you wait," he told her as he climbed into the truck; she spoke to him sternly—but in a motherly fashion—and he was sure he was being chastised for his lifestyle.

"Ah, Maria, you know you can never stay angry with me," he teased.

He smiled at her—she smiled back. Begrudgingly.

CHAPTER 4

As they drove, he read the article in the paper. It was beautifully written, he thought, and humorous as well. The article focused on the census taken in the U.S.—how people were asked about their color, religion, and ethnicity. Yet, the article stated, there should be only one answer that anyone should have to give, whether they were born in the country or naturalized: American. Because, obviously, being born there made you American. But if you swore an oath, you were also an American. On top of all else. And being American should mean that none of the rest mattered. "Until the government and the people stop discerning between color, faith, and original ethnicity, not all Americans will truly be free to chase their dream. Still, as a foreigner, I applaud the country for the ideal of equality so many hold true—and speak to its citizens, for somewhere in there, that dream does still exist."

He thought he was in love already, just reading what she had written.

Maria dropped him off in the Gávea district near the Hipódromo de Gávea. In Rio, the track was known as a jockey club, and deserved the name. The track was beautiful and offered spectacular views. Corcovado, the mountain where the beautiful and giant Christ the Redeemer statue stood, could be seen from the track, along with other mountains and stunning geographical features. It was near the Jardim Botânico, or botanical gardens, and the area swarmed with locals and tourists alike. Gávea had taken its name from the Pedra da Gávea, a gigantic rock formation that towered above its surroundings. In Portuguese, *gávea* meant "topsail," and the rock formation could certainly resemble the topsail of a mighty sea vessel. Much of the area was affluent, but still, beer and roasted-peanut vendors were here and there on the streets, along with the restaurants and cafés. Students abounded as well—Pontifical Catholic University, one of the most important universities in the Rio de Janeiro state, was not far from the Hipódromo. Baixo Gávea, an artsty, bohemian area, was also close by.

Not only were the locals intriguing, but also the people who came from miles around, their numbers swelling with the approach of Carnaval. No one in the world—not even the Italians in Venice or those at Mardi Gras in New Orleans—celebrated the time before the coming of Lent as they did in Rio. But then, nowhere else in the world was like Rio, where joy and dance and music *were* the pursuit of life and happiness.

The track was impressive—handsomely set and well maintained.

The races had started, but with his paper in hand, River stopped first at a coffee bar, ordered his espresso, and sat, fascinated. He stared at the picture of Natal. Then, he reread the article. She was smart—and philosophical. Natal reminded people that material desires could get in the way of living. She wrote about the wonderful things in Rio that cost nothing: the sights to see, the things to do and, how, just taking a walk at night could be the greatest freedom.

He rose at last, thinking that now he'd have a way to find her. Of course, she might not be interested in him at all, but he had to at least meet her.

Feeling exceptionally cheerful, he walked the short distance to the track.

He found Theo easily enough; his friend liked to stand down by the rail. Theo was actually Thiago Norway, a Brazilian local with long hair, a scruffy chin, and scruffier clothing, thin as a reed and always smiling. His background had to have contained a mixture of almost all the people who had ever come to Brazil—Indian, Portuguese, maybe German, and probably some African. Somehow, all those genetics had combined to give Thiago a strangely compelling face. His eyes were almost golden against his brown skin, his hair dark and curly. His cheekbones were high like those of a classic Greek bust, but also broad—as if he carried the blood of ancient indigenous princes. In sum, he never had two cents to rub together and he was still the happiest, most generous man River had ever met.

They'd met at the track when River had placed a bet on a horse. Theo had been behind him—extolling the virtues of another horse and jockey. But River's horse had won the race, and Theo had been convinced that River knew something special about horse racing, horses, or jockeys. River had never been able to convince him that he didn't—but Theo had a tendency to bet on the wrong horse anyway. He liked to buy lottery tickets as well.

Most often, not a single number that he picked came in.

He didn't have a problem in the world with picking up a half-smoked cigarette someone had discarded and puffing on it as if it were one of the wonders of the world. River was pretty sure that he actually did all right working all kinds of odd jobs, but he was ever on the lookout for easy money and dreamed that one day he'd hit it big at the track or win a lottery.

Thiago had told him once that he barely remembered his parents; he'd grown up on the streets of Rio and had often survived by eating what the rich and the tourists left behind. Just as he had no problem picking up cigarette butts, he had no difficulty finishing another man's beer or the three ounces of steak a man left on a plate.

"So many men think that they must order the biggest steak on the menu!" Thiago had told him once. "I have worked as a busboy many times, and I have fared very well on the meat left over." He'd laughed. "To be a man, they must order the most meat, yes? And yet, especially as they grow older, they can't eat it all! It's the challenge, my friend, it's the challenge. I keep the world from wasting what should not be wasted!" He'd grown serious. "And I teach the new breed of street urchins to survive. It's not so bad, really. I am immune to all things—I have so many of those . . . what do they call them—"

"Antibodies," River supplied.

"Yes, yes, those!" Thiago had told him happily. "I have tons of those! And it's good, you know? They say that Americans can't even drink water in Central and South America. Me, I can eat anything, drink anything, anywhere." He shrugged. "Well, at least, I think. I haven't been that many places. One day, maybe. I wouldn't mind traveling. Maybe one day, if I'm a rich man, I will travel and then . . ." He paused to grin. "Then, I will see what Americans are like in America!"

"Would you ever want to be one of the rich men, Thiago?" River had asked him.

"Sure! Why do you think I play the ponies? But money is not life, my friend. If I have it, I will share it. If I don't have it—I will still feast and dream on."

Theo fascinated River. River counted him—as he counted Beluga—as a true friend.

"*Meu amigo!* You made it. Beluga said you were

sleeping like the dead with a big dog you stole at your side. What are you doing with a dog, eh?"

"I had to take him. He's a good dog; he was like a slave," River said. "So, you, *meu amigo,* how are you doing so far?"

"You mean betting?"

"We *are* at the track."

"One little one came in—enough to play for a while," Theo said cheerfully. "Now, see, look here at my form. There's the horse for you! He's a big bay and he's won most of his races so far. I have my money on him. You going to go bet?"

"You already put in all your choices?"

"You're too late for the sixth race but there are six more races coming up. Go put in your bets. I'll be here," Theo said. "Hey, you want my advice first?"

"No!" River told him, laughing. "I like the way I choose."

"You choose because you like a horse's name."

"Hey, if I like it, the horse probably likes it too. That means he's a happy horse—and happy horses run fast," River said.

"Not if they're ridden by a bad jockey."

"And what's a bad jockey? A man who woke up and had a fight with his wife. Who knows who had a fight with his wife on what day?"

River walked back through the stands and the crowds of people in them to reach the window. Grabbing a race form, he quickly jotted down his choices for the six remaining races. One young thoroughbred in the eighth race was rated dead last but River had seen his first race. He decided to put his money on the horse—Montalbo's Ricardo. In the tenth race, there was a horse named Chancey's Adventurous Escape. He had to bet on a name like that too.

He placed his bets and found Theo again. Theo was grumbling beneath his breath.

"Your horse didn't come in?" River asked.

"Fourth! He came in fourth!" Theo said, shaking his head.

"I told you—you can't go by statistics all the time."

The next race, River's horse came in. Theo stared at him, shaking his head in disgust. "You—I call you by the right name: Lucky Dog. You are a lucky dog, you know that, my friend?"

River smiled but felt a little chill. *Lucky?*

He *was* lucky, in a sense; he had enough money to spend his days exploring as he chose. He had friends, Beluga and Theo. He had this magnificent country to see, and he meant to do it. But he had killed people. He had seen death. And lately . . .

He started to say something casual but noted that Theo wasn't paying attention to him anymore. He was looking up at the boxes—the reserved stands.

"Tio Reed Amato!" Theo said, his voice clipped with aggravation. "I don't get it. I just don't get it. How does such a bad man get to do so well in life?"

"He has money, Theo. That doesn't mean he does well in life."

"Why can't he be caught—and stopped?" Theo asked. "Everyone knows that he is as slimy as a vat of olive oil, but they all kowtow to him anyway."

River stared up at the man. He was wearing dark glasses, a panama hat, and a pristine white suit. He was surrounded by men in dark glasses and dark suits—all standing with their arms crossed over their chests. A human shield? He was, River had to admit, an impressive figure.

As they both looked at Amato, another man, dark-haired, with a swarthy complexion and a five o'clock shadow on his chin, broke through the crowd to speak to him. Amato was not happy with whatever was said. He turned on the man; he didn't touch him but it was evident that he was either yelling or speaking sternly. At the end of his tirade, he waved a hand in the air, dismissing the man completely. The man practically bowed as he backed away from him, and disappeared out of the reserved box.

"Money. He buys everyone," Theo grumbled.

"You mean Tio Amato?" River asked.

Theo nodded gravely. "He believes that every man can be bought; every man has his price. Most often, he is right."

"Not everyone. I would never be bought," River declared. "And I'm not the only one; there are many people who can't be bought with money."

"You are naive—nicely so, but naive," Theo said.

River shrugged. "There's nothing I want so much that you could buy me for it," he said. Then felt a flicker of doubt.

There was something every man wanted badly enough to sell his soul for it—wasn't there?

But he couldn't think of what. For a moment, he

just felt . . . empty. "You are different; you're an expat walking around Brazil. And you do all right—you have the gift with the ponies, eh? But there are men who cannot resist. They are men just trying to eke out an existence," Theo said. "They are men with babies to feed, who pay bills paycheck to paycheck and run out of money sometimes before the next paycheck. Tio Amato is a powerful man. He rules the world around him because he can. Because there are those with great riches—and there are those who live at the lowest level of poverty."

"That's everywhere," River said.

"Yes—but here, there are only two kinds of people. The rich and the poor. And Tio Amato knows who is who—and sometimes he can even buy the rich. When they are rich, they are often scared. They know that he's got connections; he's in the drug trade and there are mean men in that trade. If he wants something, people give in. They don't want to be enemies with such a man as Amato."

River had been watching Amato with growing distaste. It wasn't just his physical look; it was something in his bearing. He enjoyed power—and he enjoyed seeing others broken and bowing to him. He enjoyed cruelty.

And River was pretty sure he'd killed someone.

Maybe a man who couldn't be bought.

River looked away from Amato at last, not wanting the image of his face to stay implanted in his mind. So "Tio" Reed Amato ruled the world around him. Everyone knew the drug trade came with enforcers—and lots of guns. Did that mean that Amato could get away with murder? Had he dropped a body off the bridge?

River didn't know it for a fact. He had no way to prove it.

Maybe the body would be found. Still, how to prove Amato was responsible for a body being in the river?

He stared back at the race track. "Hey, there they go!"

"Come on, seven!" Theo cried. "Seven, seven, seven! Gooooooo!"

Horse and jockey number seven raced ahead—and fell back at the loop. Montalbo's Ricardo started slow, then burst into speed at the loop and came in first.

River was silent as Theo muttered beneath his breath. He looked at River and groaned. "You had your money on that horse," he said accusingly.

River shrugged, grinning. "I'm thinking they call him Ricky for short. That's kind of warm and familiar. He's probably a happy horse."

"And you remain a lucky dog!" Theo said.

In the ninth race, neither of the men's horses came in. In the tenth, though, Chauncey's Adventurous Escape sailed across the finish line, well ahead of the others.

"And that one was yours too," Theo said. "You don't gloat, but I see it in your eyes."

"Yeah, I bet on him."

"Hmm. And what do they call him for short? Escapey? How can he be a happy horse?"

"Ah, because adventurous escapes are fun—and he knows it!" River told Theo.

Theo went on to mumble and mutter in Portuguese. His horse placed in the eleventh race and River's won in the twelfth.

They headed back up to the betting cages to collect. Walking through the crowd wasn't easy; Theo bumped into someone and steadied himself on River's arm, apologizing quickly to the man he'd run into.

"*Sinto muito.* I'm so sorry, so sorry," Theo said.

It was the swarthy man they had seen get a reaming from Tio Amato.

The man's lips curled back in a snarl. He was not appeased. "*Bastardo! Estúpido!*" he exclaimed, drawing back as if he were about to take a swing at Theo's jaw.

"Hey!" River protested, stepping between them. He stared at the other man. "He bumped into you; he apologized. Move on!"

The man stared back at River for a minute, fists clenched at his sides. Maybe he decided that he didn't want to get into it with someone in fit shape. He raised his fist again and looked at Theo as if giving him a warning, but then he dropped it, aware that Theo was not alone.

Swearing, he moved on.

"He's beaten up by Amato; he wants to beat up on someone else in turn, I guess," Theo said.

"Forget him. Let's collect."

The track was thronged as they made their way to the window. Mostly, however, people were nice.

They were in Carnaval spirit. Men and women said "excuse me" in a variety of languages as they made their way through the people grid.

Friends greeted one another.

Even strangers laughed when they bumped into one another.

The young were quick to smile and flirt a little, just in passing. River smiled too, passing others. He'd learned that flirting was a compliment, but there were boundaries. In Brazil, as everywhere, people wanted to be respected.

"Complimenting women," Theo said happily, tipping his head to a blonde. "That is good—whether she has one tooth or is a beauty! Now, pinching—definitely a no these days!" He laughed and moved ahead, winking as he lifted his hands and cast his eyes toward a derriere that he apparently thought should be pinched.

But Theo would be respectful. In his mind, only the old, outdated men of Brazil still considered themselves macho men.

They finally made their way into the line to collect their winnings. Theo took his few dollars; River had made quite a sum from his long-shot bets.

Stepping away from the line, he placed his winnings in the slot of his backpack.

"Forget him," Theo muttered suddenly. "Forget him? The creep is following us."

River looked up; the swarthy man was leaning against the wall by the windows, watching them.

"Don't worry; he'll leave you alone," River said and slipped an arm around Theo. They walked away from the windows together and out onto the streets. Theo looked back; the man wasn't behind them.

"You're a good friend," Theo told River.

River shrugged and started to say something but Theo was already moving on. He cried out, reaching down to the sidewalk to pick something up. It was a cigarette.

"Look! Just lit! Someone lit this up and . . . maybe got into a cab or something!" Theo's expression was one of pure delight.

"Theo—I just did well. I'll buy you a pack of cigarettes. Well, I'd rather not. You shouldn't smoke, you know?"

Theo grinned. "I don't need cigarettes. I just smoke them when I find them. And this one—it's good. And, say, I imagine the lips that touched them. They belonged to a beautiful and mysterious woman with big breasts, big lips—and Brazilian buns, ha-ha!"

"What if it was a big fat lousy man with sweat streaking down his face?" River asked. But he found himself thinking of the mysterious and beautiful Natal.

"My imagination is far superior to yours!" Theo said indignantly. "No, the lips that touched this cigarette were full and moist. And the woman had dark eyes that whispered of a bedroom in the night, hot passion . . . all good things!"

"Fine. You imagine those lips as you like."

"Yes, I will imagine such a woman for you too, my friend. One filled with fire and life—someone crazy enough to bet on a horse because of its name as well!"

"Hey—my horses came in," River reminded him.

"Yes. When will I learn?" Theo teased. "So, no cigarettes. But, we'll go to the café and you'll buy me lunch, eh?"

River laughed. "Yes, we'll go to the café, and I'll buy you lunch."

Theo's favorite café in the area was about three blocks from the track. It was situated in a side alley, off one of the major streets where today, men and women in business suits carrying briefcases hurried about—in between stilt walkers and beautiful women in colorful festival shirts and studded, scanty bra-tops advertising menus for Carnaval. On a corner, a group of children from a samba school performed—causing even some of the harried businesspeople to stop, watch, and applaud.

It was business as usual—in Carnaval season.

The restaurant they chose was local and modern—the tables were veneered pine, the kitchen was gleaming chrome, and sheet-glass windows afforded the same view as the race track from the back. They found a table toward the rear with a clear line of vision to Corcovado. The waiters were dressed in suits here, the waitresses in full skirts and tuxedo shirts. Theo ordered a *churrasco,* choosing *batatas,* or potatoes, over rice and beans. River asked for the local *peixe,* or fish and a *chope,* or draft beer. When their waiter left them, Theo shrugged and took a deep breath. "Ah, a friend buying you lunch—because he likes a horse's name! That is life. So, what is that you're holding as if it was so precious? Looks like a paper to me."

River realized he'd been carrying the paper he'd taken that morning tightly between his arm and his chest, and he showed it—along with the thumbnail picture of Natal—to Theo. "Speaking of Brazilian beauties—do you know this woman?"

Theo studied the picture. "No, I have never seen her. I have never heard of her. But, I do not read tourist papers, you know?"

"No, I guess you don't."

"You have that drawing pad of yours in there?" Theo asked.

River nodded, and Theo said, "Draw me a picture while we wait. Draw me anything that comes into your mind."

River shrugged and took out the sketchpad and his pencil. Looking through the giant, plate-glass windows and beyond, he thought for a moment and then began to draw. He could still see the race track in his mind. He drew the track and as he did so, he saw the background and the horses and he began to sketch a race. Their *garçom,* or waiter, brought their food and he thanked the man but kept sketching.

"Hey, your food is here—fish is no good cold," Theo said.

"Sushi can be great cold," River murmured.

"We're not having sushi," Theo pointed out.

"But fish can be fine cold."

"Better hot," Theo argued.

River didn't respond.

Theo savored a bit of his meat, but then tapped on the paper. "You've drawn one horse in the race. Symbolic, you think? One horse—your horse, which wins so often! But the jockey isn't so happy."

River looked at his sketch. It was true. He had drawn a jockey that wasn't looking where he was going; he was looking back, as if he was running away from something rather than trying to run a race.

He set the sketchpad down. "So . . . hey, it's a sketch," he said.

"A good one," Theo told him. "You should be an artist. A real artist."

River laughed. "Well, if I draw and it's decent, I'm an artist. Doesn't the act of drawing make me an artist?"

Theo waved his fork in the air and shook his head. "No, no. I know many men who think they can draw. They cannot. Well, I know of men who throw paint on a canvas—and they do become great artists—because some idiot thinks all the splashes are artistic and they see everything about the human soul. But you—you can draw. You should have a great gallery with all your work."

"Eat your meat, Theo. I don't want a gallery. I want to roam Brazil, steal dogs, drive Beluga crazy, and go to the races with you."

"One day . . ." Theo said.

River shrugged. "One day. I have many sights to see before that day. I like my days right now."

Theo nodded, chewing the last of his meat, sipping his water, and then savoring the last of his potatoes.

He leaned forward. "You really don't mind buying my lunch?" he asked River.

"You know that I don't."

"When I have fortune at the track, I will buy you anything!" Theo said.

River grinned. "I don't want anything, my friend," he said softly.

"Then I will buy you lunch!"

"That's a deal," River agreed.

Setting his napkin down, Theo rose. "I must rudely leave you now. I have some work this afternoon. They are filming a commercial down by the Convento de Santo Antônio. I have been hired to hold microphones, you know? I will make more money for the track."

"I will see you—when I see you," River told him.

"Thank you." Theo left. River paused, thinking that he wanted to keep sketching. Here, they would never rush him. They would never tell him that it was busy and that his table was needed. There was no hurry in a Brazilian café. You weren't urged to leave if you weren't ready to leave.

But River knew that they were busy and he paid the check and left. Out on the streets, he felt the life of the city. It seemed that there was always a palpable pulse to be felt in Rio, but never so much as at Carnaval. Now, a float was going by in the midst of the busy car traffic. The revelers atop were in samba dress, bright yellow puffy shirts and dresses. They sang to the crowd and invited them to the Genovese party the next night—at a very reasonable cost, of course!

River loved the throng of people in Rio but at the moment he still felt the burning need to draw. He made his way through the colors and the sounds and the scents until he wasn't sure exactly where he was. The streets were not so well paved; alleys were not paved at all.

But there was a charming little hut with a sign that advised, in Portuguese and English, that the finest coffee in the world could be found there.

It was at the side of a little alley with windows that looked over an overgrown garden that separated it from the next street.

It seemed perfect.

River was greeted warmly by a pudgy proprietor.

He was led to a table, where he ordered a *café*, and then pulled his sketchpad back out and studied what he'd been doing. He didn't like the picture he'd been sketching of the track; he started over again.

As he did so, he heard children laughing and he looked up. Through an open window he could see through the garden area and foliage to the little street beyond. It was definitely a working-class neighborhood. Mothers were bringing their wash to a Laundromat. The children were playing, kicking a plastic bottle across the stone path.

He watched them for a moment, then smiled and began to sketch them. He looked at the street scene and then at his page as he sketched, then at the street again.

His pencil paused midstroke and he felt that thump in his chest again—his heart double-timing, stopping . . . and then beating again.

There she was.

Natal.

He knew her name now. It was a beautiful name.

She walked with a sway of her hips as she carried her basket of clothing. She wore jeans that hugged her lithe and perfect form, and her hair waved down her back and around her shoulders. She paused to tease one of the children, laughing. She looked up at the sky as if she drank in the sun.

He watched her enter the Laundromat.

For a moment, he sat there. He heard the clink of forks and knives against dishes, the musical quality of the Portuguese language spoken around him.

He saw the children and the doorway.

"Senhor?"

The *garçom* stood before him, questioningly. "Um, nothing, thank you, I'm done. *A conta, por favor,*" he said.

The waiter nodded and walked away to get his check.

River stood, stuffing his pad into his backpack.

He couldn't wait for the waiter. He drew out his money, estimated the total, and dropped a generous tip on the table.

Then he crossed the tiled back patio of the restaurant and moved slowly through the trees and foliage to the little stone road before the Laundromat.

What the hell would he say to her?

What did it matter?

He had to meet her.

He made his way through the children and into the Laundromat. At first, the room seemed like a misty parlor after the brightness of the sun. He heard the washers swishing and the dryers humming. He looked around.

An old woman was sorting clothes. A man was leaning back, half asleep in a chair as he waited for his laundry. At another table, two old men played cards and puffed on cigarillos.

And then he saw her.

Natal.

She seemed like beauty in motion. She made the room come to light with her every twist and turn as she transferred clothing from her basket into a washer.

She turned and looked at him and he saw her face. She seemed like a goddess, her features so stunning, her eyes so large and dark, her lips so full, and her cheekbones so elegantly sculpted.

The moment seemed perfect.

Then someone smacked him on the arm.

"Hey, *estúpido,* jerk, *americano*!"

It was the old woman. "You—you are standing where I need to work. Idiot—move! Move! I have work to do here."

Natal smiled slowly.

He moved quickly for the old woman.

And he walked toward Natal, his beautiful Brazilian mystery woman.

CHAPTER 5

River felt his heart as if it pounded in his throat. She was smiling at him. *Natal* was smiling at him.

Natal.

He loved the sound of her name.

His own smile was awkward. He felt like a high school kid, trying to flirt for the first time.

"Hello," he said.

"Hello."

"You speak English?" he asked hopefully.

"Of course." She smiled a little.

He didn't know what to say next.

"I see you're having a bit of trouble," she told him, a nod of her chin indicating the older woman who had spoken so roughly to him.

He shrugged. "I didn't mean to offend her."

"Hmph!" Natal said. "She was being offensive to you." She moved closer to him, mischief dancing in her eyes. "I say we snatch her coins and run away. Teach her to be rude!"

Stealing wasn't something River did—but he glanced at the coins. They didn't equal one American dollar.

It didn't matter. Natal didn't give him time to protest. "Get them!" she urged.

"But—that's stealing!"

"Less than an American dollar!" she said.

River couldn't help it. He set down a dollar—but then snatched up the coins as she had commanded. She was lightning out the door.

He followed her and looked back—the old woman hadn't noticed.

Natal was gone.

He pushed onward, throwing his backpack over his shoulder, suddenly much more worried about losing Natal than he was about the morality of taking the coins.

He caught up with her in the street; she was laughing as she waited for him.

"So," he said. "We have coins—what about your clothes?"

She waved a dismissive hand in the air. "Ah, well, they were old. Maybe the old woman will find them and take them—a fine trade for her coins, don't you think?"

River laughed. "Yes, I imagine she'll have the better deal with that."

"And you left her more." Natal started forward, leaving River to scramble after her. "So now we have coins," she said. "What will we do with them?"

"Not much; they'd hardly buy a few cups of coffee."

A ball bounced toward them, and a boy ran up to retrieve it, thanking River when he tossed the ball back.

"Poor thing," Natal said, some of the light leaving her eyes. "The children here . . . they have so much promise."

She cared about the children on the streets, he thought. Little urchins, most of them shoeless as they played.

Dirt poor.

Her face was filled with expression, her movements full of grace. He thought that the sculpted lines of her profile could rival the finest Greek or Roman face ever sculpted in marble. Her eyes were dark with a streak of wickedly beautiful mischief—and compassion.

And yet . . .

For a moment, even as he watched her, the street scene seemed to fade before his eyes. He didn't see the children here.

Instead he saw a little girl with a cherubic face and great blue eyes. She stood before him in a pinafore dress, white socks, and black patent leather shoes. She held a bottle of bubbles, and she blew one, laughing delightedly as they drifted off into the sky.

The little girl turned and smiled at him with glee, then—

"Mister! *Senhor!* Mister!"

The vision of the little girl faded, and his memory returned. He was on the street on the outskirts of Rio; children played and shoppers moved about, buying fresh meat and vegetables for their dinners. A pair of lovers walked by; a man with a guitar hurried on, probably to join up with his group for a Carnaval celebration.

A little boy tugged at his shirt.

"You have change, *senhor*? Any change?"

He smiled at the child and dug in his pocket, producing a coin. The child smiled at him.

He trembled inwardly, and then shook off the feeling.

Natal was observing him silently.

They were in an older, poorer section of the city. Shops were worn and needed paint. The people also appeared to be worn—and in need of paint as well.

Ahead, there was a rustic arcade, filled with old machines.

He touched Natal's shoulder. "I know what to do with the coins we have," he said. "Come on!"

Catching her hand, he ran ahead for the arcade. There were a number of children gathered, looking longingly at the machines.

"Here." River looked at Natal and gestured to the coins. When she saw his intent, her eyes lit up.

She handed out all the coins they had taken. River reached into his own pockets, drawing out what coins he had. Within a matter of minutes, the kids were laughing and chatting with one another, careful as they determined the merits of each game they might play.

"Worth leaving the old crone my old clothing, don't you think?" Natal asked quietly. She studied him for another moment. "Tell me your name."

"River."

"River," she repeated, a smile playing at the corners of her mouth. "In English, you are water!"

"My parents liked the name," he said with a shrug.

"I like it too," she assured him, seeming to reach a decision. "I'm Natal."

"I know. I know your name. I know that you write."

She drew her arms across her chest. "How do you know my name? And that I like to write?"

He flushed. "I've seen you. In a picture. It was with an article you wrote for the tourist magazine." Her eyebrows shot up. "It was wonderful—and so true," he continued. "The article I read. You wrote so well about America."

The small smile returned. "I was not insulting your country. It is a melting pot—but sometimes, they don't seem to want the contents to melt, right? But here," she said, lifting her arms to encompass her surroundings, "we enslaved people, yes. The New World was all about sugar and, in your country, tobacco and cotton. But here, when the wars for independence began, all fought, and all were free. Oh, I'm not saying there aren't people here who are still prejudiced—against the native populations, against this one or that one for a color or religion or sex or sexual choice—but not our society at large. Everyone is here—gay, straight, black, white, Indian—and we tend to just love one another in the streets. We're happy!" She laughed. "We dance—we samba. We live for music and . . . life!"

He smiled—the last thing he wanted to do was argue with her. And yet, he was fascinated by her mind and equally certain that she might be testing him.

"Brazil," he reminded her softly, "was the last country in the western hemisphere to abolish slavery—that was 1888."

"Ah, so you aren't a 'yes' man," she said, pleased. "But, you see, that is the point! The original Portuguese settlers were mostly men, and they looked for companionship among the indigenous people and, yes, the slaves. So we are truly all mixed up—a big mix for many hundreds of years. And we think nothing of it. As a whole, as a society, that is," she added, sighing a little. "Well, we've had our bad. In the thirties the government encouraged workers to come from Europe—but not Asia or Africa. But, that was the thirties. We are a browner society in general—and our constitution prohibits discrimination by the government and by the people!" She shrugged. "Still, sometimes it is hard. Prejudice exists everywhere, but . . . I will always work against it. Women may not be discriminated against, and yet, for some old men, it's hard. They think that the woman's place is, as your people say it, barefoot, pregnant, and in the kitchen. But, we toss our hair at those who carry cultural weight and think they are macho men." She

paused again. "And I think we try here. We love life—
and I love to write about all life, the good and the
bad—and what makes it special."

"Life?" he asked her, bemused. "What is it to you
that makes life so special?"

"Art, pictures, and music—traveling. Dancing,
and meeting people, the people in the streets, little
children, pets . . . everything. The grass, the sun, the
mountains and the valleys. Nature's beauty, all of it.
The oceans and lakes and . . . and rivers."

He smiled. "Nice. And you make your points
beautifully, with words that make people smile and
think."

"Thank you," she said. A slight frown creased her
brow.

"What is it?"

"Here, sadly, sometimes, money talks," she said.
"The color of money—that is what sometimes mat-
ters."

"I believe that's the whole world," he told her.

She refused to be down.

"Life is what we make it, right? Come on . . . let's
hop on the bus."

"We just gave away all our coins."

"We'll slip in the back."

There was no way he could resist her.

"Come; it will be an adventure," she persisted.

"I'm into adventure," he assured her.

"Then follow me; I know how to do this."

And she did. She grabbed his hand and pulled him
along to an overhang on the side of the road where

people were waiting. She nodded and smiled as they joined the throng. The roads here were dusty; farmers and women carrying belongings in rolled-up scarves waited.

Then the bus, spewing all kinds of smoke and noxious fumes, pulled up. A horde seemed to step off—and the group they were part of moved on. Natal led him through the back doors, where they were swept up in the sea of people and pushed toward the back.

He wasn't sure about not paying people—just as he wasn't sure about stealing coins. But she had left her clothing—probably worth much more!—in lieu of the coins—and, of course, he had set down the dollar bill.

The bus was going where it was going anyway. And if anyone noticed they were not paying, he did have bills in his backpack.

Natal looked at him and smiled as if they were conspirators. She leaned close and whispered, "Don't worry, River, Mr. Water, my friend. I will see to it that I pay double a few times; we aren't taking anyone . . . let's see—as you would say it—for a ride!" She laughed softly.

The sound was like music.

For a while, he held on to Natal and stood next to a man clutching a chicken. Natal smiled at him and spoke to the man—and River patted the chicken on the head. Natal laughed and the man grinned, and River thought that, all around Natal, people seemed to brighten. The man with the chicken left the bus. More people got on and off. At one stop, the driver pulled the bus off the road and came striding down the aisle. He began a rapid explosion at them in Brazilian Portuguese. Natal listened gravely; the driver reached for River but Natal grabbed River's hand and lifted her chin in the air—and headed for the exit of the bus, pushing them both past the driver.

As they exited, River heard the riders who were still on the bus booing the driver for his actions.

Natal stood by, watching, hands on her hips, grinning and satisfied.

"You know, we could have just paid him," River pointed out.

"Yes, but what is the adventure in that?" she asked.

"Getting where we were going!" he said, and laughed.

"Did you even know where we were going?"

"I guess I didn't," he admitted. "Do you know where we are?"

"In Brazil?" she teased.

"Even I know that!"

"We are close," she told him.

"Close to where?"

"To where we are going."

It wasn't as if he had to be anywhere, River reminded himself.

And it wasn't as if there was anywhere else he would rather be.

"How do we get there now?" he asked.

She lifted her two hands, presenting both thumbs. "We hitchhike."

River wasn't sure any sane person would pick up a

scraggly backpacker like himself, but Natal had no doubts.

A car was coming down the dirt road. She did nothing. He thought that maybe he was supposed to be doing the thumbing. He started to step out but she caught hold of him and pulled him back. "Wrong way, silly! Just wave nicely!"

Embarrassed, he stepped back. But as she had encouraged him, he waved.

The farmer waved in return.

They both coughed in the cloud of dust left by the passing vehicle. But another quickly arrived, going the other way. The vehicle was a beat-up old Ford truck. Natal headed for the road before he could stop her—he ran quickly to put himself in front of her.

The truck stopped, and the driver, a friendly-looking white-haired fellow, waved them on back to the bed of the truck, offering them both a grin that showed his few remaining teeth.

River nodded his gratitude profusely; Natal said something in Portuguese.

They hopped into the back of the truck, squeezing between crates of clucking chickens.

"Chickens—it had to be chickens!" he murmured.

"What?"

"Bad joke," he told her. "There's an American movie—"

"Indiana Jones!"

"You know it?"

"Of course. He hated snakes—and he encountered snakes. Do you hate chickens?" she asked.

He laughed. "No—we're just encountering a lot of them!"

She grinned and leaned against him a little. "It's a bit of a drive," she warned.

He didn't care. Her leg brushed against his. The sky was blue above him. A *cluck* here and there meant nothing.

But they got there—though even when they did, River wasn't sure where they were.

When they hopped out of the truck, Natal rewarded the driver with a kiss on the top of his white-haired head. They both waved their thanks as the driver drove away.

"Now?" River asked.

"We walk," she told him.

"Walk where?"

She pointed to a small footpath that led upward. It was largely obscured by bracken, but she knew where she was going. He followed her.

He loved so much of the landscape in Brazil. The rainforest here was geologically ancient—way older than the Amazonian rainforest. When explorers had first come to the coast, they had seen nothing but green, the forest so rich it eclipsed all else. It had been called Mata Atlântica, or Atlantic Forest, and in places, it had stretched inland for 125 miles. But that had been then, and now, civilization—and the twelve million plus people who currently lived on the coast—had changed it. Only special, wonderful places were left where the flora and fauna—as uniquely diverse as the people—reigned supreme. In these wilds, a man could catch a glimpse of a woolly spider monkey, a lion tamarind, or a sloth. Not always, since the animals were wary of human beings. But the monkeys could sometimes be seen up in the trees; their cries to one another could occasionally be heard. It was truly a wonder—like stepping back in time.

"I feel like I'm on safari in Africa!" he called to her, getting smacked in the face by another branch.

"And wouldn't you like to be on safari in Africa?" she asked. "I would."

He laughed. "Okay, so yes, but, I don't think I'm prepared to run into a lion."

"Some beautiful birds, a few wild dogs—no lions in this stretch. Monkeys!" she added, grinning. "We are not so in the wild here, really. Or, at least, if we are in the wild, it is a wild that others have found too."

He was surprised when they broke into a clearing, where a few vendors were selling cheese, fruit, bread, and some dried fruit.

"Now," she said.

"Now?"

"Dig into your backpack for some bills for these people!"

He did. He walked behind her as she pointed out her selections and at the end, she must have argued about the price of the items because the old vendor continued to haggle with River.

He just grinned and paid the man, and then followed her over to where he was certain she was haggling over the price of a blanket with another old man.

He simply paid what was asked, grinning all the while. She shook her head and rolled her eyes; haggling was an art, he realized.

He shrugged and tried not to smile too stupidly. He was with her. They were having a picnic.

They headed off again, climbing. There were clear patches, areas of rock, and stretches of scruff and even heavy brush.

"We are about to find the treasure!" she called back to him.

A moment later, he followed her out into another clearing. They had climbed fairly high, but nowhere near as high as Corcovado mountain, which they could see in the distance. The Christ the Redeemer statue, in the late-afternoon sunlight, seemed to glisten and gleam and look down at them with a holy light.

"Christ the Redeemer," Natal said. "A magnificent sight, yes—and from here, far from the crowds that throng around it every day."

He turned to her. "This is breathtaking," he said. "Truly beautiful."

She smiled and flushed. "Set out the blanket, please."

He quickly did so, doffing his backpack. Natal set to opening their little containers of food. "This place is good. You can see the statue. You can feel love and forgiveness—but you don't have to see the tourists."

"Are we in the national park now?" River asked her. The statue was in Tijuca National Park, he knew. He'd been to it before.

He'd never seen the statue as he was seeing it now.

She shook her head. "No, but we are near. There is a chapel under the statue and there are so many tourists, but . . . I will tell you a little secret. There is a pass—an old mountain pass—and it will take you there when you wish. I prefer it here."

"Where we're alone?" he murmured.

She rolled her eyes. "We are not alone. See there—by the gnarled old tree? Right beyond, there is an old couple, gnarled like the tree. But they come here for their lunch. Maybe they come to remember when they were young. When they had adventures, yes?"

"Maybe."

"And over there," she said. "There is a young couple—escaping a harsh papa, perhaps!"

She was right. They weren't alone. But that, of course, was why the vendors were in the clearing: they sold their wares to those who liked to escape to this quiet place where they looked up and into the distance and saw the giant Christ—His arms outstretched to encompass all and, perhaps, forgive all.

Natal looked up at the sky. "Eat, you must eat. Enjoy what you see. We can't stay long."

He rolled over on the blanket and looked at her. "Why?"

"Because I must be back."

"Why must you be back?"

She wagged a finger at him. "I am a free spirit—I don't answer questions. Adventurers make no promises, and they give no explanations or excuses."

He reminded himself that he had never really expected to meet her, much less spend an afternoon with her.

"No questions," he said. "You need give me no explanations."

She smiled at that. "So! I will tell you the story of the very old couple. She was a child in Germany—a Jewish child. He was an American soldier. When the Americans and Russians rolled into Brazil, he found her hiding in a field. She was terrified because she was Jewish; she was afraid to say so. But he showed her his Star of David and said, 'But, fräulein, I am *Juden* too.' They kept in touch; when he was twenty-eight and she was twenty-one, they married. That's beautiful, yes?"

"Very."

"Now you. The young couple."

"Me?"

"Yes, now it is your turn. You must tell their story."

River stared at them thoughtfully. "Hmm. Every man and woman has a story, and in beautiful tales, their stories combine—and they become one tale to tell. Let's see. I will tell you their story. Their fathers are at odds with one another. They were business partners when the children were young. They had a huge fight. The mothers were friends too, but they were no longer allowed to talk. The children found one another at a football game. He is a star player. They met and flirted and teased and at a dance, they fell in love. But then they realized who they were—who their fathers were—and they knew they had to meet secretly."

Natal clapped her hands in delight. "That is their story?"

"Okay, so it's kind of a Romeo and Juliet rip-off," he admitted.

"It's a lovely story about the couple meeting in the rainforest beneath a canopy of trees and nature. Yes. Or, we could go back."

"Back?" he said, swallowing his disappointment. She'd said that she couldn't stay, but he hadn't thought to lose her quite so quickly.

"For the story, we can go back to the days when the Portuguese came here." She rolled toward him, mischief in her eyes.

"Oh, back to the colonial days, of course. Sure. Wonderful. Then, what is the story?"

"It's always the same, for all peoples. In 1550, Pedro Álvares Cabral arrived at Puerto Seguro. When he came, there were many native tribes living here. Two main groups spoke Tupi, but they were very different. The Temiminó were fascinated by the newcomers. And they were a lovely people—they were fishermen, they farmed the land, and they hunted. And they bathed. They made the explorers bathe too. They were hospitable and welcoming to those who came, but . . . There were also the Tamoio. They hated the newcomers! They were bitter, brutal enemies from the beginning!"

"Terrible," River said. "Imagine that—they didn't like giving up their land!"

Natal sighed and shook her head. "We are all guilty of that, eh? Anyone of European descent in the New World. That, however, is beside the point. You are ruining their beautiful love story."

"I would never ruin a love story!" he protested.

"She was the daughter of a Temiminó chief—he was a great warrior of the Tamoio tribe, son of a great war leader. He could have swept her up and made her his slave, but he was in love, yet he was not allowed to be in love. He knew that he couldn't force her to return his passion; he had to win her love. What he didn't know was that she did love him. He was beautiful, and she knew that no matter where he came from, or what he had been taught, he was a good man deep inside. And so, though her people deplored him as the enemy, she wanted to be with him. But it would be horrible if they were caught; she might be thrown out, denied by her family forever. And he could face death for such a betrayal! So . . . they came here."

He smiled. "I think I like my story best. I think my couple have a better chance at making it in the end."

"Ah, well, love is always a beautiful story. There is a rich history here, yes? Next, we could tell a tale of love between a native girl and a Portuguese—she teaches him cleanliness first, so that he learns to bathe and keep his body fresh and beautiful, eh? Ah, when the explorers came at first, they were horrified and amazed. The native people did not think of their bodies as evil. They danced naked. Or maybe the explorers—men at first, of course!—were not so horrified. The women must have been very beautiful, eh? And that's how our hero fell in love: he saw this beauty, dancing. She was naked, and as rich and beautiful as the earth, and he believed in all the freedom and music in her soul. But that's for another day. Now . . . we must go."

"No matter what year, no matter what nationality or tribe—he would protect her from all things, even to his own death," River assured her.

"And she would lie down and die for him," Natal said passionately. "We must get back."

He couldn't seem to dissuade her. He told himself that he had to be grateful for the time he'd had with her.

"We still have food," he noted, even as she started to pack it away. But she was ready to go; they would go.

And he would pray for another time together.

"We will give it to the old people."

"Just to the old people? Why not the young people too?"

"Because they are young. They will go to their separate homes and their parents will feed them. Even in Brazil, not every child cares for an aging parent."

He folded the blanket and took the bundle of food from her, following her over to the older couple. He didn't know what she said—he only knew that the old couple smiled and nodded and seemed grateful as he handed over the food and the blanket.

He flushed and nodded when they thanked him profusely.

Again, Natal caught his hand.

It was strangely more difficult going downhill than it had been coming up. Probably because while going up, he'd looked forward to the time with her. Coming down meant that she was going to leave.

She seemed to have grown a little tense as they reached the road again. She didn't wear a watch so she looked at the sky.

He wanted to hold her; he wanted to tell her not to worry. He would be there, he would protect her . . .

He would be that lover, from any tribe, any nation, who would fight and die for her. Preferably not die, of course, since that would mean he wouldn't be with her anymore.

And yet, how foolish a thought. He would protect her.

From what?

He didn't know that she needed protecting from anything or anyone.

River was careful to remain easy. He desperately wanted to see her again. He had the feeling that if he tried to hold on to her—to the magic of the day—he never would.

He learned that people in this part of the world on the outskirts of the massive city of Rio de Janeiro were just nice—and accustomed to helping one another. They easily got a ride all the way back into the center of town. They didn't have to slip onto a bus and slip off unnoticed; the appeal of more adventure seemed to be gone for Natal.

But when they stood in the square together, looking at one another, the noise of the shoeless children running around them seemed to disappear; the horns and laughter and music faded. Everything seemed to go to a distant place as he stared at her.

"I can see you home," he said.

She shook her head. "No . . . free spirit, remember?" Her words were light, but there was an edge to her voice.

"A free spirit, and your perception, what you see . . . it becomes your writing?"

She shrugged.

"Can I see you again?"

She opened her arms, mimicking the open gesture of the Christ the Redeemer statue. "Of course. We are in Rio. We welcome you with open arms. I will see you again."

"Where?"

"Where?" she repeated. "So many places, and all beneath that welcoming embrace!"

"So, somewhere, perhaps, to see the statue?"

"There are many places to view the statue. You can see it from almost everywhere." She came to him and he felt the sweetness of her breath on his cheek. "I do love the Christ the Redeemer statue. You love the statue. But, tomorrow, you will find me at the beach."

He smiled at that. Rio was all coast and lagoons and beautiful beaches. The coastline seemed to stretch forever.

"Which beach?" he asked her.

"Ipanema," she said. "You know—I will be the girl from Ipanema!"

"Okay, Ipanema it is," he told her.

"No! Wait, while I promise that I can find you any-where, I will make this easy for both of us. The Copa-cabana," she said. She set her hands on her hips in a charming gesture as she explained her plan. "If we head to Copacabana, you can find me easily. Just look for me in front of the Copacabana Palace. You know where that is, yes?"

"Yes."

"Bring a suit or some trunks. Okay? We'll soak in the sun and lie on the sand—like real tourists. And natives," she added with a laugh.

"Anywhere," he told her softly.

She seemed a little troubled by that; maybe he was coming on too strongly.

But her smile quickly returned.

"The beach is good," she said. And then she waved, and she was gone.

River watched her go.

CHAPTER 6

He was in the center of town, by one of the plush hotels. He watched her for so long as she left that he was barely aware of the people in rich costumes going by him, dressed in high Renaissance apparel. English, German, Portuguese, and more languages could be heard in constant and heady murmurs; a grand ball was being held somewhere nearby that night.

And yet, even as the lavishly costumed group moved by him, he heard a drumbeat; a parade float was approaching. A handsome man and women in a colorful tribute to colonial native wear were dancing atop the float. They called out to the crowd. Music poured from a boom box on the float; it was good and it was catchy and people in the street danced and laughed with them. Even those who were so richly garbed, heading into their posh ball.

River smiled. The beauty of Rio was in the people, in the beat, in the fact that the rainforest encroached on the city, just as the native pulse of freedom forever touched upon all that might be rigid and structured.

A middle-aged woman grabbed hold of his hand; he was suddenly jumping to the beat of the samba himself in the middle of the road. Partners swirled and turned and traded—he danced with a teenage girl, and then a youth in drag. He didn't care; the youth didn't either. They both laughed. Breathless, River broke away at last. He was happy—exhilarated.

It was Rio.

And he had found Natal.

He would see her the next day. And that sent his heart soaring. He would be careful; he wouldn't cling to her. He would force himself to remember that they were both free spirits—and that meant that he couldn't pin her down or make demands.

But just thinking of her . . .

He realized he was standing dead still while others danced around him, a stupid smile on his face.

He gave himself a mental shake and began the walk back to Beluga's hostel.

CHAPTER 7

"You're whistling," Beluga told him the next morning.

"I am."

"So, let's see. There's only one reason a man whistles like that. A woman," Beluga said sagely.

"You told me to find a woman. Beluga—*you* need to find a woman."

Beluga laughed. "Maybe. But I'm a happy man. I'm at peace with who I was—and who I have become. I like people and people come to me. I make them happy; that makes me happy."

"There must be something in the air here, in Rio. It's Brazil, city of joy, right?" River said lightly. "Our friend Thiago—he's happy too. He never has money—except for the track—and he's always happy."

"Thiago learned to survive on the streets. He

doesn't hate money; he just knows that he can survive without it. If he had it—he'd give most of it away."

"Best thing to do with money," River assured him. "Except for what you need, of course." He wasn't a big believer in money—but he did want enough to keep Convict fed now, and to buy coffee or vinho and bread and cheese when he was with Natal.

"Ah, well—the burden of life. Yes, we need so much. But I learned years ago, my friend, that the more you have, the more you spend. The more you spend, the greater your debt. Then, suddenly, you're a slave to money. So, Thiago is smart. He will never be a slave to money. If he ever has it, he will be good with it—he will give it away. But . . . he's not so good at the track!" Beluga broke off, laughing. "He will probably never have it. And still, he'll be a happy man. And you are happy today. So tell me—where are you off to? The track again? Will you see Theo?"

"I'm going to the beach," River replied.

"A good thing to do in Brazil. But leave me the dog again. People can get picky and nasty sometimes. Convict, he does well with me. Though maybe he loves Maria more. She has better scraps of food!"

River laughed. "Today, okay, if that's what you wish. But, you know—"

"You owe me nothing. I can feed a dog."

"I'm not sure if I'm coming back tonight," River warned.

"Of course you're coming back. This is more or less your home right now—even if you're wandering and seeing the sights. But," Beluga wagged a finger at River. "When I don't know for sure, I can't save you a bed."

River grinned. "Beds are kind of like money, Beluga. If you're accustomed to not having a bed, you don't have to have one."

Beluga didn't return the smile. Instead he studied River, concern in his eyes. "You're really going to the beach?"

"Yes. Why?"

His friend hesitated for a moment before replying, "I worry about you—because of what you feel about Tio Amato."

"Oh." River felt his face burn and quickly lowered his head. Something did need to be done about Tio Amato. He had forgotten about the man, forgotten everything but Natal.

And the thought of being with her again.

What if he did go to the police? Even if they were honest and honorable, what did he say to them? *I think I saw Reed Amato have a body thrown off the bridge?*

There was no way to prove anything.

Maybe, with Natal, he would think of something.

"I'm not going near Tio Amato today—I promise you. I'm going to the beach. And when I make my way back, I'm going to dance in the streets with all the Brazilians who love the samba music so much."

"Then go with God, my boy. I will trust Him to watch out for you—because He knows that it must be Him to take care of you, because you are so reckless." Beluga rolled his eyes.

River sipped his coffee, too anxious to eat the food that Maria offered him. He thanked her with a kiss on the cheek, and she flushed, happy.

Convict intercepted him on the way out, head up, tail wagging. Gone was the frightened, abused creature that River had rescued only two days ago. River knelt before him, taking the dog's head in his hands and touching it to his forehead. "Hey buddy," he murmured. "Stay put today, okay?" Convict licked his nose, and River laughed, giving him a quick scratch behind the ears before leaving the dog to his new home.

Rio—beneath the benign blessing of the Christ the Redeemer statue and the mountains—was mostly coastline, and beaches abounded. He was glad that Natal had chosen the beautiful Copacabana Palace. The hotel had opened its doors in 1923; before that, the beach had pretty much been deserted except for locals who might come and bathe and swim at times. But the hotel had been an immediate hit—as planned by Octávio Guinle when he hired a French architect to design the place. Guinle had wanted a grand hotel—similar to the likes of those to be found in Paris and Nice and Cannes. Fred Astaire and Ginger Rogers had put the hotel on the map—and increased the fame of Rio itself—in the movie *Flying Down to Rio*.

Looking up at the magnificent façade, River smiled.

He'd studied Brazil and Rio, and he knew that Astaire and Rogers had never danced at the Copacabana Palace at all—the movie had been filmed miles and miles away—and that only the magic of the movie industry had placed them at the Palace. That didn't matter; the movie had made the place famous, and Rio had suddenly been known here, there, and everywhere. If Fred and Ginger had danced there, it was a fabulous place, filled with sun and fun and wonders.

And, of course, in River's mind, it was.

And Natal was one of its wonders.

Except, as he idly cruised the sidewalk in front of the Copacabana Palace, he didn't see her.

Time meant little here, he knew. Especially to Natal. They hadn't set a time; she had just said that he could find her there.

There were wonderful restaurants in the hotel, and he considered waiting in one. She probably loved little cafés and charming little shops. But what if she missed him? No, better to wait until he found her.

He walked and looked into shops idly, pausing to examine an English-language book that covered the breadth of the country of Brazil and its history.

Then he walked back and began to pace in front of the Copacabana Palace again. A few little street urchins found him there; they were begging. He smiled at them and found a few bills to give them from his backpack.

The kids were delighted and disbelieving as they ran off with the money. River's knowledge of the language was enough to buy food and find the men's room—or an appropriate clearing in the rainforest. But he thought that he understood what they were saying and was angry with himself—even as he felt badly for the three little boys.

They were the forgotten children—little scamps, just as Theo had once been. But Thiago had not hurt others; he had learned that people were wasteful, and he had learned that another man's leftovers were treasures to him.

Did River have a right to judge?

These kids had gone in a different direction. They weren't begging for themselves; they brought their money back to someone who offered them minimal care—and possibly abused them—for whatever they could bring in.

He should have followed them; he should have risked arrest to pound some sense into whoever could be so cruel.

He would never catch them.

There was nowhere in the world where such men didn't exist, he told himself.

But the incident made him think of Tio Amato again. At least the children hadn't looked abused or beaten; they had even appeared to be happy.

Tio Amato hurt people.

Killed them.

He gave himself a mental shake. He could not solve the evil that existed everywhere. He was only one man—a drifter, no less. There were also people out there—law enforcers—who were decent. It was their problem.

And he was waiting for Natal.

He looked up and down the street. As he did so, he caught sight of a man just slipping into the front of the hotel.

Tio Amato?

Maybe he just had the man on his mind; there was no reason to believe that Tio Amato and he were following all the same paths in Brazil.

But, as he peered closer at the entrance, he thought he saw someone else—the other man who had been at the race track. Amato's henchman, his enforcer—or so River believed.

No. It couldn't be—or it was extremely unlikely.

He almost went in to look. But what then? Stare at Tio Amato and his big henchman and then walk away? He couldn't just start a brawl in the hotel.

And he might have imagined that Tio Amato and part of his posse were there. Tio Amato was way too big in his world to have a workforce of begging children.

Maybe he was an overseer, taking money from the man who used the children.

And maybe, River thought, *I am making all this up in my head because I despise Tio Amato—and despise the fact that it seems I can do nothing about the man being a killer.*

He walked on, telling himself to shake it off; he was waiting for Natal. She was everything bright and beautiful in the world while Tio Amato was everything dark and evil.

But still she didn't come.

As the afternoon dragged on, he began to fear that something had stopped her. They should have arranged a time. She wasn't going to come.

The sun beat down with a fervor that demanded reprieve. When at last the heat and sweat had become too much, River yielded and made for the water. Only for a little while, he promised himself. A few minutes to cool off and come back—and pace some more.

He'd pace until it was late, until the sun began to wane, and probably beyond that.

Heading to the sand, he stopped to purchase a *canga*—or towel-like, almost-sarong—to bring with him. The nearly toothless vendor tried to strike up a conversation, but River found it difficult to concentrate on anything the man was saying. A feeling of hopelessness had begun to overwhelm him. He couldn't stop Tio Amato. He couldn't find the woman who intrigued him so. What was he good for anymore?

A flash of violence in his mind. Guns and bombs and shouting and death.

No. River was more than a killer. He had to be.

The vendor looked at him strangely, and River wondered if he'd spoken without realizing it. He thanked the old man and slung the *canga* over his shoulder.

Dark images still stalked the edges of his mind, but he forced himself to focus instead on the sight of the ocean, the sound of the waves crashing down. The sight of bikinis and swimming trunks and unbridled joy. He thought about Theo, who could find comfort in anything. He'd come to this beach with Theo before;

he'd taken his friend to Cipriani—one of the nice restaurants in the Copacabana Palace. Theo had been in awe. Since River was with Theo, he'd easily been able to say, "It's just money, Theo. If we don't spend it for a nice night, what is it for?"

"Lucky dog!" Theo had told him.

He wasn't feeling lucky. He was feeling lonely.

He spread his newly purchased *canga* and set his backpack on it, half covering it with sand.

He sat for a minute, watching children play and build sand castles. Sandcastles were a common art form here and the children were often very good at it.

Boats were out in large numbers, close to the shore, many with music blaring and passengers dancing away before they jumped into the water or jumped out.

River remembered that he had come to the beach because he was hot. He pulled his shirt over his head and went running into the surf. It felt good. The water was cooling. He couldn't really swim; there were too many people splashing and playing around him.

It was while he was in the water, though, that he remembered the children he had given bills to—and how he had heard them talking about the "prize" they had gotten from the silly American and how pleased "Uncle Juan" would be.

He stood, dripping, and walked from the water, thinking he shouldn't leave his backpack—even if he wanted to be a free spirit like Natal. It was good to give; it wasn't good to have what he had stolen.

He rose from the water, sweeping back his hair,

water dripping from his physique. At that moment, his mind on his backpack.

But there she was. Natal.

She was wearing a full skirt, sandals, a white peasant blouse, and a huge sun hat. She took off the hat and waved it when she spotted him.

As she stood there, dazzling beneath golden rays, he thought that she was the most beautiful thing he'd ever seen.

And she had come to meet him; she had somehow known to come down to the sand and the water when she hadn't seen him in front of the Copacabana Palace.

He forced himself not to run at breakneck speed toward her; he smiled and waved in return and trotted out of the water.

As he neared her, he saw the little scamps he'd seen earlier—heading for his backpack. He veered off his path.

Natal followed his gaze and saw what was about to happen. She turned quickly and raced toward River's little *canga* station on the beach. He could hear her telling them that they were little robbers and would wind up in jail.

He shouted loudly—emphasizing that Natal was not alone, and that he was on his way back.

By the time he reached the *canga*, the kids were gone—but Natal was there, tall and indignant.

"The urchins know you are about. When will they learn not to steal?" she demanded.

"When they're taught not to do so."

She rested her hands on either side of her waist. "You mustn't think we're a bad people."

"I don't think that at all; I think you're wonderful people," he assured her.

She flushed. "I sneak on buses. I take a few coins—but only when I leave something behind, and the bus is going where it is going whether I sneak on or not. I like the challenge, you see—but never to hurt anyone else. I try to help people."

"I know that you do—please, I don't think badly at all of the Brazilian people. I'm here because I'm fascinated with your country."

"There are just some people . . . sometimes children wind up without homes and the system can't always manage or isn't really in place. And they are taken under the wing of men who are less than scrupulous. And taught to steal. I hate that it happens in my country."

He nodded. "Natal, it's not just Brazil. Think about Charles Dickens and Oliver Twist. Poor Oliver! First, he's in a workhouse, then he's with an undertaker, then he finds the Artful Dodger—and the next thing you know, he meets the evil Fagin! Please, I know—it's not just Brazil."

"Dickens," she said. "Yes, I have read Dickens. He knew people, eh?"

"The bad—and the good," River said. "I gave those kids money earlier; my fault. They know that I have bills in my backpack. I'm usually more careful."

"It's good to give—it's not good to steal. I'm sorry.

They are young, but . . . the young get lost. Dickens, though. Yes, you're right. And I love his work. You love his work?"

River nodded. "*A Tale of Two Cities* is my favorite."

Natal smiled at him, tossing her sun hat on the *canga*. "And mine." She slid her hands down his bare wet arms. "You've been swimming. Very good. We'll have to bury the backpack—no! I will ask the older lady with the blanket on her knees to watch over our space. I want to feel the water and the sun."

She pulled her white blouse over her head and shimmied out of her skirt, revealing a bikini beneath.

River struggled not to stare.

"Wait one minute," she said, seemingly oblivious to the effect she was having on him. "I will ask her to watch."

"For thieving children?"

"Don't underestimate the goodness in people either, my friend," she replied.

She took his hand and hurried over to the woman she had referred to—an older lady sitting under an umbrella who, despite the heat, did indeed have a blanket on her lap.

He waved to the woman with a smile and as Natal spoke, he indicated his backpack. She nodded at him and looked at Natal.

Natal came back and caught his hand. "Come, let's get in the water."

"She's pretty old," he said quietly, indicating the woman. "Think she can guard my stuff?"

Natal laughed. "She carries a mean cane, my friend.

She will stop any little rascals. Trust me—they will know to fear her."

Something about the day still seemed to tug at River's mind. In the far reaches, he knew that he couldn't forget Tio Amato.

But with Natal before him . . .

He had to let it go.

"Come!" She released his hand and ran for the water.

He ran after her, splashing back into the cool surf, laughing as the saltwater hit his eyes, as the sand oozed through his toes. She was swimming with long, easy strokes; he swam after her.

She paused suddenly, turning back to splash him.

He splashed her in return. There were some children, perhaps between the ages of eight and twelve, in the water. They laughed and got into the splashing game. Soon, everyone was splashing everyone and having an all-out water war and tremendous fun.

River dove beneath the water and came up directly in front of Natal. She couldn't quite manage a splash that didn't get her too. The saltwater stung River's eyes but he didn't really notice. Natal was so easy in the water. The children were children.

"Hey," he said softly, treading water hard with his legs and slipping his arms around her.

"Hey," she said in return. "Behave—there are children."

"Of course. I always behave."

"I doubt that," she told him, but she remained in

his hold for a minute before pointing to the boats farther out.

"They are partying—we should join them."

"Do you know them?"

"No," she said. "Do you?"

"No, so perhaps—"

"Perhaps we shouldn't join them?" Natal supplied. "Don't be silly."

"They may not want us."

"But they will. This is Rio—and it is Carnaval season."

She escaped his hold and swam straight out toward deeper water. He followed her and saw that she was heading to one of the boats.

There were people partying on the boat, their music playing loudly. They had cups of wine and beer and food spread out on one of the back cushions.

They waved to him and Natal.

Natal spoke to them in Portuguese—she spoke quickly, and he didn't think that he could follow what she was saying. River, not wanting to look like a fool, greeted them with his broken Portuguese.

But the people on the boat were young and welcoming—and in a party mood. It seemed the more the merrier; there were two young men and three young women aboard. Before River knew what was happening, the partiers were insisting that they join them. Natal swam for the ladder; he did the same.

A pretty young woman with light hair and eyes helped him onto the boat.

"*Americano!* Join us!" she said.

Someone had given Natal a glass of wine; he quickly found one in his hands as well. Those on board were all chatting and moving to the music and having fun.

"Samba!" Natal exclaimed.

Suddenly River was balancing his drink, trying not to spill it, as he found himself hopping in rhythm to the music—as Natal was doing.

He was perturbed; the blonde was in front of him, then, and Natal called out to him, "It is just dance; we all dance. Come, River, this is nothing wrong. It is Brazil!"

And so he danced. He thought about the night before and he thought that he loved Carnaval and Brazil. The people could be very religious; they honored their Catholicism. But they seemed to believe truly in the guidance that they should love everyone. They didn't seem to have any hang-ups; the men danced with one another, laughed, changed partners, and had a good time.

"You will have dinner with us?" the light-haired woman asked him.

He realized that it was growing late; yes, even in Brazil, it was time for dinner.

"No, no, we cannot—we must go back," Natal said.

"No, but thank you!" River said.

The blonde looked as if she would plead; Natal laughed, and thanked them all again—and dived over the side of the boat.

River did the same.

Natal swam hard for the shore and he followed behind her. She turned to splash him, her laughter ringing lightly on the air.

He splashed in return.

For a while, she played in the water. He caught her to him, treading water, holding her close, feeling her heartbeat. All around him he could hear the sounds of talking and music and the sounds of children playing. Splashing and enjoying the water, as they had.

But all he could see was Natal. Her eyes as he held her close. Her smile, as she looked back at him.

Then, something shifted in the sky; darkness was coming.

"I must go," she said.

He closed his eyes and lowered his head; he had sworn that he wouldn't push this. If he did . . .

She might not agree to see him again.

"As you wish," he told her, releasing his grip. Natal swam toward shore. He followed.

When they reached his *canga,* his backpack was right where he had left it. The old woman nodded gravely to him as he thanked her. She smiled. He smiled in return.

Natal had slipped her clothing over her bikini. He swept up his own shirt and put it on and threw his backpack over his shoulders.

"Time to go," he said.

She placed a hand on his chest. "I leave you here."

"We can head back toward—"

"No, no, I must go now. From here. But I will see you tomorrow?"

He believed her. She had promised to be here today; she had come. And he had held her, even if just for a moment.

"Yes. Where?"

"A museum?" she suggested. "We have magnificent museums, art—history. Natural treasures."

"A museum is fine."

"No," she said. "I know what you love. The statue. The Christ the Redeemer statue."

"But where by the statue?" he pressed, remembering where lack of planning had gotten him earlier today, pacing for ages. "The place we sat last time?"

She offered him her most dazzling smile.

"I know how to find you. Don't worry; I promise you—I will find you."

She turned and scampered away off the sand.

And he was left alone, looking after her.

Even so, he was happy.

CHAPTER 8

Beluga was sitting in a chair out in the night, smoking a cigar and sipping what appeared to be scotch. He frowned when River came walking up. "You told me you had no schedule and might not be back—but you are. Why are you so late? Now we're full tonight— I have a troop of Canadian backpackers and their chaperons here, kids on top of kids! I'm sorry—I didn't think that you were coming back."

"That is no problem, Beluga," River told him.

"No? You want to sleep under the stars—with the bugs and the cold damp earth?"

River laughed. "No—I want to sleep under the stars and the velvet of the night sky."

Beluga sniffed and muttered in his own language beneath his breath.

"The world is what we see it as, right, Beluga?" River asked. "Tonight, I see the beauty of the sky."

"And the bugs of the earth, eh? Well, sit. Join me for a while."

River did so.

"Nice night, eh?" Beluga muttered.

Everything in the world is nice—after the day I've spent, River thought.

"Yes, beautiful night."

Except . . .

"You're frowning," Beluga pointed out. "What's wrong?"

Beluga was right; a dark shadow had slipped over his mood. Of course, he knew why—when he allowed himself to really think. The world was beautiful with Natal. But the world should be . . . good. When things were wrong, a decent man was supposed to fight them. And to be a truly happy man, he needed to be a decent one.

And one thought haunted his mind far too often. Tio Amato—and the murder River was certain the man had committed.

"What is it?" Beluga asked again, turning to face him.

River was silent another moment before replying. "I saw Tio Amato yesterday at the track," he said. "To-day, I thought that I saw him again."

The expression on his friend's face turned grave. "Where?"

"Walking into the Copacabana Palace."

Beluga groaned. "You didn't go accuse him of dumping a man off a bridge, did you?"

"No." River was silent a minute. "He's a bad man, though, Beluga, a very bad man. And he taints those who are around him."

"River, I have told you, I have explained what I know. Stay away from him."

"I'm not a Brazilian peasant. He can't touch me. I'm sorry; I'm not calling you a peasant. I'm just saying that I'm not native to this area; he can't threaten me as he must others."

"I'm not offended; I made my place here, I chose my place here. And no, you are not from here. But don't deceive yourself; your American citizenship is no protection here. He can hurt those he chooses to hurt. Do you want to be the next body that he tosses off a bridge?"

"There must be a way to stop him."

"He buys the authorities; leave him be."

"Surely every policeman can't be bought. I know there are those out there—from here—who believe in decency, who don't believe in the innocent disappearing or being killed."

"Sure. I believe it too. I just don't know how you tell the good from the bad. Or even those who are good but afraid." He was quiet for a minute. "You see many blondes in Brazil, my friend. Many your age. And do you know why?"

"There are many blond Portuguese people," River supplied, not knowing where this was going.

"Yes, that's true. But many of them are newly arrived. They came after World War Two. Some were war criminals who were terrible and cruel. Some might have been taken for war criminals—they were good people, but they didn't want to go to the workhouses or the gas chambers themselves. They knew that terrible things were happening and many of them wanted to do something, but they were afraid. They came here or escaped to other places as quickly as they could. Some came here when they began to see the changes and they came rather than starve. But in all people, those who are evil can't always be distinguished from those who are just afraid. Do I make sense? It's often hard to see what lies in a man's heart. So, you may find good police officers—but they have wives and children, and while they see things that horrify them, they will be too afraid to do anything. Do you understand?"

"I understand. I still believe in the brave—and I believe in strength when enough people see what is going on and determine to face it together." River thought about his afternoon with Natal. He was falling head over heels for her, but still—he liked her so much because she was free, because she believed in justice, because she would never be cruel. "I believe in the brave—who will risk everything."

"Then you are just silly, my friend. This isn't your war; you don't need to fight it."

He didn't want to think about war—even the word could make him smell gunpowder and see the earth as it exploded around him.

River fell silent for a moment, then said, "Well, my friend, I'll collect Convict. We will find a place under the stars."

Beluga sniffed. "Stay awhile; have a shower, relax. Then go sleep under the stars."

River grinned. "Thanks, Beluga." He had rinsed off after at a freshwater spray station at the beach. But it hadn't been much. He was going to see Natal again the next day. He would be clean—even if he did sleep on the ground after his shower.

He headed to the main house. Maria chastised him for being gone so long—and leaving her with a dog. But her hand was on Convict's head, and when River had showered and was ready to leave, she seemed loath to let Convict go. She told River that he could leave Convict with her any time.

"Maria, you are the best," he told her.

"Yes, I am," she said, wagging a finger at him. "Don't you forget that."

He smiled, about to start out. But then he paused and said, "You really are the best. Always so nice." He hesitated, not sure how to ask the question. "Are you happy?"

Maria's eyebrows shot up. "Happy? No one is happy all the time. But mostly, yes."

"I need to find you a man," he teased.

She rolled her eyes. "You think a man is all it takes to make me happy? Anyway, I have one already."

River chuckled. "But you work with Beluga. I mean a man to love."

"I do love Beluga."

"I mean as in a great romance."

"I had my great romance and it is still here," she told him, a hand on her heart. "Now I have Beluga, like a brother. Are we ecstatic every day? Maybe not. But we are content. We like what we do. Yes, maybe . . . yes. I am happy. Why do you ask?"

He hugged her and spun her around, causing her to squeal, "River!"

He set her down. She was grinning and flushed.

"Just wanted you to know you really are the best," he told her.

"*Obrigado!*" she told him. "Thank you."

Grinning, he left her at last.

The hostel was full; there were one or two older guests, a group of young counselors, and what seemed to be a tribe of twenty-some teenagers. They were cheerful and smiled when they saw him; they were on a group trip, he learned, and were anxious to see the countryside and Rio.

One of the boys told him in a whisper—because it was a church group—he mostly wanted to see the half-naked women getting ready for their Carnaval dancing.

"Enjoy; it is a beautiful city," River told him, winking.

"I like the women; Reverend Thornberry says we must see the Christ the Redeemer statue," the boy whispered.

"There is nothing wrong with appreciating the beauty of a woman," River said. He noted that Maria had come from the house and the reverend was speaking with her in halting Portuguese. "And you won't have problems doing that. They are everywhere. Just be respectful."

"Of course!" the boy exclaimed, shocked.

River grinned. "Are you going to any of the beaches?"

The boy nodded. "Ipanema."

"You'll see plenty of lovely women," River assured him.

"And we're going to see some of the parades—we're staying through Carnaval."

"Then you'll see beautiful dancers too."

"Samba!"

"I promise you—you'll see plenty of samba dancing."

"Do you like the beaches here?" the boy asked.

River nodded, a little hesitantly. When he thought of beaches, he thought of Natal . . . but he also thought of Tio Amato. He was becoming somewhat obsessed with the very thought of the man, he realized. But, maybe he couldn't help it.

Tio Amato just hurt—even killed—people.

God alone knew where the man might be. He'd surely be smart enough never to prey upon a North American religious group.

Still, River found himself warning the boy. "Don't wander from your group. You'll see all the wonders you can imagine—but listen to the reverend as well."

"Oh, yes, of course," the boy said quickly.

River grinned. "Really."

The boy flushed.

"Yeah, of course. I mean, I'm not like you—you

know what you're doing here. You know your way around. You know what to watch out for."

Yes, I do, River thought. The problem was that the whole thing with Tio Amato seemed to be eating at him.

Let it go, he told himself. *Just let it go.*

Think about Natal. Just Natal.

"Tomorrow, the Christ the Redeemer statue," the boy said.

The very thought of the statue—where he would soon see Natal—made his heart race. "You'll love it. It's all amazing, the trip, the statue—everything. It's so big and so high in the mountains, you can see it from many places. But go all the way up to it, if you can— that's the most spectacular. And who knows—you may see half-naked women along the way," River teased.

He left the boy's side to go collect Convict. Maria seemed almost sorry to see the dog go.

"You bring him, back, River," she ordered. "You bring him back when you go off again. No crazies will take the dog—he is a good dog."

River gave Maria a kiss on the cheek. "We'll watch out. Of course, I'll bring him to you when I have business where a dog cannot be."

"You had best, River. Beluga—he loves that dog now too, you know."

"I know, and I'm grateful," River assured her.

Natal had said that she'd find him by the statue; the area, of course, was massive. He decided that he'd head there like any tourist the following day, but for the night, he'd find a stretch of plateau near the mountain—he could see the statue and the stars that way.

When he stopped for the night, he thought that he was surely on a farmer's land. But he'd learned that day—really learned, through Natal—that the people in the outskirts of the bustling city were nice. They were friendly. They wanted to know others.

"What do you say, Convict?" he asked the dog. "Have we found the right bed?"

Convict barked and wagged his tail.

River made a pillow out of his backpack and lay down on soft grass and earth.

Convict quickly curled up beside him. The warmth of the dog next to him was nice.

For a while, he stared up at the statue. Then he looked at the stars, noting the Big Dipper for Convict.

How far did Natal's love of adventure extend? There was so much of the country he hadn't seen. Maybe they could go off together on a long excursion through the countryside; they'd tour the mountains and the valleys. They'd find out about native tribes. Every day would be . . .

"I really just met her, Convict," he told the dog. "But somehow, I feel like I've known her for years. And when we wake up—well, the two of you will become great friends."

As he dozed, he began to imagine the map in his bag and made a mental note to check out the train stations and schedules. He didn't want to fly anywhere—flying, they wouldn't see the country. He would have to convince her that a free spirit would come with him. He didn't have to hurry; there were still so many places they could go together here—so many things to do. He thought about the Jardim Botânico—exquisite! They could imagine what it had been like when João VI had created the gardens, determined to have cinnamon and spices and fruit from around the world at his table when he chose—not just when the ships came in. They could make up stories about him and his son, who had opened the magnificent gardens to the public. They could sip espressos at the D.R.I. Café by the pool, walk by magnificent fountains and falls. Maybe, when she trusted him more, he could introduce her to Theo—and they could all go ziplining together through the rich canopy of the rainforest trees.

And then they would travel on.

With dreams so sweet, he slept, and slept deeply.

When he awoke, he did so slowly. For a moment, he thought he heard laughter—a child's laughter.

And he smelled . . .

Pancakes. Pancakes and maple syrup.

He hadn't had pancakes and maple syrup in Brazil . . . he was in Brazil. And yet the aroma of the food was so real . . .

He was somewhere else—somewhere far away. He could hear—as if from a distance—the tinkling sound of a woman's voice.

And the laughter.

The laughter of a child. It was delighted laughter, the kind only a child could ever create. It tore and tugged at his mind with a sweet sense of nostalgia . . .

Then Convict barked—a bark that was loud and anxious. Instantly snapping out of the memory, or dream, or whatever sweet illusion had filled his mind, River was wide awake and leaping to his feet, ready to face whatever danger might lurk.

But it was just a farmer—chiding him for sleeping, River imagined, on his property.

The man wasn't really angry; he shook his head more from confusion. River figured that the farmer just couldn't understand why people would sleep in the open.

River's Portuguese wasn't anywhere near good enough to begin to explain.

Convict barked again. River calmed the dog and apologized in his broken Portuguese.

The farmer looked at Convict, and River assured him that the dog was a good dog. After another glance at River, the farmer came forward and petted Convict.

River was careful when he reached into his backpack—it was never a good idea to let anyone see just how much money was in it—and handed the man a few bills.

The man looked at the money in surprise. River knew that he hadn't had to offer the money. But after his conversation with Theo the other day, he thought that the few dollars might be something important to the man.

Maybe they were. The farmer smiled and nodded and tipped his sun hat to River.

River grinned and thanked him. He turned, calling to Convict, and made his way to the road.

He found a farmer's market where vendors were selling meat pies and bought some for himself and for Convict. The dog was grateful—and well-mannered. But as River considered the day, he stroked Convict and said, "I think I'll take you to Maria for the day—there just might be a few places they won't let me take you. Sorry, you'll have to meet Natal another time. Maybe Maria will give you a bath—you could use one, you know."

Convict looked at him, gave him a strange, friendly howl, and thumped his tail.

Maria accepted a few dollars for keeping and bathing the dog, though, at first, she protested. He didn't understand her Portuguese—she could speak so quickly!—but it seemed that Maria was saying that she had fallen in love with Convict too, and didn't need to be paid to take care of an animal she loved.

He had to remind her that she was doing him a favor that meant a great deal to him, and that she needed money for soap for the dirty dog and for food—and for some trinket for herself.

She was a widow, he knew. Beluga didn't let her want for the things she needed in life, but she could always use a little extra for something special that she simply wanted rather than needed.

He gave her his most winning smile, and she finally accepted the money.

"I work, I make money, you know." She paused. "You asked me if I am happy. I forgot to mention—my children who survived come and see me. They work in Brasília, but Rio is their home, and they are good children. I am grateful I have them still, though I mourn those I lost. But every life is precious, yes? And I still have my two. A girl and a boy."

"I'm sure you have wonderful children, Maria. They have you for a mother!" He winked, and she rolled her eyes in response. "And you work very hard. To do me another favor, you must take this money. Perhaps you should even use it for something fun or pretty. Perhaps for a hair comb or a bracelet—or a scarf, maybe. Or a scanty costume for Carnaval."

"A scanty costume, eh?"

"You'd be beautiful."

"Once!" she said softly. "Once, yes. Now—maybe a hair comb."

"Maria, you are truly beautiful now," he assured her.

She laughed briskly and waved a hand in the air. "Go and see Beluga."

But River was eager to slip away to meet Natal. He told Maria he'd be back soon for Convict. Then he hopped a bus and headed into the city.

And from the city, he looked up at the statue.

Today. Today, he would see her again.

And perhaps, come closer.

But, all he had to do was see her . . .

And life was suddenly good.

CHAPTER 9

River stood on a busy street in the city, listening to the sights and sounds of crawling traffic, motorbikes, motorcycles, music leaking from a dozen venues, horns, and shouts. So many people—how would he find her?

As Carnaval neared, it seemed that the population of Rio had doubled and then tripled.

There seemed to be more music, pouring from every venue.

There were performers in the streets.

There was dancing, and women in colorful costumes with bare midriffs.

The city itself was incredible; it had a life of its own.

And from each peak that surrounded it, he knew, the view was spectacular.

But it was time to get to the statue—to find Natal.

He felt someone standing close behind him and turned. To his astonishment, it was Natal.

In a city so insanely large and crowded!

He smiled and cast his head at an angle. "Were you following me?"

"I don't follow any man!" she said, laughing to keep any sting from her words.

"How did you find me here?"

"Well, maybe I followed you. A little."

She was beautiful and as light as a summer day in a white embroidered peasant dress with a white flower in her hair. His heart beat faster.

"So . . . here we are. In a city that truly never sleeps. So many neighborhoods, so many museums, shopping . . . dining." She threw out her arms as if offering the beauty of Rio to the world. "What shall we do today? I know! Rob a bank!"

He laughed. "We are not robbing any banks."

"Then we should hop the metrô and see where it takes us."

"I thought we were going to the Christ the Redeemer statue. I was about to head that way and try to find you."

"But I found you."

"Yes, you did. How?"

She ignored his question. "So—we do both love the statue. We can go there. Yes," she said, rolling her eyes and sighing softly with a teasing lilt to her voice. "I will act like a tourist."

"You know," he reminded her, "I am a tourist."

"Ah, yes. But you come here for a long time, right? There's no place you have to be? You're staying in Brazil."

He shrugged. For a moment, something seemed to tear at his memory, but he dismissed it.

Yes, he was staying in Brazil. He wanted to see wonders with her here in Rio—and he wanted to travel the country with her. He walked to her, took her hand, and looked into her eyes. First, he had to really win her. Earn her trust. Make her feel for him . . .

That absolute need he had for her.

"Want to indulge me?" he asked. "You've shown me Rio as a native might see it. Let me show you Rio as a tourist might see it."

She groaned softly. "I will not walk around with a city map and stare up at tall buildings."

"I don't expect that," he assured her. "But—I won at the track the other day. Let's take a tour. Let's take the cable car up Sugar Loaf Mountain. Stop and see all the views. We can look down on Copacabana Beach and I'll imagine the swimsuit I saw you in when we were there ourselves. We can view the Rio-Niterói Bridge and see Corcovado mountain. Then we can take the cog train all the way up to the Christ the Redeemer statue . . . stop in the little chapel and act like tourists."

She dipped her head at an angle, offering him a half smile as she mulled over his proposition.

"Okay."

"Okay?"

"Yes—you will be the tour guide today."

He caught her hand. "Come, then, we'll catch the subway to the cable car."

He was oblivious to the people around him—people of many different nationalities—as they hurried through the busy business district to catch the subway.

Natal, however, pulled back. There were stiltwalkers in the street. There were clowns and regal women dressed in colonial clothing, throwing candy to children. They were led by a vehicle playing music for them as they walked about and stooped here or there or paused for pictures.

"I love Carnaval," Natal murmured. River had to lean close to hear her. "We've not yet come to Fat Tuesday, and already, the city is so alive."

He paused with her and realized that half of what intrigued him so much about her was her ability to see all around her, to appreciate everything that she saw.

"Stop to smell the roses," he replied.

"What?"

He smiled. "You. It's a saying. Never become so embroiled with what you're doing and where you're going that you forget all that is beautiful."

"Well, that would just be stupid, eh?" she asked, knocking his shoulder.

"Indeed."

The stiltwalkers passed on by.

"You see, we were just like tourists, distracted by what is going on. But now—ready for the next adventure."

He caught her hand, thinking that his face might freeze in the silly smile he always felt when he was with her.

"Onward," he agreed.

CHAPTER 10

At the station, he produced his card—which, he realized, he could have used on the bus with Natal—and slid in with her close behind him. He was afraid he'd lose her if they stopped for another car.

She seemed amused. "Ah, so we are robbing the subway."

"If you wish."

They were jostled between others. But each time the subway car weaved and waved, he caught sight of her face and the smile she gave him—and the way she rolled her eyes.

Before following a line of tourists who seemed to be composed of Americans, Canadians, and an Italian family, they paused for dark, rich coffee. The Italians argued with the others about the size of their mountains. The Canadians reminded them all about the Canadian Rockies. Natal and River laughed with the others.

"You're traveling Brazil alone with a backpack?" a Canadian woman asked.

The question was jarring; it seemed to take River from time and space. And then he saw the twinkle in Natal's eyes.

"Ah, not really," he said. "I have Brazilian friends."

"Indeed, he does!" Natal said.

"And where are you from?" the woman asked.

"I'm an American," River said. "Seeing the sights. Making my way around the world—with friends."

"Lovely," she said.

The cable car rose to the first height—seven hundred feet above sea level. Everyone rushed to the glass windows to look out. From there they could see the city with its teeming life, Guanabara Bay, Corcovado mountain, and the Rio-Niterói Bridge. And, of course, rising high on Corcovado, the Christ the Redeemer statue. From their vantage point, the magnificent mountains seemed touchable; the water in the bay was sparkling as if a thousand diamonds rested upon it, and the heights and valleys and water were all remarkable.

"This land—so beautiful!" Natal whispered.

"Nothing here is more beautiful than my friends," he teased.

She flushed and grinned.

Soon, the cable car began to rise again. River found himself sitting next to an American man who appeared to be in his mid-fifties or perhaps sixty. He told River he was there with his wife, his son and his son's wife, and their teenaged girls.

"The trip of a lifetime for the wife and me," he said.

River nodded. "For me too."

The man studied him briefly.

"You served in Afghanistan?" he asked.

"Iraq," River replied, turning away. He didn't want to be asked about his service; he didn't want to answer questions about it. There was always something painful about it that seemed to burn in his gut. He'd see the flashes of fire, hear the screams of men.

"Take care of yourself," the man said.

River nodded, disturbed. The air seemed to be filled with the scent of pancakes and syrup once again.

But Natal turned to look at him then, and he was back in the moment.

The cable car made a stop at a higher level. They went on to ascend the peak of Sugarloaf Mountain to see Copacabana Beach, the Santa Cruz fortress, and the beaches of Niterói.

Everyone *ooh*ed and *aah*ed again. The teenaged American girls pestered their parents and grandparents to take them to the beach as soon as possible. The mother reminded them that they were due to see the National Museum of Fine Arts that afternoon.

The grandfather said, "Perhaps the museum will wait for tomorrow. A beach will be pleasant today, don't you think?"

The girls kissed and hugged their grandfather; the mother shook her head but smiled and gave in.

Natal nudged River. "When we have our children, we will be strict. With our grandchildren, we will just delight in them at every step."

He smiled at her as she curled into his arms. So he wasn't the only one dreaming of a future. Her hair was silk and her perfume was exotic. It almost cleared the day of that strange hint of pancakes and maple syrup.

"We'll be doting grandparents," he promised her.

When they alighted from the cable car, it seemed that they had become friends with everyone who had been with them. It was nice.

Natal knew a little out-of-the-way restaurant where they could go to eat—where his attire and backpack would be readily accepted, she told him.

It was down an alley in a residential section of the city where children played barefoot in the street, where the smell of spices and broiling meats was heavy in the air and music played badly from ancient sound systems.

The restaurant walls looked like old adobe. Windows opened to the street, and a little brook trickled by just behind the restaurant. The kitchen was in full view of the restaurant, behind a counter where the one waiter moved about, shouting orders to the cook, collecting plates as they were prepared. Huge copper pots hung from the ceiling.

The prices, River could see, were ridiculously cheap. The waiter spoke little to no English but that didn't matter; Natal gave him her order and River grinned and pointed to the menu; the waiter laughed with them both, shaking his head at the American tourist, but doing so good-naturedly. River and Natal had a delicious local red wine and *empadinhas*.

River actually knew what he was ordering. Bars where busy Brazilians picked up a few *empadinhas* to eat while walking on their way filled many of the streets. *Botecos*—or street-side restaurants with just a few stools—also served them. They were pastries stuffed with beef, fish, chicken, or cheese, and maybe even vegetables. But Natal told him that these were the best he would ever have.

And they were.

As was the wine.

It had no name. It was from the owner's own little vineyard—and his basement winery.

As they ate, Natal teased him and taught him words in Portuguese, laughing at his pronunciation. He teased her back for her accent.

The little restaurant only seated perhaps twenty, and still it was loud, with the waiter calling his orders, the cook calling out what was ready—and a single entertainer, a guitar in his hands, walking from table to table to croon out a number. Natal told River that he was singing old Brazilian favorites. One song was by Chico Buarque, and it was called "Roda Viva." Natal explained to River that it had been written in 1968 and protested the dictatorship that had existed in the country in the 1960s and '70s. The protest was subtle—but if you knew the language and the words, you knew that it was a protest. Chico Buarque had been one of the most exceptional musicians to come out of Brazil.

"We try—but as you know," Natal said, "politics can be very ugly. We were, of course, colonized as a Portuguese holding. We were all colonies—all in the New World."

"Yes," River agreed. "Moneymaking stepchildren of great European powers."

Natal grinned. "And not that we don't want to be friends with all those European powers. The United States claimed independence and went to war in 1776, yes? Here, we were much the same. Simón Bolívar's determination and leadership gained independence for Venezuela, Colombia, Ecuador, Peru, Bolivia, and Panama—he was probably the greatest general South America has ever known, and he tends to be the general people know of in other countries. He had pretty much defeated the Spanish and made most of the Spanish holdings independent by 1822, and that was when Prince Pedro de Alcântara, who was the son of King John the Sixth of Portugal, proclaimed independence—by popular demand of the people. Our people fought for independence and won. Of course, we all know that just winning independence does not necessarily make a perfect place for all."

"I don't think there will ever be a perfect place," River said.

But being here with you—that might be as perfect as it can get.

He refrained from saying the words—he didn't want to scare her away.

"No," Natal agreed solemnly. "In 1889, Marshal Deodoro da Fonseca carried out a coup d'état and declared we were a republic. The power was in the hands of the rich, yes—as it was in most places."

River smiled at her—glad he'd loved her country enough to read up on it in plenty of history books. "A 'bloodless' coup happened in 1930," he said. "Getúlio Vargas came to power. Then, during the late thirties and early forties, the *Estado Novo* were up in the driver's seat—with some ties to fascism, right?"

She cocked her head, grinning. "So, you really do read. And study."

"Of course. I love Brazil."

"We still have problems."

"Every country out there does."

She laughed. "The Swiss? Not so much, I think. We struggled along. We had a mess of wavering and instability between 1946 and 1964, and, of course, tons of European immigrants, including those who were running from rightful persecution—those who did horrible things in World War Two. Still, in 1945, the modern constitution was passed, and we had what they called the 'populist years.'" She made a face. "Not so good, really. And sadly, we then had the bad years that Buarque sang about—the military dictatorship from 1964 to 1985." She looked at him oddly. "I believe that documents have shown that the United States might have been involved in some choices there."

"I love my country too," River told her. "But loving it doesn't mean that I believe we have always been right. After all, we massacred much of our native population."

"Conquerors conquer," she said. "Anyway, the dictatorship was defeated by a vote in 1985. Then we had terrible economic times, but since then, we've had a few good men and now, today, we try very hard for a stable government and to be a part of the world that is equal and humane and growing and we . . . we are a good people, really, living in a beautiful land! We're different, very different. We were colonized by the Portuguese—not the Spanish, English, or Dutch. Our men were, hmm, I think the term is 'hard up,' but it led to good things—a real mix of people! We celebrate our European heritage, our native heritage, and our African heritage all at once."

He laughed. "You don't have to sell me—I've told you. I love Brazil very much."

Toward the end of the meal she grew somber. "So. Will you just wander forever?"

"Maybe. Maybe I'll live here."

"Why do you hate your own country?"

"I don't hate my own country," he told her. "I—I told you, I love my country."

She sat back straight in her chair as if she were a stuffy doctor. "Yet you have . . . issues."

"Everyone has issues," he told her.

"You don't talk about war."

Had he mentioned his occupation as a soldier? "No one should talk about war," he said.

The air seemed to be filled with smoke.

There was no smoke in the place. None at all.

River tried to sit still; he tried not to duck, not to appear a fool. But he could hear the whistling again—the whistling that meant a bomb was coming.

And through it all that weird scent, not of fire now—but of pancakes.

She set her hand on his. "I'm sorry. We'll not talk of war. We'll talk of the goodness of man."

He forced a small smile and wagged a stern finger at her. "When we're good, we don't steal coins."

She pouted. "I left her all my clothes."

He shrugged. "What if she didn't want clothes?"

"She did—my clothes were much better than hers."

"Okay, but we pay from now on."

She shook her head. "I didn't think . . . I didn't think you had much money. I wanted to do things with you—it seemed best."

"I have money," he told her.

She tossed her hair back with a lazy hand. "Okay," she said. "Okay. I like this word—*okay*. Easy. Nice."

"It became popular in America when Van Buren was running for president," he told her. "He was nick-named 'Old Kinderhook' and his supporters formed the OK Club. But some say it's from the Scots—*och aye*—and some say it's from the French—Aux Cayes—which was a port in Haiti with excellent rum. I don't know—but it is a good word."

She stared at him, her surprise obvious.

"Hey, I read." He grinned. "I like *obrigado*."

"Thank you," she translated. "And you just like

that word because you use it often. You're nice." Her gaze flickered to his mouth. "Too nice, really." She traced River's hand with her own, sending a shiver down his spine.

The wandering musician appeared suddenly at their table. Natal leaned closer to River. "Robert Carlos—a song from the early 1970s. Very beautiful. 'Detalhes.' It is a love song," she added, her eyes twinkling.

The strumming musician sang a little off-key. But what he lacked in vocal grace he made up for with enthusiasm and drama. He seemed a little old and a little worn, just like the restaurant, and yet he was perfect.

When he was done, he stood there grinning at them—waiting. River tipped him handsomely, and the man moved on.

Natal squeezed River's hands. "Let's get our bill—we haven't taken the cog train yet and you said that we would do that."

"Yes, yes, of course, let's do that."

They did, enjoying every minute on the cog train that took them up to the Christ the Redeemer statue.

When they were close, the statue was even more immense than he remembered. Getting off the train, Natal wanted to take the 220 steps that led to the base of the statue rather than the escalators. He tried to keep up with her—she was fast, but he caught her as they reached the base. She laughed. "It's one of the new Seven Wonders of the World, you know," she told him. "It's damaged—and it's fixed. Now, it means Rio!"

"It's immense, it's majestic, it's wonderful—and I've never seen it as I'm seeing it now, because of you," River told her. "My friend."

They were close, so close he could have taken her in his arms and kissed her. She would have fallen into them, held him in return, kissed him back.

And yet, suddenly, she backed away, looking at the ground. "We—we are friends. I tease too much."

"No."

"I am a free spirit. You are a free spirit."

"Of course."

"Let's just . . . have fun. Have fun with me. Let's enjoy our time."

He'd pushed too hard. River took a step back, though he wanted nothing more than to draw her to him and demand to know what was going on with her life, what caused these sudden moments of gravity.

He knew that he couldn't. If she walked away . . .

"Just fun," he said, though it pained him to do so.

She grinned and seemed easier. "I will write about this," she told him. "I will write about that little girl—the one craning her neck. I will write about the wonder in her eyes. I will write about the statue—how beautiful it is, and how it has become the icon of Rio."

"Will you write about the government too?" he asked.

"The government has always seen to it that the statue is cared for."

He nodded. "But the government doesn't always see laws as being the same for all men."

"In any government there are those who serve—and those who wish to be served."

"And there are corrupt police who are blind to the antics of some men."

Her eyes narrowed. "Here—and everywhere."

"But we can't let them get away with what they do," he pressed.

"What are you getting at?" she asked sharply, crossing her arms tightly.

"You've heard of Tio Amato?"

Something flashed in her eyes, gone before River could interpret it. "I don't want to write about people like him. I prefer to write about *the* people." Her voice changed. "The farmers. The men with their fields and their trucks and the women who raise their children and bake and create families. I like to know how they think and feel. They are real—not those who posture and . . . never mind. Let's not think of anything bad or evil now. We are almost in the arms of the Redeemer."

For a moment, he was tempted to argue back, to make her understand that evil couldn't be so easily dismissed. Yet, wasn't that exactly what he'd been doing? Using Natal to distract him from his darker thoughts?

What sort of man did that make him?

"Well, technically, we're nowhere near the arms," he said at last, not ready to reveal himself as a hypocrite. "They're way above the ground!"

She wrinkled her nose. "I don't like technicality. Feel the arms—so good. So kind. Welcoming all—welcoming all to Rio." She grinned, and suddenly backed into the crowd that had formed behind them. "Hide and seek!" she mouthed.

She disappeared. River tried to smile—to enjoy the game.

But she'd disappeared so easily.

What if he couldn't find her?

He began to mill through the crowd, seeking her out. He walked the entire circumference of the base. He didn't see her.

And then, as he rounded a corner one more time . . .

She was there.

Grinning, laughing, delighted that she had eluded him for so long.

"Now you," she insisted.

"No, really," he said.

"But it's your turn."

"I'm afraid that you won't want to find me."

"But I will, of course. I will always find you," she told him. "We're both free—but I'll always find you."

He nodded, watching her. "Freedom is good. As long as it's not used to hurt other people."

She cast her head at an angle, studying him. "I live to please myself—but never to hurt others," she told him.

"Let's get in line for the cog train," he said. "There is someone I have to pick up—someone we need to be with."

She hesitated. "I don't—I don't wish to meet others. What we have together should just be together."

"You won't mind this friend—I know you won't. It's my dog, Convict."

"Dog? And you named him Convict?"

He shrugged sheepishly. "I stole him. But he was being mistreated."

She smiled and touched his arm. "I would love to see your dog."

"And I would love for you to meet him."

She seemed a little tired as they made their way back, quiet, content just to hold his hand or lean against him. When they reached the city, no one seemed to pay any attention as they hopped on the bus to take them to the outskirts and Beluga's place.

She stopped on the road, pulling back. "You stay here?" she asked him.

"Often."

She smiled. "I'll wait for you here. Don't stay long," she added softly.

"Beluga is the nicest man and Maria, who tends the place, is lovely too."

"I believe you."

"So come with me."

"No, I'm a little tired. Not my best. I'm happy to meet a dog tonight. Dogs don't judge. I will meet people at another time," she assured him.

"As you wish."

He didn't understand why she was loath to go with him, but he didn't push. He believed that if he gave her room, he'd come to know her better.

He saw Beluga—the big man was speaking to a young couple beneath one of the beautiful old trees by the main building. But tonight, River didn't want to wind up in conversation with his friend, so he slipped by, anxious to avoid him. He found Maria in the kitchen; she greeted him warmly and told him there was room for him that night. He smiled, gave her a kiss on the cheek, and told her that he had an adventure planned that night but promised that he'd see her later—without defining what *later* might mean. Convict was delighted to see him, and yet, a little hesitant about whether or not he should leave Maria.

"Your master is here!" she told the dog. "Go with River."

Convict barked happily. He wagged his tail. He was ready to go. River thanked Maria and she told him, "It's okay. Convict is a good dog. Even Beluga likes Convict. He likes to call him, 'mangy dog,' but then he sits with him with his big old hand on his head and they're both happy, like two old men!"

Convict raced ahead of River and out to the road, pausing and looking back now and then to make sure that River was with him. The dog greeted Natal as if they were long-lost friends, as if they had known one another forever.

Natal laughed and petted the dog and made a fuss over him—delighting the dog.

"He's a good friend, right?" River asked.

"A very good friend," Natal agreed.

"And now?"

"Now we wander. We find food. We find a place on a hill where we can look up and see the statue and the stars. But first, let's picnic somewhere special."

"And where is that?"

"I will show you. We'll buy some food first—even if we're not hungry right away, we now have a good friend to feed," she said, patting Convict.

He was all for that.

And since they were just heading into evening, there were many vendors on the road. River stopped a truck carrying produce; they went to a local shack of a store and bought meat and bread and a bottle of wine.

Natal led the way.

"We're going to need another blanket," he told her.

She grinned. "So we will. But it's not a bad thing, is it? You pay for the blanket—and you give it away to someone who needs it. That's a good thing."

He touched her face and smoothed her hair back. "Yes. Why not? A good thing. Well—do we hitch a ride? Take a bus?"

"We walk. Down an old path."

River purchased a blanket from a vendor, and then he and Natal took the road to a drive that was barely discernible in the grass and brush that was encroaching on it.

And halfway to their destination, River saw the house.

He paused and whistled softly.

It belonged in the pages of a book for those touring "haunted" places; it also belonged in a book where a digital company could wipe away time and the elements to show one of the most beautiful old Victorian houses ever.

"Abandoned? That's abandoned?" he asked.

Natal was silent for a moment and then said, "The owner couldn't pay his mortgage; I believe he angered the lender. He's not been gone that long—this is Brazil. Greenery grows quickly; rains take their toll."

"You mean that it went into foreclosure?" he asked.

"You could say that."

"And no one did anything with a place this beautiful?" River asked.

"Oh, the lender is doing something with it—he's leaving it as a warning to those who do not pay their bills. Who do not pay homage to those in power. Come—you must see it inside."

She headed quickly down the path; he followed. Dusk was just beginning to fall; the house with its balconies and beautiful gingerbread porch was cast in mixed tones of violet and gold and orange.

She was up the steps and through the door before River could catch up with her. When he passed through to the foyer and the grand parlor, he paused again. The house had been beautiful. Now, leaves cluttered the floor; there was a broken window right in front. And yet, the grace of the curving stairway, the charm of the fireplace and hearth, remained.

"Come upstairs—we'll picnic there!" she said.

As usual, she scampered ahead of him.

He caught a glimpse of her as she hurried into a room. He followed.

The shadows of dusk sat over the room, erasing some of the cruelty of time. Large French doors opened to the balcony.

Natal threw open the doors. The rising moon was full that night; patterns of light swept in from both the dying sun and that newborn orb, and there seemed nothing as beautiful in the world as the room, the open doors, and Natal—standing out on the balcony, her hands on the rail, caught in the mixture of light.

He walked out to her, aware that Convict followed him. He slipped his arms around her. For a moment, she leaned back against him. He was certain that he physically *felt* her scent, light and yet sensual, sweet and evocative. He *breathed*—and it seemed that the very scent of her filled him and touched him.

"We'll picnic," she said, spinning away from him.

Deftly and swiftly, she threw the blanket out on the hardwood floor. It was evident that she knew the place and that she had come before. She found a lantern in the closet and set it at the edge of the blanket while she set out the food.

"Convict, for you—sausage!" she said.

Convict stayed beside River on the edge of the blanket, so River grabbed the sausage and fed the dog while Natal made plates for them. "We could come here again—light a fire in the fireplace and cook!" she said.

"We could," he agreed softly.

He watched her for a moment, then opened the wine he had bought and passed the bottle to her.

"We forgot cups," he realized.

She laughed. "This is not America; no red Solo cups. You know that."

He nodded and handed her the bottle; she took the first swig.

They ate. She talked about writing, about Brazil, about the wonder of Carnaval. Her eyes were bright as she described the dancing and the parades and the merriment. "We must go into the city for some of the parades," she said. "Remember I told you about the natives who danced naked when the first explorers came? Well, maybe that adds something to the sensuality of what happens here now, all the time. You must see some of our Carnaval dancers—they are so beautiful. They dance with scant costumes but move with such fluid grace and skill. Fast. They shake and rotate and move so that everyone who watches is mesmerized. I think perhaps we are so special and so free here because of those early people; they lived in their environment, as part of it. They welcomed the sun."

"We will," he said.

Those were the words. Spoken in a whisper. She set the bottle down and crawled to him on the blanket, her eyes filled with mischief as she looked into his. "River . . . like water. Cool and smooth." She put a hand on his chest.

He'd been afraid. Afraid that if he touched her, she'd disappear. But he reached out and cupped her chin in his hand, leaned toward her, and kissed her.

It was as if he actually breathed in her essence still; the longing for her filled him and became a physical ache as they kissed, hot, wet kisses, deep and insinuating, sweet and sloppy, and then impassioned.

She wore nothing under the peasant dress. Her flesh was as sweet as her lips. She was as giving and passionate in making love as she was in seeking life. He lay against her trembling, and he felt the silk of her hair and her flesh, felt the fever and fire in her lithe, leanly muscled body. She teased and touched in return and whispered.

And the sound of her whispers drove him further . . .

She rose over him, leaning down, the mischief in her eyes. And even in the midst of his hunger he reached up and touched her hair.

"You are freedom," he whispered. "The spirit of love and life . . . and freedom."

She grinned and eased against him. "And you are the spirit of a hot volcano," she teased.

"Volcanoes can be great adventures," he said.

"So I have discovered," she said. Then she kissed him. One of those hot, liquid kisses that seemed to awake everything in him, that made him everything she might want him to be.

They made love through the night. And at some point, spent and exhausted, he slept.

CHAPTER 11

When River awoke, he was newly aroused.

She was outside, standing on the balcony, naked and perfect in the rising sunlight, totally indifferent to her nudity and her beauty.

He walked over to her and slipped his arms around her.

"I am a liar," she said softly.

"A liar?"

She pushed away from the balcony and walked back into the room, finding her peasant dress and her shoes.

"Not so much a liar," she whispered, pausing for a minute and then meeting his eyes. "A dreamer," she said at last.

"Natal, what are you talking about?"

"I have to go," she said.

"Go—go where?"

"Home," she told him. She looked away from him. "I should not have been with you because . . . because you are . . . different. You are somehow . . . real. When I saw you, when we met, it was so spontaneous and, I don't mean to turn this into a cliché, but it seemed . . . right. I'm a free spirit, yes, but I'm usually decent and honest."

"You are beautifully decent and honest," he assured her.

She looked at him sadly. "No. Usually, but I wanted . . . I wanted what I saw in you. At first, it was just fun. But then, I had to keep seeing you. It was like reaching for a star that I couldn't have, but there you were and . . . I reached." She paused. "River, I have deceived you."

"I still don't understand."

"I live with a man," she said in a broken whisper.

He felt as if he'd been slapped, as if the air had been knocked out of him. As if *life* had been knocked out of him. "A man?"

"His money is why I can write, why I can go where I please, and why," she added, "I can say I am a free spirit."

River just stared at her. He felt frozen. She lived with a man. "Who? Your husband?"

Natal shook her head but looked as miserable as ever. "His name is Reed Amato."

No. Surely not.

Amato. She lived with Amato.

He wasn't angry; he was desperate. There had to be a way to get her to leave such a man.

He strode toward her but she put up a hand and said, "I'm so sorry. You have a right to be angry."

"I'm not angry. I don't want you to go. I can . . . help you. I can get you out of there."

"No. Please, let it be as it is now. If you don't want to see me again—"

"I will always want to see you again."

"Even if I'm not as free as . . . as free as I pretend?" She looked down. "Even if I am a liar?"

"Natal, I swear, I will always want to see you."

Her eyes searched his; she believed him. She smiled sadly. Her voice was soft, barely a whisper, when she said, "Then I will see you again, but now . . ."

"Natal—"

"Please . . . don't try to stop me. I am going home. There are many reasons. And you are not to follow me there. Reed Amato is . . . he's not a nice man. Not to others. You are not to follow me—I will never see you again if you do. Do you understand? It's dangerous."

"I'm not afraid of Tio Amato. I'm not afraid of any danger he offers. Leave him. I will be there for you; I will see that you can live and write and dream. I can see that you are truly a free spirit."

She shook her head and stepped back. "No, don't you understand? This house—it stands as it does because of Reed Amato. Because the owner didn't listen to him and Reed ruined him and his family. I don't know exactly how he does what he does, and

I don't want to believe he does what he does . . . I don't see what happens. I wouldn't have lived with him, ever. If I had realized just—just how he had come to be so rich and have so much power. But, River, listen to me. I don't know what I want yet, but I don't want you near him. Don't you understand me yet? Those who cross him sometimes lose more than their houses. They—they disappear."

"And don't you understand me yet?" he asked softly. "I'm not afraid of him. I'll get you away from him."

"And if you're not afraid, you're stupid."

"We won't be stupid—we'll just get the hell away. Look, I believe you. I believe that he's a very dangerous man. I think I saw . . . I think I know that you're right and that he does kill people or have them killed. Natal—you have to get away from him!"

He tried to walk toward her again. She threw her hands up and stepped back again. "No! I am afraid—but not for me. For you. And right now . . . now I must go. And I must think and try to see if I believe . . . never mind. Right now, I simply must go. And tonight—for me, if you ever want to see me again—you must leave it alone. I'm sorry—I'm so sorry."

And with those words, she fled.

Convict barked as River flew from the house, racing after her.

But as quickly as he could move, he didn't catch up with her.

She was a free spirit—or so she'd said. This was her home. It was as if she could disappear into thin air.

CHAPTER 12

River made his way to Beluga's hostel. His old friend was sitting outside with one of his cigars.

River found himself thinking that Beluga would have made an excellent action star. He might have given up professional fighting and used his money to buy his hostel, but he was still in ruggedly fit shape. He envied Beluga for having found his place in the world. He was happy in it. He loved the people who came through and he was happy to provide affordable accommodations for young people—and for older people too, who might not have been able to travel if it weren't for Beluga and men like him.

Beluga grinned lazily at him, enjoying the cool breeze. He pointed to a nearby chair and waved his cigar in the air as he said, "River. You sleep here? We have plenty of room tonight."

"I don't know yet," River replied, hedging. His feet had taken him here, but he felt restless. It tore at him to know that Natal was with Reed Amato. She called herself a free spirit, but she wasn't free if she was tied to that man. And yet she'd been with River.

He didn't like the idea of being with another man's woman—and yet, he would take whatever Natal had to give. He wondered if he'd be as disturbed—since they had barely met and he had no right to jealousy—if it weren't a man like "Tio" Reed Amato.

"You don't know? It's already afternoon," Beluga said. "Late afternoon."

River shrugged. He was tempted to go into town. He wanted to look through the gates to the great house where Tio Amato lived and reigned over the countryside.

Why?

Would he see her? Would she be laughing, smiling, talking about her freedom and her free spirit with the man? Or would River see something that he didn't like—something that would hurt him? Natal looking miserable as Tio Amato ordered her around.

Most likely, he thought, he wouldn't see anything at all. There were gates and a high wall and within his mansion, Amato probably kept his draperies shut.

"What do women want in a man?" he asked Beluga.

"You've found a woman?" Beluga asked.

"No, not really. I've found a . . . a minor flirtation." Minor flirtation was nothing compared to what he felt for Natal. "She's otherwise engaged. But I'm curious—what is it that they want?"

Beluga loosed one of his hearty laughs. "I say, I don't know what a woman wants since a woman has not stayed with me in years. I had my great love . . . now, I have what the world allows me now and then. Ah, yes, there is Maria—she is the woman in my life and she is like my sister. A good worker and she looks after me. But as to love, my friend? Love is for the young. For the adventurous. There is that wild and wonderful feeling that teases the heart and the senses—it is wanting what one doesn't have. Then there's the magic of that feeling—and being loved in return. Glorious days. Sunshine fills them even when it rains. But, alas, then there is marriage or commitment and the real world. No matter how much of an adventurer a man may think himself, the world intrudes. Bills and babies, my friend, bills and babies. If the two are good together, that feeling of *being* in love deepens and grows and there is still love. But the scent of flowers and perfume is replaced by baby poop, and romantic dinners become a struggle to budget."

River laughed. "I didn't ask what happened to love, my friend. Love is something that we feed and foster, and we hurt one another, but then . . . we are still there. If the love isn't real—or strong enough to survive life or someone better who walks by and seems to promise more—then it all falls apart. It can be real—and last. But that's not what I'm getting at. What I asked is, what is it that you think women want? Or, perhaps, why do they say they want one thing but become bound to another?"

Beluga gave that grave thought. "What do they want? Ah, maybe, when the tender teen years are gone, they want to know that they will have a life. I saw a funny picture on Facebook once—"

"You have a Facebook page?"

"Of course—and you should too. It helps you maintain ties with people."

River didn't want any ties.

"So what was the picture?"

"It was of a beautiful woman in a little tiny bathing suit. Nothing to it in the rear—a very nice rear, by the way."

"A thong," River offered.

Beluga nodded. "This woman, with long dark glossy hair and a beautiful body, is walking with a man who looks like a thousand pounds of ugly. And there's a caption to it that says, 'Yes, he has more money than you.'"

"Very cute," River said. "But I don't believe that. Not all women want money."

"No, they don't," Beluga agreed. "What can I say? All women are different. I don't know what they want. Maybe some of them want a nest—somewhere they can make their home. Perhaps they want to fly and party and play. But they want a home to go to when they're tired. More than that, maybe, they need to feel that they are adored and needed. Yes, just love. Real love. If you love a woman with all your heart—but maintain your soul, the *you* she fell in love with—

you will find what you're looking for. That's it in this world, River. We need to care, and have others care for us. That's what is good about us, eh? 'Cause there's a lot that's very bad in human nature. Love—give her love. Honest love. And then, I believe, a good woman will be there for you."

River stood up. "Can I use the shower and maybe get some coffee?"

Beluga seemed to consider his request. "Yes, but I need payment."

"Of course."

"Not in money. I would like a drawing."

"A drawing of anything in particular?"

"Yes—your woman."

"Well, sadly, she's not my woman."

"Your flirtation, then—I would like a drawing of this woman, yes? Maybe I'll see the future in your drawing. Or, at least, tell you if she's a good woman or not."

"You know her, Beluga. Or you have seen her. I first saw her here—she must have taken a bed for the night just a day or so ago."

"I don't remember a beautiful woman," Beluga said. "But maybe Maria let her in."

River drew out his sketchpad. For a minute, he closed his eyes. He envisioned Natal. He saw the sun in her hair and saw the laughter in her eyes when she teased. He saw everything that he loved about her—he thought that he saw her spirit and her sense of freedom.

It wasn't real.

Or, it was. In her heart, it was real. But perhaps Beluga was right. She liked to fly—but return to a nest where she knew that she was loved and protected.

He drew. Beluga, at his side, watching him, drew in a breath now and then.

River's fingers began to fly. He shaded areas, drew back, smudged in others. And when he was done, he knew that the drawing—done so quickly with night falling and Beluga looking over his shoulder—was one of his best.

It was Natal. And while it was nothing but pencil on paper, it captured the essence of the woman as River saw her—as he had fallen in love with her.

Mischief was in her eyes—as well as kindness. The beauty of her face and perfection of her features were enhanced by the light that seemed to shimmer from her. The likeness was so real, River almost expected her to come to life and speak to him.

"It's magnificent," Beluga said. "I can't take this for just a shower and some coffee."

"Then take it because you're my friend. It's a gift. I can draw her again. I could draw her forever."

Beluga, holding the picture, looked down at him. "One day, I believe, you will be a great artist. And I will be rich too, because I will have your early drawings. But this one I will never sell."

River grinned. "I'm taking my shower now."

Convict whined when River approached. River patted his head. "Stay with Beluga for a bit—then run and see Maria. She'll have something for you, I'm sure. Then we'll be on our way."

Convict curled up by Beluga.

River showered and dressed, taking more care than usual. As he suspected, by the time he came out, Convict was in the kitchen with Maria and the woman was feeding him scraps.

"He is the best beggar in the world," Maria huffed, stroking the dog while he ate.

"He's not begging, not really," River said.

"Oh? Then, what?"

"He's performing for pay—his performance happens to be a sad face and a lot of whining, but it's a performance."

Maria laughed. "And I suppose you have come for coffee? Will you eat something?"

"I would love coffee. But you don't need to feed me."

Maria felt a need to feed everyone. He wound up sitting at the table with a bowl of delicious stew. He didn't know what it was—he didn't ask. It was good.

As he ate, he asked her, "Maria, do you remember Natal? The beautiful young woman who was here a few nights ago?"

"*Americana*?" Maria asked.

"No, no. Brazilian."

Maria frowned. "We were very busy, many pretty young girls—ah, Canadian girls, yes, I think. But, a Brazilian woman . . . ?"

"It would have been before the night you were so busy," he said.

Maria shook her head. "No, I don't remember a Brazilian woman. She was here? You are certain?"

He was about to say yes. Then he lowered his head over his stew, smiling.

It was Natal.

She had somehow snuck in without paying. That was her way; she simply liked the game of it. Or, perhaps financially, Tio Amato held her on a tight leash.

"Maybe I'm mistaken. I thought I saw her here first. I might have just seen her likeness in the paper," he said.

Maria shrugged and went about her work. A few minutes later, River thanked her, called to Convict, and was on his way.

He and Convict easily hitched a ride into the city. When they arrived, they had to walk the final leg to the giant compound that was Tio Amato's, but River didn't mind. He didn't even know what he was doing—or why he was doing it.

Convict liked the walk too.

River reached the compound and stood across the street. For a long moment he just stared at the grandeur of the little empire Tio Amato had created for himself.

The structure and property were beautiful—truly fit for a king. The architecture was fairly modern; River thought that it had been built perhaps in the early seventies. The estate had to cover an acre or perhaps two within the city. The wall surrounded it all. The house itself had to have been about ten thousand square feet. It was three stories high, painted not white but an opaque color that would set it apart. A porch led to the front door and the door itself was arched. Above it were elegant carvings and what must have been Amato's coat of arms.

The yard was equally splendid. Matching fountains—with Perseus shooting an arrow—stood on either side of the elegantly tiled walk that led to the porch.

Great gates were the only break in the stone wall, which stood about ten feet high, keeping visitors out. The gates, ornate and also topped with the coat of arms, opened and closed for cars to come in and out and sweep through the arc of a driveway that allowed for visitors to get out at the front porch and the door.

It seemed that while people were meant to be kept out, they were also meant to be able to see in.

See the wealth, perhaps.

See the power.

Because it was easy to see the house—at a bit of a distance—from the street.

Elegant etched-glass windows adorned the double front doors.

Picture windows allowed those inside to look out on the world.

Out on the little people.

But those picture windows allowed those who looked through the gates to look right into the center of the house as well.

The people of Brazil could look in—and see how the king reigned in his glorious mansion.

And River could see—he could clearly see. The windows opened to the elegant living room, which seemed to be filled with fine plush chairs and sofas and antique shelves and tables and a sumptuous chandelier.

All seemed to glisten in the myriad crystal light of that chandelier.

There were windows in the back of the living room as well. The room was lit up—but so was the patio and the charming pool and grotto beyond.

Tio Amato had to have arranged it all so that even the back could be seen from the street. Passersby might look in on his shimmering parties. They might see the beautiful people who lived there, or played at the pool or by the grotto.

Now it was quiet, though.

Through the windows, River could see that Grecian urns sat amid flower beds behind the crystal waters of the pool; tables and lounge chairs were set on a tiled porch that led to the pool, all of it enviable—all of it like a fantasy, especially as seen through the windows.

Standing there with Convict obediently seated at his side, River viewed it all.

He didn't envy Tio Amato a thing.

The house was ostentatious, and it wasn't something that mattered in the least. It was a showplace—because Tio Amato felt that he had to prove himself to the world.

River thought that the man was such a fool, because he himself knew what was important. River didn't care about the mansion or the property or the flowers and silver within; he cared about Natal.

Natal was more beautiful than any piece of crystal, more precious than a house or land or any *thing* that a man might own.

He smiled.

But, of course, Natal could not be owned.

Tio Amato didn't realize that yet; River was ahead. He knew. Even if Natal didn't fully know it yet herself. Her words that she would really free herself needed to reach her soul and her will.

And they would.

But while River saw Tio Amato—sitting in his great plush reading chair, the day's newspaper in his hand—he didn't see Natal.

Amato was wearing an elegant crimson silk smoking jacket—how apropos. He was indulging in a large cigar and a snifter of brandy as he read. His feet rested upon a pillow on a footstool before him.

River must have stood there—just watching and waiting—for an hour. But Natal didn't appear. She was asleep, he thought. She was asleep—and avoiding Amato because she didn't want to be with him.

In his heart and prayers, River knew, she wanted to be with him.

At last, he left his vigil at the house, his heart heavy.

"I couldn't see her," he said, looking down at Convict. The dog perked up at River's voice, tail wagging.

And what had he expected? For Natal to leave the

house and fly toward him with open arms? She had a home and a job. She had a life outside of her relationship with River. And she'd told him not to come.

River remembered the way she'd fled from him that morning, without looking back.

Maybe he should have listened.

CHAPTER 13

But as they walked down the street away from the house, River paused and turned. He'd heard a car he'd paid no attention to at first.

Now, he did.

A large black limousine came out from the property.

He couldn't help but wonder if the car was following him.

The windows were tinted; he couldn't see within.

The car shot by him, and he told himself to relax. No doubt one of Tio Amato's paid men was leaving the estate on some errand. The drug lord was not having him followed.

Tio Amato didn't know that he existed.

"It's all in my head, huh, Convict? The man doesn't know I covet the woman living with him."

Convict barked.

He was halfway back to the road out to Beluga's, back to where he could try to hitch a ride for himself and Convict, when he noted the public bathrooms at the rest station off the main highway. He figured he'd make a quick stop—he might or might not get a ride and it would be a long walk.

"Convict, you're going to have to spare me a minute. It's not as easy for me as it is for you."

He tied the dog to a bike post by the men's bathroom and went in.

He was washing his hands when Convict started to bark. Glancing up in the mirror, he saw that another man was entering the restroom. He was about to apologize to the newcomer for the dog barking when the words froze in his throat.

He knew the man.

He was suddenly certain that this guy had been driving the black limo that had left Tio Amato's house.

It was the man he had seen at the race track; the same man who had given Theo so much trouble.

He started to turn but the man was fast. Before River knew it, the man was at his back—and his knife was at River's throat.

"Is the money all in the backpack?" the stranger asked, his English heavily accented.

"The money?" River repeated.

"Yeah, the money!"

"You're after my money?"

"All of it, rich boy. All of it. And if I don't get it the easy way, I will kill you. I'll drag your body out and dump it and no one will even notice for days that you're gone. You're nothing but a drifter, drifting here and there . . . and when you drift into a shallow grave, no one will know."

River was stunned. He'd been so certain that everything in life had to do with Natal—and through Natal, Tio Amato, and through Tio Amato, this man.

"You work for Tio Amato," he said. "You don't need money."

"That kind of money you have—I saw you at the track. Yes, I need that kind of money. Stupid—this is our place; this is my turn. Give it to me."

River could see the man's twisted reflection in the mirror. The waves created by the dull old glass seemed to emphasize everything that was ugly inside the man: the curl of his lip, the dull blades of his eyes, and the greed within them. He worked for a murderer—for a man so consumed with himself that the lives of others meant nothing to him.

"Now!" the man demanded.

River's training kicked in. He shifted in a split second, shoving the man against the sink and wall before hurling himself backward.

The fellow grunted in surprise, the breath taken from him, as River sent him crashing back into the far wall. The knife clattered from his hand as he stumbled for balance and to clear his head.

River quickly reached for the knife, stepping back.

"You're not taking anything of mine," he said evenly. Hadn't Tio Amato already taken from him the most precious person possible?

But that wasn't logical; this man was an extension of Tio Amato. Natal had been with Tio Amato before they had met. This man had nothing to do with his feelings of longing and frustration.

Logic didn't matter—this man, like his employer, thought that he could take whatever he wanted. He was just as bad.

He wasn't taking River's money—or his life.

"Get out of here—now," River demanded.

But the man let out a bellow like a raging bull. He thrust himself from the wall and came thundering across the few feet that separated them.

River never meant to stab him. He'd asked the bastard just to walk out.

But the stupid bull had plowed into him so quickly and with such impetus and venom that the knife . . .

It sank right into him. Right into his fat belly.

The man's eyes—stunned and glazing—stared up into River's with horror.

River was certain that he stared back at the man with equal dismay.

What have I done? he thought.

And he watched the man fall to the ground, the knife hilt protruding from his gut.

A sensation of panic filled him—*Run!* he told himself.

Then logic swept through his mind. He'd stabbed the man in self-defense. All he had to do was tell the authorities the truth.

No. Not where they were. Tio Amato, according to

Beluga, owned a number of policemen. He didn't want to call the police or be caught by them. Not here. Not in Rio. He needed to get the hell out. He slid the knife free from the man's gut—it would have his prints on it now—and slid it into his boot, wincing at the hot slick feel of the blood on the blade. Then he turned and calmly walked out, untying Convict as he did so. "Come on, boy," he said. "Time to take a long walk home, I think. Through the forest."

He looked up as he heard a sound.

Someone else was heading toward the restrooms.

Another man in a suit, this one blue with a matching blue fedora.

Did he see me? River wondered. *He was still at a distance.*

He might be another strongman for Tio Amato.

"Hey, excuse me!"

The man was calling out to him. With Convict's leash in his hand, River skirted around the restroom wall to the rear of the facility. He was lucky—he was facing one of the first richly forested regions that edged the city. He quickly slipped into the trees with the dog. In a matter of minutes, the growth was so dense that he could barely see himself.

His heart was pounding as he struggled through the vegetation.

He didn't even know if the bleeding man had been dead or not.

If he wasn't dead, he soon would be, the way the blood had been seeping from him.

River listened intently as he quickly put distance between himself and the restrooms. No sirens; no sounds of an ambulance or police.

Finally, he paused. He had to get across the road to walk the distance to the hostel. If no one was coming for him—at least not now—he needed a place to wash the blood from him.

He stopped in the forest, wiping the knife blade clean with a bandanna from his backpack. When he was certain he'd wiped away every possible fingerprint, he discarded the knife in a thick batch of prickly bushes.

His head was thudding.

He hated the fact that he might have killed.

For a moment he paused, clasping his hands to his ears and falling to his knees on the earth. He could hear it again, feel it again. The thunder in the earth when a bomb exploded.

The screams of men as they were hit by the shrapnel . . . as their limbs exploded along with the earth.

This time, the vision, the daydream—whatever it was—seemed to stay with him a long time. *Kill or be killed.*

He hadn't caused the fight; hadn't brought it on.

He'd begged the ass to leave him alone. The idiot had killed himself, rushing River—and meaning to kill.

The ground seemed to steady beneath him. The acrid scent of powder and ash left the air. He staggered back to his feet. Convict stood by him, licking his hand tentatively. He patted the dog's head reassuringly. "I'm okay, Convict. I'm okay."

Eventually, he made his way back to Beluga's.

To his surprise, Beluga was still outside.

He stopped a good distance away. He'd thought that he'd tell Beluga what had happened. Now, he wasn't sure.

Quickly, River tore off his shirt, stained with flecks of blood. He wiped his hands on it before pulling a clean shirt from his bag and throwing it on.

He kept the bloody shirt bunched tight in one hand as he approached his friend.

Say nothing. Say nothing.

"So, you didn't meet up with your lady friend?" Beluga asked.

River's heart sank. "And you didn't get off your butt and do anything else?" he responded, casually moving the hand that held the shirt behind his back.

"Indeed. I got up. I checked in on some people, helped Maria with the dishes."

"You did dishes?"

"Okay, so—no," Beluga admitted. "I brought them to the sink. And don't look at me like that. I work, I help with the laundry. Maria does the dishes because when she does them, they actually come out clean. Now, you. What of your great romance?"

"I'm trying to have a grand, sweeping, beautiful romance," River said. "It's not all that easy, you know?"

"Ah, love is never easy. But it's not going so well?" Beluga asked, frowning.

"No, not brilliantly, not at this moment. But it's going—it will just take time."

He was always open and easy—and honest—with Beluga. Tonight felt . . . wrong. He'd never lied to the man. But he couldn't tell him what had happened.

"I can still have a bed?" he asked.

"Yes. You can have the back room in my house all to yourself tonight."

River thanked him.

"Let Convict stay with me for a bit. He can enjoy the night air. And, you know, the longer he's out here, the less you have to worry about him using the bathroom, eh?" Beluga asked.

River forced a smile. "Convict is a good boy. He knows that his bathroom is outside."

"He is a good boy. He's a good dog." Beluga hesitated. "He's a good companion. I'm glad that you brought him."

"I'm sure he's glad too," River said, watching the way the dog sat at Beluga's side—and the way Beluga's giant hand fell gently on Convict's head.

"You look tired. Go. Go in."

"Thank you, Beluga. Good night."

Once inside he dropped his pack on his bunk and headed straight for the shared bathroom. Luckily, it was empty.

He washed his hands studiously. The blood seemed to be gone—but he kept washing. He checked his leg and his pants where the knife had been.

The blood was gone.

But he could still *feel* it.

It had been a long day. Emotionally searing. Funny, he could walk forever—hell, he could *run* forever—fetch, carry, tote, and haul, and not feel so tired.

He moved his pack and fell down on his bunk. For a while, sleep eluded him.

And then the dream came again. The awful sound of the explosions that seemed to ricochet in his skull. The stink of burning powder.

And burning flesh.

The screams of dying and injured men.

He fought to escape. To escape the dirt and the powder and the death . . .

The dream itself, perhaps.

But he didn't wake. He remained in the horrible mist caused by the explosion and he saw men—men everywhere. Armed and ready and hunting and then . . .

She walked into view. Light seemed to surround her. To break the mist. But the men saw her too. And then turned, as if they were hunting her . . . stalking her.

His men? The enemy? He couldn't see.

He shouted her name; he could hear himself, but even her name sounded strange in his ears, as if he were saying it wrong.

They were everywhere—men. The enemy. He had to fight them off—he had to reach her.

"River!"

He woke suddenly in a blind panic—fighting still.

"River!"

For a moment, he was still too dazed from his nightmare to react.

And then he saw a stranger standing over him.

A stranger in the uniform worn by the police of Rio de Janeiro.

Memory returned.

Panic seized him again. Instinct said that he should fight.

Logic warned him not to. He heard another voice speaking.

"River, calm down, it's me, Beluga!"

He blinked—and saw that Beluga stood by the officer. And he realized, just as he saw Beluga, that he had reacted by instinct. A soldier's instinct.

He'd reached into his bag and drawn his gun. A gun he shouldn't have had as an ex-pat in Brazil.

Again. Again—he'd drawn the gun again!

"He's all right; he's all right. Post-war stress—that's all. The gun isn't even loaded," Beluga told the officer. "Right, River?"

It wasn't right, but River nodded.

The police officer smiled sympathetically. *"Olá. Bom dia,"* he said. He seemed to struggle searching for words for a minute, seeking English in his mind. "You're a friend to Beluga. It's all right. He's friend, I'm friend. I did not see."

"Ricardo just stopped by to see me to say hello. And to help me get bums like you up and out so that we can clean for the day," Beluga said.

River scrambled up, tucking his old service weapon into his backpack, and quickly took the police officer's hand. *"Bom dia,"* he said. It was his turn to struggle, trying to remember his Portuguese. *"Como está?"*

Ricardo was pleased. He shook River's hand.

River looked at Beluga. "Ah, well, I'll get Convict and get out of your hair," he said. "Where is he?"

"Where do you think? In the kitchen with Maria."

River nodded to the policeman, smiling.

Backpack over his shoulder, he realized that he was almost bowing as he left the two men in the back room.

He hurried out to the kitchen.

"*Café*?" Maria asked.

He really needed to behave normally. "Sure. Thank you, Maria."

CHAPTER 14

It was a good thing, River supposed, that Beluga's police friend Ricardo had been at the hostel—and that River was up and getting on his way.

There was no telling when police who knew about the dead man in the restroom would come around. And if they came around when River was there, it wouldn't be good.

But he did his best to act normally. Beluga told him he could have a shower and his coffee and have a few minutes, but everyone else was up and gone and River needed to be gone too.

River tried to behave as he always did. He thanked Beluga, grabbed his pack, and he went to accept coffee from Maria.

While he was in the kitchen, Beluga came in. Convict trotted over to his friend, who slipped him a piece of sausage.

"Where's your friend?" River asked, trying to sound casual.

"Ricardo? He went on to work." Beluga was quiet for a moment. "I thought about telling him what you told me the other night. About the body. Ricardo—he's always been a good man. But . . ."

"You didn't tell him."

"No—because you never really know another man."

"No, you never do," River agreed.

"Hey," Beluga said, "you know, the dog doesn't take up a bed. He can stay."

River allowed himself to smile at that.

"I'm not sure when I'll be back," he warned. He hated leaving Convict, and yet . . .

It might be best, under his present circumstances. What if he was picked up and thrown in jail? What would happen to Convict? He could be put in a pound—or he could wander the streets and starve or be hit by a car or . . .

"Doesn't matter," Beluga said with a shrug. "Convict is okay. He'll be here when you come back—and I know you. It won't be that long."

It could be forever, River thought.

And if so, wasn't that best for the dog?

He nodded, squatting down and patting his companion. "You're the best," he told Convict. "But Beluga needs company. He talks about a woman, but he hasn't gotten one for himself yet, so . . . you keep him company."

"I can find a woman, you know."

"One to keep!" River teased.

Beluga waved a hand at him.

He'd tarried too long at the hostel, River thought. He thanked Maria and Beluga and then headed out.

"You're going to find your woman today, you think?" Beluga called as he was leaving.

"There's always that dream!" River called back to him.

Natal.

He winced as he hurried down the path from the hostel.

Natal.

Would she miss him?

Would he ever find her again?

He had to believe, he thought. Belief kept a man going.

As he hurried away, he was glad that he hadn't said anything to Beluga about the previous night—he would hate to ever put Beluga in a bad position. Beluga was probably a lousy liar—and River didn't want his friend to have to lie for him anyway.

He took the road toward town; he needed to hear what had happened and if the police had or hadn't found the man and if they were after him—if they had any idea that the act had been carried out by an American drifter.

He wasn't going to get on a bus and he wasn't going to hitchhike. Not today.

Nearing the city, he kept a sharp eye out for police. He zigzagged his walk, ever vigilant.

He passed one coffee stand where several policemen were enjoying an espresso. He thought about
sprinting quickly to the other side of the street, or
into traffic—anywhere—but controlled the impulse.

The policemen didn't even notice him.

He decided to find an out-of-the-way café where
he could buy a large coffee and scan a newspaper. He
chose one he knew and ducked into it.

It was a busy place. They had newspapers there
that were in Portuguese and English as well as Spanish, Italian, and German.

So many people, of so many nationalities, came
to Rio.

And many stayed.

He bought a double espresso and a pastry and almost bought another for the dog—and then remembered that Convict wasn't with him.

He found an outside table where he could keep his
back to the wall and his eyes on the street. As in many
areas of the city, he could look up—look up to the
Christ the Redeemer statue. When he did so, the sun
seemed to be brighter and golden light streamed back
down at him. In the light, he could see Natal, see her
smiling face, and hear her laughter.

The laughter seemed to change suddenly. It was a
child's laugh—as sweet as only a child's laugh could
be. Natal, he saw, in his golden-sunlit vision, was
holding the hand of a little girl.

For a moment the vision was so sweet and beautiful and *real* that he felt he could almost reach out
and touch the two. Something stirred in his memory.

Something he should be able to grasp—but just couldn't. The sun shifted—he was looking at nothing but the distant image of the statue. Everything—the tinkle of laughter, the golden visage—was gone.

He gave himself a mental shake and quickly began to read the paper. There was no mention of a death or a murder the night before.

Tension began to ease from him.

Then it returned.

His eye fell on an article stating that someone had found the body of the big man who had served Tio Amato, left in a pool of blood. Could the witness have been the other man who had been going to the men's restroom, the man who had hailed him?

River leafed through the paper, searching for the rest of the article. At last he found what he was searching for.

"'Victim of assault hospitalized; comatose, he can give police no leads to his attacker.'"

River quickly scanned the article. The police were not giving out information regarding the victim pending notification of his next of kin. While he remained unconscious, his vital signs were good and doctors were hoping for a recovery.

Relief flooded through him.

I didn't kill him. I didn't kill him. River reread the article, searching for anything that would indicate the police were looking for him. There was nothing.

Just as he was beginning to feel a bit at ease, a hand fell on his shoulder.

He instantly froze.

Instinct kicked in; the instinct to jump to his feet, grab his knife—which was no longer there!—and swing around to fight.

Somehow, logic intervened. He was in a busy coffee shop on a busy street. A fight would get him nowhere—and innocent people could be hurt.

"So, here you are!"

Only seconds had passed while he'd considered his options. And now, he was glad he hadn't moved.

It was Theo. Theo, who took the chair opposite him, grinned, and helped himself to River's double espresso.

"I've missed you, my friend!" Theo said. "Where have you been? Not at the track. And let me tell you—the track is not good without you. But I tell you—today is my day, now that I have found you. I have a lottery ticket. You must touch it—blow on it for me. Give it some River magic!"

River let out a breath. "Okay, hand over the ticket."

Theo did so. River put it between his hands. "This ticket—I give my luck to this ticket. Well, I give my gambling luck to this ticket—not the rest of my luck."

He held the ticket up then and softly puffed out a breath, then handed it back to Theo. "There you go—lucky ticket."

"You didn't need to give me all your gambling luck," Theo told him. "I wanted you to come to the track with me."

"Not today, my friend."

"Why? You suddenly decided to get a job in the

city? What—are you going to become a member of the nine-to-five establishment?"

River shook his head. "No. And I'm not sure there is such a thing anymore. But, I'm just not in a gambling mood. I am in a rambling mood. You go to the track. You have luck now. You'll do well."

"I'll do well to keep my head down. What if that big gorilla is there—Tio Amato's henchman? What will I do without you?" Theo asked.

River felt the tension sweep into his muscles. He willed it away.

"It's your lucky day. I've decreed it. If it's a lucky day, you won't see him. How's that?"

Theo sighed. "All right, but I will miss you. Ahha!" he said suddenly. He laughed, got up, and ran to the street. He stooped down where a group of people had just passed. He came up with a cigarette that had barely been lit. He grinned and walked back to River's table. "Smokers—and supposed smokers who have quit smoking—they light up and then see someone they know. Then they toss the cigarette down as if they were never holding it—as if no one can smell the smoke." He inhaled deeply. "Ah, this is good, very good. American and very long."

River folded the paper. "Enjoy. And enjoy the rest of the espresso."

"*Obrigado.*"

River grinned and looked around. He'd been sitting in one place too long. And he'd made a decision. Maybe he wasn't being pursued.

But maybe he shouldn't take chances. He was going to get a train ticket and move on for a few days.

As his eyes roamed the crowd, he suddenly did a double take.

Maybe he *was* being pursued!

There, at the service window, was a man. A man wearing a blue suit and a blue hat.

The same man who had been heading toward the men's restroom last night.

The same man who had called out to him.

The same man who had seen him.

He got to his feet abruptly.

"River, you okay?" Theo asked.

"Yeah, sorry, didn't mean to jiggle the table. I gotta go."

"You got a train to catch or something?"

"I just gotta move. You know that feeling."

Theo shrugged. "No, not really, but—"

"Bye, Theo," River said, starting to weave his way through the tables.

"*Ciao,* my friend!" Theo called.

River waved. He headed quickly down to the street and along it.

Turning back, he searched the crowd again.

There was no sign of the man in the blue suit.

Maybe he was just having coffee.

He had seen River the night before. Had he gotten a good look? River didn't know—it didn't matter. He had to keep moving.

He saw more police on the street and noticed every

officer he might not have paid the least heed to in days gone by. One officer directed traffic at a broken light. Two more walked the street. He saw a patrol car pass by.

He walked directly in front of a police car when he crossed the street to the train station.

No one paid him the least heed.

River zigzagged through the streets until he arrived in front of a kiosk offering train tickets. He stared at it a moment, then walked to the counter and in his faltering Portuguese asked, *"Fala inglês?"*

He noted the girl behind the counter. She was young, perhaps in her early twenties. She had a beautiful face with elegant cheekbones, long sweeping auburn hair, and friendly hazel eyes.

The girl looked him up and down and cracked a smile. "Oh, yes. I speak English. In fact," she said, lowering her voice, "it's the only language I speak halfway well. I should speak Portuguese better—I'm a grad student here. But I'm not that great. Still, I'm okay with advice about Brazil and I can crank out a train ticket easily enough."

It was nice to hear her voice and see her smile. She seemed the best of those to be found in his homeland. "Where are you doing your grad work?" he asked.

"Observatório Nacional," she told him. "Actually, one day, I want to work at NASA. And I will have a chance to go back and work at the Goddard Space Flight Center. But, I mean, I want to study the universe, so studying what's learned in other countries seems important too. Anyway, where would you like to go? São Paulo?"

São Paulo was a huge city—a great place to get lost. But it was also a place with a large police force, and perhaps too obvious a choice. Many people went south to São Paulo. "No, I think I'll go north."

"Ah, toward Natal—Rio Grande do Norte, Brazil!"

His breath hitched in his throat. "Pardon?"

"Natal, Rio Grande do Norte—it's a very beautiful area."

He lowered his head for a minute. Of course. He'd seen the area on his map of the country. He hadn't been there yet. But Natal. That was perfect. While he laid low, he could dream of the woman who had captured his heart and his imagination. He could enjoy the place that bore her name—and conjure a way to win her from Tio Amato. Even if the venture was doomed.

No. He could do it. He knew that he could—convince her she needed to be free of her fears—and she'd then be a truly free spirit who would come with him.

"You like it there?" he asked.

"I love it there. Beautiful beaches. I mean, it's Brazil. Beautiful beaches are everywhere. But I can promise you, it's nice, even more laid-back than it can be here. The people are very bohemian, very artsy. And friendly—natives and tourists."

He leaned closer to the window. "Where should I get the train?"

"I've convinced you?"

"Yes, sounds great."

"Well, there are three stations."

River's brow furrowed. "Not a lot of tourists—not where people would usually go," he said. "I like the smaller, local stations or stops."

"Go to the little station right on the outskirts of the city; the train makes a brief stop there. Don't take the train out of Méier station—not if you want to avoid a mass of preppy types. There will be throngs of tourists and suit wearers."

He lowered his eyes.

Yes, let me avoid the suits, he thought.

She produced a map. "You can slip on here at nine. Locals take the train here. It's very charming."

"Thank you," River told her. "How much—and when?"

"I'll sell you a ticket that you can use any time in the next twenty-four hours. Will that work? And I'll show you on the schedule where you should get on."

"When is the next?"

"Not until evening, I'm afraid. It is a 'night-owl' train and it will be there at five tomorrow. It seems like you're in a hurry, but if you miss the train you'll have all day tomorrow to pick up another. It leaves at eight; you must be on it."

River dug in his backpack for the money to buy the ticket. He paid her and she smiled.

"*Obrigado* to you, sir!" she said.

He left her and looked at one of the clocks atop the façade of an old building.

He had hours to kill even to take the first train.

Walking in the direction of the station the American girl had suggested, he sought out another coffee shop. It was in an alley shaded from the sun. If he sat in the back, he wouldn't be noticed. And there was a large clock on the newer building across the street—nowhere near as pretty as the old one, but it seemed to tell time correctly. He could watch it while he waited and not miss his train.

He bought more coffee—Theo had managed to snag most of his espresso anyway and he had a long time to stay up. He hadn't slept well; his sleep had been plagued by dreams.

Rio, he thought, had always been a dream for him.

For a moment, he paused, hearing the child's laughter in his mind again. Then it faded, as sweetly as the last savoring of a sugar drop on the tongue.

He gave himself another shake, opened his backpack, and took out his sketchbook.

He was secluded; he felt safe.

He began to sketch, not knowing his intent. Most of the time, he didn't.

Sometimes, he did scenery. And he loved to draw people. Beluga had always made a good subject. And Maria too.

No one had been as easy to draw as Natal. No drawing had ever come out as beautifully as the one he had done of Natal.

But he didn't draw her then. His pencil moved rapidly over the paper. He began to draw a scene of upheaval and horror. There were servicemen in it—

cold, dusty mountains in the background. The ground was exploding again, men flying in the air as if they'd been tossed as easily as basketballs.

A chill seemed to have settled over him as he drew. Then, as suddenly as he'd begun, he stopped. He studied what he had created. It was a war scene—one he knew too well. Combat had often been hand to hand; they went into villages where insurgents had dug in. And when they did . . .

There were grenades exploding, buried mines bursting into flames, men . . .

Dying.

But, he had survived. And come home . . .

Home was a blur; he'd had to get out.

He'd come to Brazil.

River blinked, staring at the page. He'd put things in there that didn't belong there.

Walking into the chaos was a man in a business suit. A business suit with a hat.

He was the man coming for River. The clock across the street bonged. Once, twice . . . it kept going. It was 7:00 P.M.

He couldn't believe so much time had passed. He looked around—even the waitstaff at the café had changed over. And if he didn't move, he'd miss the train.

He got up, stowed his sketchpad, and hurried down the street.

Rio tended to be a late-night city, and with Carnaval on the way, dusk seemed to arouse the city as if it truly woke up and found life when darkness came.

There were people everywhere, thronging the streets. As each day brought them closer to Mardi Gras, with Ash Wednesday to follow, people seemed to be in a greater fever to party as wildly as they might.

There were jugglers out on the street, musicians too many to count, dancers, clowns, all vying for a piece of the action—and attention.

Music blared from every nightclub.

River took in the sights and sounds as he hurried toward the station as best he could through the crowds. Everywhere, he looked for the man in the blue suit.

But when he glanced into one club that he was passing, he paused. His heart seemed to stand still before speeding into double-time.

He didn't see the man in the blue suit.

He saw Natal.

CHAPTER 15

She wore a colorful crop top with a brilliant red skirt that swirled and waved about her perfect legs as she moved to the music of a samba. Her dark hair traced her skirt's movements. Others in the room had stepped back.

All to watch her.

She moved with such joy. With so much life. She seemed to epitomize all that was right and wonderful and vibrant in Rio.

For a minute, he just stared, enchanted.

And then, hardly aware of what he was doing, he entered the club.

Natal spun, her dark hair flying and draping around her like a velvet cape.

And she saw him.

The smile she gave him seemed to radiate throughout his entire body. He felt as if that smile gave him light—and life.

Swaying to the music in the most sensual walk he'd ever seen, she came right up to him, slipping her arms around him and toying with his hair.

"Can you dance, drifter man?" she teased. "Can you move—like Brazil, like Rio?"

He should have felt awkward. He could barely find his tongue—a way to speak. But if he didn't, he feared she would go away.

"I can do anything," he said, "when I'm with you."

He knew, at the back of his mind, that he needed to get to the train station.

He knew he should leave.

He couldn't.

She drew him closer and he discovered that he could feel the music through her, move as she moved. It didn't take much. He'd seen the samba before . . . he'd played at it before. He'd never considered himself much of a dancer.

But the crowd around them was dancing too, drinking, laughing—and calling out in encouragement. Suddenly, he discovered that they had moved out into the streets, in the midst of a massive party. Bright, vibrant lights and colors abounded; fireworks went off over the water and streaked across the sky.

Someone handed him a slice of lemon, salted his hand, and gave him a shot glass. Natal had one too.

She laughed and sucked the lemon and then placed her lips on his hand to taste the salt there. "Quickly, drink!" she told him.

And he did. They thanked those around them and the music continued to throb like a pulse inside of him, but they weren't moving anymore.

They were just standing in the street, staring first at the sky bursting above them, then at one another.

"I thought you had to be home," he said softly.

"I do what I wish," was her response.

"Then you wish to go home?"

She looked him square in the eyes. "There are times I must."

He shook his head. "No. Not to him. Reed Amato is a bad man."

"Yes," she agreed.

His eyebrows arched. "But—"

She pressed her finger to his lips. "Not tonight," she said passionately. "Not tonight. We will not speak about him."

Every muscle in him seemed to tighten at her words. He couldn't push—he would lose her. But he had to make her see the danger she was in.

"I am with you tonight," she continued.

As she spoke, in the whir of colors around him, River found that his eyes suddenly focused on one.

Blue. Dark blue.

The man in the blue suit and the hat was there, just beyond them. He seemed to be intrigued by the celebration.

But he was looking.

Looking for River.

"I have to go," he said.

She stared at him, puzzled.

"From me?" she whispered.

"From here."

She studied him a moment, then caught his hand and tugged at it.

"Come," she told him.

Together they hurried through the crowd. Natal knew what she was doing; she led him swiftly and managed a unique pattern through the dancers and celebrants in the street. When he turned back, he saw people filling in the gaps their bodies had made—no one could follow them.

Natal led the way through street vendors and entertainers and then down a quiet street where there were few lights in the houses. Finally, they came to a gate. Behind it he could see a children's playground set and beyond that, paths through the trees and brush.

"Come," she said before climbing quickly over the gate.

He followed.

When they had both landed softly on the other side, she caught his hand again.

"Come—I know a place."

They ran across the children's play area, over a manicured lawn, and through to the trees. There were trails here, made up of soft earth and grasses and what looked like pine needles. She kept going until they broke through the trees to a small lake.

Lights from the now-distant city fell gently here, casting a soft white glow upon the water.

Natal stopped, gasping for breath and smiling at him. His own breathing came just as heavily.

"Here we are now," she said. She slipped off her shoes and headed down to the lake. Sitting by the water's edge, she tapped the surface with her foot, sending ripples onto the calm surface.

He sat beside her.

"We're safe now, safe here?" she asked.

"I think," he said softly.

"What were we running from?"

River hesitated, not sure how to answer. To tell the truth would mean admitting to having stabbed a man. He ran a hand behind his neck. He was supposed to have been on a train. As long as he remained in Rio, he wasn't safe—not with the blue-suited man following him.

Who was the man? Not a cop—he seemed to be alone as he came after River.

It occurred to him that the man might be another goon in the employ of Reed Amato. That he'd been sent to find River—and take the matter of revenge into his own hands.

"River?"

"It doesn't matter," he said. "With you is where I want to be. Even if you insist on being with a drug lord."

"I'm not with him," she asserted angrily.

"You go home to him."

"We argue," she said. "I am not his—he does not own me. No one can own me."

He wanted to believe that she hadn't *been with* Amato again since she had been with him—that he was what she needed, what she wanted.

"We'll stay here tonight?" he asked her.

She smiled at that. As her eyes met his, she untied the knot to her crop top, nestled between her breasts. She slowly removed the top, leaned forward, and kissed him. He drew her into his arms and slid his hands over her flesh, her bare breasts, as their lips met in something passionate and forceful and tender, liquid and intimate and beautiful.

She rose to let the skirt slip from her hips and was caught in the white light that gleamed in from the city. He looked at her body, lithe and graceful and beyond beautiful. Then he tossed his pack aside and scrambled out of his clothing, rising up to meet her.

But she leapt aside, avoiding him.

"Catch me!" she said softly, smiling broadly, and raced into the water.

He paused at the edge of the lake. She had swum out and was treading in the deep water, looking back at him. "Come in, *americano*!"

"Is it swimmable?"

She snorted. "Children swim here all the time."

River stripped off his clothes and stepped in and cursed at the frosty bite on his flesh. He could hear her laughing at his discomfort.

"Move about and it will not be so cold!" she told him.

"If I catch you, it won't be so cold," he assured her. When he was finally within reach, Natal dove, swimming away from him. They played the game several times.

She was laughing with delight when he finally caught her. She turned in his arms and their naked bodies touched fully, their legs entwining as they kissed and tread the water. The kiss broke and she swam from him again quickly, heading back to the shore.

He followed with all speed, and hurried out of the water to her.

She had no intention of eluding him then.

As they stood, naked, alone, surrounded by the pines and the whisper of the night, she had never appeared more beautiful. The moon played upon her sleek, damp skin, and she seemed like something out of a magical tale.

She stepped closer to him so their bodies touched and her warmth seemed to engulf him. He tenderly touched her damp hair, smoothing it from her face. They kissed again and sank back to the earth together.

There, upon the soft grass of the embankment, with the gentle lap of the water nearby and the music and the life and pulse of the city distantly behind them, they made love. And in the moment, in the loving, River dreamed that this was his life, that this could be his life . . .

Perhaps it had even been his life, but they had lost it somewhere.

He dozed without dreaming. When he awoke, she lay at his side, leaning on an elbow, studying him. He loved the look of her, the beauty of her every line and curve, the way her hair, just beginning to dry, curled around her shoulders and her breasts.

"I have to sketch you," he said. "You won't move?"

She grinned. "I will try not to move—that's the best I can promise."

He found his sketchpad and began to draw. She was stunning. It seemed that her life and vitality went into every movement of his pencil.

When he was done, he showed it to her.

"That's how you see me?"

"Yes. Perfection," he told her.

"But I'm not perfect. I have a funny little mole."

"In my eyes, you are perfect. You are a dream. You're life itself."

She rolled her eyes and shoved him playfully. "Now I'll draw you," she said, crossing her legs in front of her, natural and uninhibited. She took the pad and began to draw.

"Let me see," he said, when enough time had passed.

"Wait, wait . . ."

He forced himself to be patient. Then he looked. She burst into laughter.

She'd drawn nothing but a stick figure.

"Worth waiting for?" she teased.

He laughed, caught her by the shoulders, and bore her back down to the ground. He kissed her but then held his face above hers as he whispered, "You'll always be worth waiting for."

She caught her breath for a moment. "If you're ever looking for me . . . the statue. The statue of Christ the Redeemer. It's my favorite. I always go there."

"I don't need to look for you. I have you here, in my arms," he said.

She smiled and told him, "There is nowhere I would rather be."

They made love again. Slowly. As if they had all the time in the world.

And then they made love again.

When he fell asleep next, it was the deep sleep of someone truly, utterly at peace.

River woke slowly to the sound of birds chirping. He felt the grass and earth beneath him and opened his eyes, squinting at the sunlight shining through the trees.

And there was a boy there—a kid of about ten—staring at him.

It occurred to River that he was stark naked, lying by a lake. He leapt to his feet, looking for Natal, trying to cover himself and find a way to cover her too.

But Natal wasn't there. He quickly scanned the entire area.

Her clothing was gone; she was gone.

He grabbed his clothes and quickly stumbled into them—pants first. The kid continued to stare at him. River waved a hand in the air.

"Hey, leave me alone, will you?" But the boy didn't move.

Dressed once more, River grabbed his backpack and his drawing pad.

He saw the last drawing done—the stick figure, by

Natal. He grinned. He loved stick figures. He had once drawn them for . . .

The thought eluded him and it didn't matter.

Because printed on the drawing were the words *Christ the Redeemer.*

Had she written it? Was it a message to him—to come and find her?

He thought about his train ticket. He could buy another.

"Hey, kid, show's over—scram!" he said, packing the sketchpad in his pack and throwing it over his shoulder.

Without warning, the kid screamed something. River fought through the blurry scramble of his mind to translate the Portuguese.

"Here—he's over here!" the kid had called.

River looked up. Halfway around the lake, he saw a man. A man wearing a blue suit—and a blue hat.

He turned and started to walk in the other direction, his heart quickening.

He quickly came to a dead halt, staring straight ahead in disbelief.

Another man in a blue suit was right in front of him. There was more than one?

It was impossible for it to have been the same person—absolutely impossible that any man could have come around so quickly, impossible for one man to be in two places.

He couldn't go forward and he couldn't go back.

River hopped past the kid and tore onto one of the pine-needle-laden trails through the trees.

CHAPTER 16

What the hell? Was the damned man a clone?

No, he had to be logical and not be so panicked that he went off and got himself caught by letting facts confuse him. There were two of them. They were both tall and well-built—muscled—River thought, diving through the trails. He didn't know how, but he was determined to lose both men and find a place to study them.

Eluding them came first—and he managed that easily enough. He could hear them thrashing about but they were at least a quarter of a football field away from him. Dodging behind a tall, thick tree, he paused to breathe, adjust the backpack, and watch them.

They weren't wearing identical suits—and neither

were they clones or identical men—but they were damned close. Only one was still wearing his hat. The other was clean-shaven and bald. They both appeared to be in their early thirties or a little older.

Hitmen? Henchmen? Did they work for Tio Amato?

Or were they just a branch of the Brazilian police that he didn't know? Why would they be—why would a special police force be after someone who had beat up a lowlife like the man who had tried to kill him?

He didn't know—he just knew that he needed to get the hell away from them.

The park, he saw by daylight, had a number of entrances—he could see that none of them had closed gates now that morning had come. He walked away from the direction the men were searching and hurried out into the street. With only a couple of days to go now to Carnaval, the streets were bursting with humanity—the population having grown incrementally every day of the last week. In a number of the city squares in all the *bairros*, River quickly saw the entertainment was just about nonstop.

It was easy to blend in with the crowd.

But then what? he wondered. *Would the men in the blue suits be after him forever now?*

He could feel his train ticket in his pocket. He still had all day to catch the train. Except that he wouldn't be catching it until that night.

He would head up to the Christ the Redeemer statue.

Because Natal might be there. And he knew he'd let his ticket go—and that he would go there every day until either she came or the men in blue managed to catch up with him and subdue him.

Who the hell were they?

So far, at least, it didn't seem that any of the city's regular officers were after him.

It was just these men in blue. Two of them now.

How many of them might there be? he wondered.

He was careful as he made his way through the streets; he was in a hurry, but he wasn't rude. A few people spoke to him in passing. Music seemed to come from every shop and restaurant doorway.

Small parades were already making their way through the streets, and eventually River had to pause to let one pass. The parade was being put on by one of the many samba schools in the city. The last float was the most amazing. It was filled with beautiful dancers, moving about their platform with grace and beauty, the women dressed in skimpy white costumes, the men in black tuxedos. The sight was mesmerizing, and as the float passed, people stopped and stared, awed at first, then clapping enthusiastically. Samba seemed to be imbedded in the very blood of the city, but the dance being performed on the float seemed to transcend the concept of human motion. It wasn't that difficult to be caught up with the crowd, to blend with the crowd. The beauty of the movement was almost hypnotic. He imagined Natal in such a costume; she could, he was certain, move with equal grace.

Of course, she would have him as a partner, but he could learn. There were samba schools on almost every corner in Rio—he could find the right one. She loved dancing and music and he did too; for her, he would really learn how to dance.

He shook his head. For now, he had to avoid the men following him and find Natal. They would have to leave until he could figure out the real purpose of the men in the blue suits. Until they were rid of Tio Amato. First things first—then the dream could begin.

At last, the float passed. River looked around—no blue suits that he could see. He hurried on through the city, headed to the cog train that went up to the Christ the Redeemer statue. No one followed him; he was certain of that.

The cog train was full; to keep his mind firmly in the present, he watched those who had never been on it before. It didn't matter what language they were speaking—their appreciation of the glorious views from the train were evident in their wonder.

The human condition, he found himself thinking. Men and women were so much the same, no matter where one went. There was the instinct for survival. There was whatever it was that lived in the soul that made people long for love, for that feeling of being together, moving forward, dreaming together, just seeking that happiness that has nothing to do with money and everything to do with the feeling of being as cherished as you cherish that special person.

There was nothing like sharing the wonders of the

world with someone you loved; he saw it in the faces of the happy couples on the train, saw it as they pointed to one another. There was nothing like striving for a family, for that complete feeling . . .

He heard the laughter of a child. A sound that was happiness itself, one of the pure beauties of life. It was a sound like water dancing over stones, light and melodic on the air.

And yet . . .

It touched something deep inside of him. And, for a moment, he forgot the men in blue, forgot even his quest to find Natal. And he felt . . .

Pain. A staggering sense of pain.

The cog train stopped, shaking River from his thoughts as he followed the rest of the passengers off.

When he arrived at the statue, he walked around the base. Twice. Three times. He listened to a guide telling visitors that the statue was ninety-eight feet tall and that it had been dedicated on October 31, 1931, but was not consecrated until October 12, 2006. River wondered if it mattered when it had been built—it was an icon in the world. But more than that, there was something in the statue's artistry that touched the human heart. It was the welcoming arms, he thought.

Staring up at the statue, something flashed through his head.

For a moment, he heard that sweet sound of laughter again. He pictured a house that was warm and smelled sweetly of something baking . . .

He would be welcome there; outstretched arms

would greet him, loving and encompassing arms like those of the statue.

Someone bumped into him and apologized profusely. He thought she might have been Scandinavian; her English and Portuguese mixed with something entirely different. He waved away her concerns but didn't engage in conversation, still clinging to the edges of his vision. It was so close he could touch it . . .

"I've seen the one in the Florida Keys," a young man said, walking along with a girl, his arm around her. "Underwater—it's a copy on one of the reefs. It's cool, really cool—you dive down to see it. But it's nothing next to this."

They walked on by.

River looked around for men in blue suits; he didn't see any.

And so he started around the base of the statue again with the throngs of people visiting. Not everyone came for Carnaval, he thought; some came just to see the Christ the Redeemer statue.

It was when he had just about given up hope of finding Natal in the crowd that he suddenly felt arms sweep around him. He turned, and she was there. Her face was radiant.

"I knew that you would find me," she said.

He laughed. "I think you found me."

She was oddly grave for a minute, looking up at him.

"You and I—we will always find one another," she said.

He needed to tell her what was going on with

him—she had trusted him last night. She had simply run with him. She had brought him to the lake in the park and then . . .

Then they had made love and he had sketched her. He hadn't even remembered that they had been running—his concentration had been on her.

He needed to tell her what had happened.

Her name left his lips and then he paused, looking at her—really looking at her. He felt as if something were boiling up inside him—anger so hot he could barely contain it. Not against her—but against anyone who could do such a thing to anyone, much less a woman.

Natal had tried to cover it with makeup, but she had a black eye.

"He hit you?" River demanded, shaking.

She shook her head.

"You didn't run into a door," he told her. "Natal, please, don't lie to me."

"River, don't look at me like that. Listen to me, I beg you. Don't waste your anger on such a man; he isn't worth it. I'm begging you—let it go. I told him that I'm leaving him. In a way, it was my own fault. No one should ever strike out in anger, but I . . . I went a little crazy and I struck him first; he is so accustomed to violence that he struck back. He was sorry for that and all I wanted was to get away. Please, River—let it go. I couldn't bear it if you were hurt because you tried to retaliate on my behalf. River—I have broken with him. I am free—please don't ruin that. There is nothing you can do but be with me. Don't ruin my new life by losing yours."

He held still. He felt the sweetness of the sun falling down upon him and the cool touch of the mountain air.

She was right. What could he do? Go to Tio Amato's house and burst in and beat the man to a pulp?

He would never get past the doorway. Amato had many men—with guns.

That left walking in with his own gun blazing and then there would be nowhere that he could run.

And he'd never be with Natal.

He took a deep breath, touching her hair gently. "I would die before I hurt you."

She smiled, took his hand, and pressed a kiss to his palm.

"I know that you would never hurt me," she said. "I know that you never will."

He was staring into her eyes when something distracted him. Frowning, he looked around her and gritted his teeth.

Now—now when he needed to concentrate on Natal's problems, and not on his own.

One of the men was back.

There he was. One of the men in the blue suits. This time, it was the hatless bald guy. "We have to go," he said huskily.

"All right," she said. She seemed puzzled, concerned.

He looked at her quickly. She didn't know anything about the men in the blue suits. She didn't know what he had done. It was in self-defense; she would understand.

But right now, she didn't know.

"We have to go, now. I'll explain; I'll tell you everything," he assured her. "As soon as we have a moment, I'll tell you everything."

"I trust you—whatever it is, I trust you," she said. "We are running from the police?"

"I'm not sure . . . I'll explain later. We've got to go."

"This way!" she said.

Natal was good. She was quick with a smile and her words were soft and polite and charming. She managed to get them into a crowd. And somehow—while it had seemed that there were dozens of people ahead of them to get on the cog train that would take them back down the mountain—they managed to get on the next one, the passengers around them chatting merrily enough. No one seemed to realize that they had pushed their way through to the front.

Then again, it was Carnaval in Rio, a city that prided itself on its joy.

River kept smiling and thanking people and nodding and agreeing when one of the wonders of the city seen from the cog train was pointed out.

Soon enough, they were back at the lower station. Afraid that the men would be behind them again soon, River kept moving with Natal's hand in his.

"Where should we go?" she murmured.

"Away—no matter what the crowd in the city, we need to go far. Where those who are not part of the farmland and the native population don't go. I'm afraid . . . no matter how many people are doing a samba and no matter how many floats or dancers or parades may move through the city, they will see me. We have to go far."

"Then we must take a bus. And you have a transportation card. I will slip in behind you. We'll be fine. But we must hurry, lest they realize we are truly escaping. Come on."

Once again, she knew her way. They took back streets, winding along through alleys and staying off the major boulevards until Natal cried, "Here!"

They caught a bus that River hadn't taken before.

But she was just letting that bus take them to a different stop, where they hopped another bus. And then another.

And then they were headed out of the city, toward the land reclaimed from the rainforest, where native Brazilians lived and worked, where it was still possible to simply disappear behind the crops, into a rich and fertile landscape with sheltering trees.

He discovered that they were back on the farmland where they had gone the first day they had been together. Where they had enjoyed their picnic—and given the remains to the old couple, along with their blanket.

"No one has followed us," Natal said, carefully looking around. "No one exited the bus when we did; no one was on the road; we're safe."

"I think so," he agreed.

But would he ever really be safe? And though she

had left Tio Amato, could he ask her to run with him for . . . as long as it took?

Maybe forever?

"Come, it's time to talk. But we must have something. We'll buy from the farmers. No one from the city comes here."

They paused to buy fruit juice from a vendor. When they walked out into the field, River knew that he had to talk to her then.

"Natal, I have to tell you what happened—why I keep running."

She stood by his side as they stared at the sun setting over the fields and the distant mountains.

She squeezed his hand, not saying anything.

"I stabbed a man," River said. He was afraid that she would wrench away from him. That she'd seen all the violence she could bear.

He waited for her reaction, barely daring to breathe.

She looked up at him. "If you stabbed him, he needed stabbing."

Her words were flat and true and trusting. Relief flooded him so fully that he felt his limbs trembling; he had fallen impossibly in love with her. If she had rejected him, he wasn't sure if he cared what the men in the blue suits wanted.

"I didn't want to; I tried to leave," River explained. "But this man—he attacked me with the knife. I got it away from him and told him that I didn't want trouble. He charged at me like a rhino. I didn't want to do it."

She touched his face gently. "I know you; I know what you're saying is true."

"I believe the man worked for Tio Amato," he told her. "I'd seen him before. At the track—with Tio Amato."

"If he worked for Tio Amato, there is no doubt," she said, "he most likely deserved to be stabbed." She let out a breath. "God alone knows what such a man might have done to others in his life."

"But I'm an American. Ex-military. I'm afraid that the Brazilian police would never see it that way. Especially because I'm almost certain that the man worked for Tio Amato."

She nodded gravely, studying his face. "So what's your plan? What do you want to do?"

"To leave," he said softly. "To take a train." He paused. He didn't say exactly where he was going. "North—away from the city. Would you come with me?"

The world seemed to stop then. Every second that passed seemed like an eternity. He felt like a schoolboy, praying that she would agree, knees like rubber, hands shaking.

"Of course," she said.

He thought that he would collapse, he was so relieved. It was as if his entire body had turned to liquid.

He fought for composure. "Then we need to get back to the city. I will get another train ticket. I was supposed to go last night, but I saw you. I couldn't leave once I'd seen you. Not without saying good-bye."

That made her smile. Despite her black eye, her smile made her face even more beautiful. Maybe it was the way her face seemed to light up for him. "Now you don't have to say goodbye." She squeezed his hand. "You wish to go tonight?"

He touched her face. "This is love," he said softly. Natal didn't contradict him. He couldn't allow himself the screams and the laughter and the exhilaration he wanted to feel and to act on—any more than he could forget that for this dream to take place, they had to escape. He had to hold on to reality and work for the future.

"I think it's important that we leave as quickly as possible," he continued. "Luckily, the city is crazy busy. This is best for now, but we'll have to go back to get the train out of Rio. Until then, we should lie low."

"I understand that, and I'll go with you," she said. "But I must get a few things."

"I can buy you new clothing," he said quickly.

"And you will, River," she said, touching his face. "But it's not clothing that I want, that I have to go back for. It's my writing. My writing is like my life, you know. It is dreams of the things I will do, memories of the wonders that I have experienced. I can't leave it behind. There is nothing material that I want or need, but what has been my soul . . . I can't leave it, River."

"I'll go with you, then," he said.

"No, you cannot."

"I'm going to protect you. If you must have such things, I must go with you."

"No, it's best if you don't. Please, River—you must stay away from Tio Amato. Let us really choose life. You can't be my great protector in the future if you are dead over such a silly thing as a black eye."

He stood, rigid; he didn't want to kill Amato. He truly hated killing.

He just wanted to give the thug a good black eye in return and tell the man he was never, never to lift his hand against someone smaller and weaker again.

Maybe it was more than that. It was true that he'd had enough of killing. Of death. But he wanted to hurt the man badly. He wanted him to feel what others did when they were in his power—desperate, hurting, terrified, and powerless.

And maybe Natal knew, or understood, just what it was he felt. Maybe she was afraid that if he were somehow confronted by Tio Amato, he wouldn't be able to restrain himself. He couldn't prove the man was a murderer. There was no way to take him to court, to make him face legal recourse. All he had was . . .

Himself.

"Here's the deal we will make," Natal said firmly. "You will not come with me. If you follow me, I will not go with you. Do you understand?"

He looked at her. She meant it.

He nodded slowly.

She was right; if he went near Tio Amato, he would act. If he acted, he'd be killed by Tio Amato's henchmen. If he weren't killed, he'd be arrested, and he'd spend the rest of his life in a Brazilian jail.

He needed an army to take down Tio Amato. He was one man.

He nodded again, letting Natal know that he fully understood her reasoning. And he took her into his arms. He just held her there where they stood, and he luxuriated in the trembling gratitude he felt.

She was with him.

"Where do I meet you? When will we catch this train?" she asked.

He pulled away and held her by the shoulders, watching her anxiously. "Are you sure you're going to be all right?"

"I don't intend to confront him; if I don't confront him, he'll not argue with me. I don't intend to see him anyway; the staff there loves me. I'll just slip in and slip out. You must believe in me, River. You must believe that I can manage myself. Have faith—as I am having faith in you," she said, her voice almost a whisper at the end. "Now tell me—where do I meet you?"

He told her about the small station where they would hopefully be able to board without seeing anyone. And he told her that the train was due to depart at eight.

"I will be there," she said firmly.

"But . . . you're going now? We should get something more to eat—we've had nothing but a few pieces of fruit. We should spend some time—"

"No. The fruit was enough for now. We must make this all work out, River, because we will leave tonight.

That is everything, my love, everything. We will get away. And then, we'll have time together, time to enjoy good food and wine and . . . all good things. We'll surf on the beaches in the north and picnic on the sands and be together—always," she told him.

My love, she had said. He nodded. "All right."

She stood on her toes and kissed his lips very gently and tenderly. He felt the stroke of her fingers on his arm.

"You understand?" she said.

"I do," he confirmed.

"I will be there."

"I believe you."

She held his gaze. "River, it's true. I love you."

"And you are my dream. You are—everything," he replied.

She kissed his lips again. It felt like the whisper of a breeze, her touch beyond sweet, a promise that the future awaited, and that it would be good.

He closed his eyes, just feeling her touch.

"I love you," she said again, and the words were part of her kiss.

He opened his eyes.

She was gone; she had disappeared as quickly as possible when his eyes had been closed; she had feared, he was certain, that he would argue with her again.

That he would want to come with her.

And he still wanted to be with her. The injustices dealt out by Tio Amato were just so wrong. Wasn't a man's role in life to fight against those things that were wrong?

He turned to call after her—to tell her that they could at least go back to the city limits together.

But she was really gone, out of sight.

All he could feel was the lingering caress of her fingers stroking his arm.

She was coming with him. Natal was coming with him.

If a man couldn't win, it didn't make sense to carry on a fight. And yet, he felt guilty. People had held silent too often through the years. They had held silent during World War II because they had been afraid; they held silent now, afraid.

And wasn't his role here just as . . .

Perhaps not bad, but not right either. He was a silent partner in guilt.

And yet . . .

There was also fighting sensibly. With a plan. With Natal, with her at his side, listening to him, giving him her wisdom, he would find a way to attack Tio Amato.

One in which he could win.

With that compromise wisely situated in his mind, he sat in the field and allowed himself his great happiness again.

She was coming with him. Natal was coming with him.

He stayed there on that farmer's field watching the sky and feeling the breeze and the touch of the sun. It was setting in the western sky.

Soon enough, they'd be on the train.

When River determined to leave, he had no intention of following Natal. He just had to get back into the city.

He had a plan. He would walk at first—he was afraid of accepting a ride from a stranger who might or might not be associated with the men in the blue suits, or the police. But a friendly farmer he'd seen before—a man with acreage just past Beluga's place—saw him walking down the dirt road and offered him a ride. He accepted it gratefully.

He thought about Beluga. Beluga had been a good friend. But River wasn't leaving here forever. He would see his friend again.

He regretted leaving Convict. He had rescued the dog; he was responsible for him. Yet, Convict was better off where he was for now. Beluga had quickly fallen in love with him. This was best; Convict would be safe. If something were to happen to River, if he was taken down somehow by the men, Convict had a good home.

River knew that he would come back; he just didn't know when.

He watched the familiar sights as they came into the city.

They were just inside the limits—where Tio Amato's massive house took up a block.

"Here's fine," River heard himself say.

"I take you further," the farmer offered in his broken English.

"*Obrigado*—but here is fine."

River hopped out of the truck, thanking the driver sincerely once again.

Then he stood on the street, staring at the house.

The gates opened; one of Tio Amato's black cars slipped out and onto the street. The gate remained open as the mechanism slowly whirred back into action.

River didn't mean to do what he did. But suddenly, he was running.

He slipped through the gate right before it closed. And then, he was in the yard.

Tio Amato's yard.

There might be security cameras—there were certainly alarms. And he still wasn't sure why he'd done what he had.

Natal had told him not to come. She had not wanted him to die over the fact that she had suffered a black eye.

But Tio Amato had killed people. Many people. The man was far more than a bully who gave beautiful fountains to his *bairro* to look as if he were a kind and generous uncle—he was a killer. He destroyed those who did not bow to his power.

Natal couldn't know; she wouldn't have stayed here if she had known.

And he couldn't just close his eyes and pretend that he hadn't seen what he had seen. He could be guilty of the crime and cruelty of silence.

Heart racing, River realized that no matter what he had promised her, he was afraid for her. Reed Amato had given her a black eye. God knew what else he might do.

Because River knew what he had already done.

The door opened; someone was coming out. River instantly slid back into his military mode, ducking low and creeping close to the wall. Thankfully, hedges and well-manicured plants adorned the place as well.

From his vantage point close to the porch and the elegant double doors, River could watch the man. He wasn't wearing a blue suit; he was dressed in black. Black trousers, a black pullover. He was shaking his right hand. River squinted, trying to see why. Then he saw that the man's knuckles were bloody—he'd hurt his hand.

That kind of injury meant one thing—he'd hurt himself beating someone.

River felt something sink to the pit of his stomach. *Natal!*

No, it couldn't be. Not even a man like Tio Amato would have someone else beat up on a woman for him.

Or would he? River had to be sure.

No, no . . . not Natal. There was someone else inside. There had to be someone else inside.

River crept around the house, heading for the back. There were wide doors facing out to the patio and the pool—and then the forest and trees that hedged the back of the property. The doors were open; the curtains blew out past them.

He heard rapid, angry Portuguese, then a thump and then . . . a cry. A man's cry of pain. Someone was being beaten—that was certain now. Some other poor idiot who hadn't paid the price that Amato had demanded of him.

At least it wasn't Natal.

Still . . .

River looked through the blowing curtains, into the house. Amato was there. He sat casually in a chair, studying his manicured nails. River frowned; it appeared that he had a bandage on the side of his face.

Another of Amato's goons was on duty, so it seemed, slamming his fist into the poor bastard who knelt on the floor, blood streaming from his broken lips.

River looked back at Amato. Yes, though he appeared calm and relaxed, there was definitely a bandage on his chin and his face appeared to be slightly swollen.

Natal had said that she'd slapped him. Maybe she'd caused the injury to Amato. And if not, this poor fellow being beaten to within an inch of his life might have been the one to inflict the injury—and now he would pay.

River's first instinct was to grab his gun from his backpack and burst in. But they certainly had guns too. And what if Natal was still in the house?

He didn't burst in. Reed Amato was talking now—his voice low and easy but River could pick out enough to know that Amato wanted money from the man. There were plastic bags on the table and Amato kept referring to them. Then River understood. The man was supposed to deal drugs for Amato. Either he had refused or he hadn't come up with the income he was supposed to have provided.

The man was begging for his life through bruised and swollen lips.

He was probably bound for the river—just as, possibly, like whatever River had seen tossed from the bridge just days ago.

He had to do something, River knew. He would never be able to live with himself if he didn't. And yet, he couldn't risk Natal.

Nor did it make any sense for him to get himself killed. He wouldn't help anyone if he did that. He had to take care and think out his moves.

The man would have to wait—and River just had to pray that he could put his plan into action before the man was hurt further or—

Or worse.

Killed.

River carefully and silently slipped back around to the front. The other man was still there—lighting up a cigarillo.

His back was to River; he never had a chance.

River was upon him in a flash, his death hold on the man's neck so intense and powerful that the man did nothing but gasp as River dragged him back behind the neatly clipped bushes.

River looked down at the man as he stared up into his captor's eyes, astonished at seeing River there—and astonished at being on the ground. "The U.S. trains its troops well," River muttered, and then moved straight into his demand. "Where's the woman?"

The man stared at him blankly. River eased the

elbow he had against the pivotal point of the man's throat enough to let him gasp out words.

"Woman—what woman?"

"Amato's woman. Is she in the house?"

The idiot still looked at him blankly.

"Tell me—tell me now. Or you'll die."

"Women, yes, Amato has women. They are all gone; there are no women in the house."

"All women are out—what about any other men?"

The hoodlum on the ground—at River's mercy—just stared at him. His eyes closed and he said. "No one."

No. No one else was in the house—not when they were torturing and possibly about to kill someone.

That was all that River needed. He was done with this man.

He didn't know what the man lying at his feet had done in his day; he had probably participated in murder.

But River didn't kill the man. He hated killing.

He grabbed a ceramic frog garden decoration and brought it down on the man's head. He was careful to hit hard enough—but not too hard.

The light went out of the man's eyes as he was rendered unconscious.

Natal had left; River was safe to create whatever diversion was necessary to get the police to break into the house. If the police came and saw the bloody man and the cocaine everywhere, they would be compelled to act. He had to be careful, however. He intended to meet Natal at the train and leave with her—forever, if necessary. Brazil was huge; there were many places they could go and live where Tio Amato's power couldn't reach them.

He created a diversion in the front—just knocking on the door. He listened and heard Amato bellow; he was directing the thug in the house with him—the one delivering the beating—to the door.

And, as River had hoped, he came to the door.

River took the man by complete surprise, springing up from behind him as he stepped up to find out what the commotion had been.

As River held him, cutting off his air long enough to render him unconscious, he felt tremors streak through him. He fought against the visions that tempted to fog his mind. Visions of black powder in the air, and men running and screaming as the world exploded around them.

Visions of fighting hand to hand; visions of fighting for his life.

The second of Amato's henchmen fell to the ground with a thud. River streaked around to the back like fire out of hell; he was able to watch as Amato rose to go to the front to find out what was happening.

River burst through the back when Amato went out the front. He dragged up the half-broken man on the floor.

"Get out of here," he whispered urgently.

The man began to mumble in Portuguese. He was too dazed and confused to understand.

River shook him, sorry to do so but determined to make him move. The man frowned, beginning to understand at last that he was being rescued; he didn't fully comprehend what was happening until he saw River grab the brandy off the coffee table and cast it over the drapes and Amato's elegant easy chair.

The beaten man ran as fast as he could toward the back as River picked up Amato's half-smoked cigar. He touched the burning embers to the chair and the drapes. The fire slowly began to lick at the alcohol-drenched fabric.

Assured that a blaze would quickly begin in earnest, River fled the house.

It was going to burn and possibly explode with whatever arms and gunpowder or more that Tio Amato kept in the house.

As he slipped out himself, River saw the man who had been beaten still stumbling and holding his head. Afraid that something might blow and explode violently, River pushed him down to the grass before running on.

When he turned back, he saw that he'd been right about explosive material in the house—there was a blast. The fire began to burn in earnest.

He had done what he could for the beaten man. He'd been down and it was unlikely he'd been hit by flying debris.

Now, there was nothing to do but hope that he would be all right—that the paramedics would find him, or that he'd be long gone by the time it all came down.

River was determined to be gone himself.

And he was. He tore through the trees behind the

house and was over the back wall by the time he heard the first sirens. Looking back, he saw that the house was quickly becoming engulfed in flames. River made his way to the street. People were rushing toward the house, and the sound of sirens was blaring louder and louder.

It occurred to him then that the men he'd knocked out would come to—and if they saw him, they would recognize him. He hoped that it wouldn't matter—that the great Tio Amato would be under arrest, that some kind of evidence would remain.

He lowered his head, praying that he hadn't made a mistake. Natal had left—for him. She had made him promise that he wouldn't take vengeance for what had been done to her.

It wasn't vengeance. He had seen what was going on—he just hadn't been able to stomach it. And Beluga had told him that the police wouldn't have investigated the possible body that had gone into the water, even if they did discover it. If the body washed up, they might suspect Tio Amato, but even if they wanted to, they wouldn't be able to prove he had been involved.

River had done all that he could do. The police would all have to be corrupt not to know the extent of the drug paraphernalia and arms that had been in the house for it to explode and burn as it did.

Still, River was afraid.

It wouldn't be a good thing to hang around and wait for whatever was going to happen next. He hurried along. He didn't wear a watch; he always knew about what time it was by the sun and the sky. But now he worried about his own abilities—he was so anxious to make sure that he didn't miss the train.

He came across one of the big building clocks and exhaled in relief. He'd been so afraid of being late, but there was still time before the train.

He needed to get away from where he was—away from the chaos that was Amato's house now. How would it go down? he wondered.

There was no way that Tio Amato and the goons had escaped burst eardrums at the least; the men he had downed were certainly going to suffer the after-effects. As to Tio Amato, he had hopefully flown pretty far after the explosion—he had to be hurting. Hopefully, he'd suffered some broken bones.

But what would they say? What would they tell the police and the paramedics?

Most likely, no one would report to the authorities that he'd been there. If the knocked-out goons were going to jail, they'd probably keep their mouths shut to the cops but tell Amato. And Amato would see that he was chased.

He was already being chased.

But by Amato's men, the police—who?

He didn't know. He did know that he couldn't wait for Natal to meet him; he couldn't wait for the train to come and the two of them to be on it.

Thankfully, the streets were wild. There were several parades going on, passing through a number of neighborhoods.

People were out and about in abundance.

Many were on the far side of inebriated. It was easy to walk with one crowd and then another; easy to appear to be part of those celebrating as he made his way through the streets.

There was a heavy police presence, but they were there to control the crowd. He smiled at one officer who smiled in return and waved to him as he crossed a parade route with a number of other people.

Eventually, he made his move across the city.

The little station was on a quiet street. River was careful as he approached it, taking twists and turns and even backtracking to make sure he wasn't followed.

He wasn't. Here, there were no trendy restaurants; he wasn't on a parade route.

No police were about and he didn't see any men in blue suits.

Breathing a little easier, he headed to the station, a little outpost of an office. He remembered that he needed another ticket for Natal. With his hood up and his head down, he approached the window. The clerk barely seemed to notice him. He only spoke his native language.

River simply said, "Natal, Rio Grande do Norte, *por favor*."

The clerk was not his charming young woman from the kiosk in any way. He barely looked up when he barked out something about the cost.

River didn't understand him but he knew what his

ticket had cost. He put money on the silver tray before the glass-enclosed counter; he received a few coins in change.

He was ready. The time was drawing near.

But there was no sign of Natal.

Fear began to plague him. There were so many possibilities. Maybe she had never really meant to come.

No, he couldn't believe that.

Perhaps she knew what had happened at Tio Amato's. She had stayed behind because of some sense of duty or obligation to the man.

That was ridiculous. Natal might not have wanted to see the whole truth regarding Tio Amato, but she knew. She knew that he was bad—that he hurt people. She'd opened her eyes and she wouldn't stay with or feel sorry for such a man.

No. She wouldn't stay out of a sense of pity or obligation. But she might not come now because she knew what had happened, and she no longer wanted to be with River. She had asked him not to take revenge. Maybe she thought that he had done so.

Maybe what was going on was even worse. Amato had more goons than the two River had tackled at the house. Maybe Amato hadn't meant to let her go under any circumstances. He had beaten her to within an inch of her life before River had gotten there and Natal was under a bridge.

Dead, her body broken and bruised.

No. God, no—he'd never believe that.

No.

The train arrived; River knew that at such a small station it would pause for only a few seconds.

An announcement came over a screeching loudspeaker—first in Portuguese, then in Spanish, then in English and in German—that the northbound train was arriving, and leaving.

He looked anxiously up and down the platform. No, there were no police.

No men in blue.

And no Natal.

The train ground to a noisy stop.

He couldn't stay there; he knew that. He had to get on the train.

His heart sank. The world was black. The world was . . .

Darkness—and blood.

A conductor came walking briskly by him. He called out—his words clearer than the announcement over the speakers.

But the announcement had changed. Now, the train was leaving.

Somehow, River managed to board the last car.

And then, miraculously, he heard her voice.

I'm dreaming, he told himself. He wanted her so badly that he was dreaming.

But, no.

He turned. Natal was racing toward the train, a brilliant smile on her face, a small bag in her hand. She'd gotten her work, her precious writing. She had gone to Amato's house, gotten what she needed, and gotten out. And then she must have stopped to say goodbye to a friend or to run some other last-minute errand before coming to the station. She looked well, and beautiful and excited.

He reached out a hand to her; the train was starting to move.

She leapt aboard and into his arms. His eyes met hers and he knew that even if he had told her what had happened, what he had done, they were together.

The adventure between them was just beginning.

"I'm late," she whispered. "I'm so sorry; it's me. I tend to be late."

He shook his head. "That doesn't matter at all. You're here."

"Truly a free spirit now!"

As the train left the station, he kissed her and held her.

He'd never felt as if his own spirit was quite so free.

CHAPTER 17

The train was moving and they hadn't found a seat. River noted Natal's hand. The knuckles were scraped and raw—bloodied.

"Natal," he said, looking at her anxiously.

"It's nothing."

"It's something," he persisted.

She shrugged. "I went in to get my belongings and of course, Tio Amato was there and he accosted me. He said I was a fool—well, he called me much worse, but he also said that I'd burned all my bridges and that he'd never support me again so that I could write. That was it, you know. When I made myself believe that he was a good man who built fountains for poor children and meant to help the world. I pretended, even to myself, that I did not see so much that made me uneasy. You see, I wanted to write. I believed that I needed to be able to write. And I'm good—they took my articles. But my articles were really all lies. I said I was free—but I wasn't. I just dreamed of being free."

"Your knuckles, Natal, what happened?"

She grinned. "He tried to stop me. I clocked him one."

"And he?" River asked, feeling his muscles tighten. He wasn't sure why his anger rose so swiftly. Tio Amato had to be at a police station by now. Unless, of course, the fire had spread so quickly that the massive amounts of what he had suspected was cocaine had burned to the ground with the house.

No, the man had to be in a prison or a hospital.

"He just looked at me. He was astounded that I had the nerve to strike him. I hurried then. I picked up my computer and other belongings and walked right out of the house," she recounted gleefully. "Such a victory—but he seemed preoccupied and said only 'good riddance.'"

She was so happy, so proud of herself.

"Where did you go when you left? You almost missed the train," he reminded her.

"Oh, well, I said goodbye to my friend Jacinto at the coffee shop and I stopped by to do the same with Anna, at the newsstand. I never meant to take so long." She frowned, looking at him. "How did you know that I left the house so quickly?"

He froze, looking down at her.

"You went to the house," she accused him.

"I had to—I had to see that he didn't hurt you," he said.

Her eyes narrowed. "You went in? You accosted him? But . . . you're here."

"I didn't exactly accost him," River said.

"What did you do? You were not to avenge me," she reminded him. "You promised."

"Well, now, wait, I promised not to get myself killed by trying to get revenge for what he had done to you," he told her. "And I did not go there to take vengeance on Tio Amato. I went to observe—just to make sure that he didn't hit you again."

"I told you I could take care of myself," she said. "And I did. River, my darling River, you must look at the bigger picture of our lives. He might have hurt you—killed you. And then where would we be?"

He shook his head. "I had no intention of letting myself get killed—trust me. And we both have lessons to learn, Natal. No one can really just take care of himself. Look at Reed Amato—surrounded by thugs, goons, or henchmen, whatever one would call his men. The strongest man needs others at his back."

"You had no one at your back!" she reminded him.

"That's true, but, honestly, I was keeping my promise to you. I didn't expect to see what I saw. They had a man in the house—they were beating him to death."

"And you thought to stop them?" she asked incredulously.

"What else could I do and still live with myself?"

"So many reasons that I love you," she murmured,

but then she added with distress, "Oh, River, what did you do?"

"I killed no one, I swear it. I simply drew them all out to the front—Amato's men first—and then, while Amato went out to see what was going on, I slipped around to the back and told the man they were beating up to get out. And then . . . well, I lit the house on fire," he said.

She stared at him, slowly arching her exquisite brows.

In that moment, he prayed desperately that he hadn't ruined everything with her.

"You . . . set the house on fire?"

"The police and the firemen would have to come. And I was pretty sure that he had all kinds of guns and ammunition—explosives—in the house. And there was so much of what seemed to be cocaine in there, Natal. No matter how corrupt some officers might be, they'll be forced to bring him in."

As she watched him, he felt as if he were composed of stone—as if the world stood still while he awaited her reaction.

To his amazement and relief, she smiled slowly and then laughed. "Oh, I can only imagine. Amato—he will be furious. He will be explosive himself."

"But behind bars," River said.

"He'll find a way to come after you."

"He may already be coming after me."

She looked at him gravely. "The men in the blue suits? But I thought you believed that they were the police?"

"I have never seen a uniformed officer paying the least attention to me," River explained. "Yes, they may be the police. But they may also be Tio Amato's men. Whichever—I believe it's best to be gone from Rio for a while. If Amato isn't already after me, for stabbing his man in the restroom, then he doesn't know who I am—by name, at least, though, of course, the goons I knocked out have seen my face. But, they don't have a name to go with my face so it will be hard for them to know who I am and to follow me. I pay cash for everything—I can't be traced by credit cards. I don't use a computer and I don't have a cell phone."

"I have a computer."

"But you use it to write—to express the joy and freedom of life and your thoughts. You're not online talking about people every day."

"I have an e-mail account," she said, worried. "But I don't think that means much. I don't do Twitter." She smiled and flicked a dismissive hand in the air. "I don't even have Facebook."

He chuckled a little. "Neither do I." His laughter faded and he looked at her earnestly. "I'm so sorry, Natal. I never meant to lie to you. And, I swear, I wasn't spying on you, and I didn't go to the house because I had to prove that I was—or could be—tougher than Reed Amato. I just couldn't let him get away with it. Natal, forgive me. I know that I saw his men dump one body. I couldn't let him kill another man."

She lifted a hand and cupped his cheek and jaw,

meeting his eyes. "No, you couldn't let him kill another man. He is all right, this man?"

"I believe so."

"I'm sure they came to put the fire out quickly," she said. She paused and looked at her bruised hand. "Well! We are both fugitives, right?"

"Just like Bonnie and Clyde," he said.

The train jolted, throwing them together. He felt the soft pressure of her body against his. She giggled, steadying herself on him.

"Just like Bonnie and Clyde—except that they didn't fall off a train."

No, they went down in a hail of bullets, River thought, wishing he hadn't.

No one was going to shoot them down. Reed Amato would go to jail. Whoever the men in the blue suits were, they hadn't been on the platform. No one knew his name—and no one knew which train he'd chosen to take. Or, for that matter, if he'd take it all the way north, or get off early.

She was with him.

He allowed himself to smile.

"Let's find a seat, then, huh?"

Taking her hand, he moved deeper into the car.

The train was crowded. He found a seat toward the front where they could sit facing forward.

There was one woman in the opposite seat, looking at them.

Natal smiled at her and brushed a lock of hair from her eyes.

The woman didn't smile back. She looked at them

both oddly, muttered something, and rose to change her seat.

River thought that she'd seen Natal's bruised and reddened knuckles. Maybe she was afraid that Natal would pounce on her.

That was fine; he couldn't help it if the woman wanted to sit elsewhere.

"Grouchy old woman," Natal said.

"Well, I guess . . . maybe years of other people being judgmental and rude have made her old and grouchy," River said.

"Maybe she works for a mean employer," Natal said. "Yes, poor thing. That's it—her husband died, leaving her with five little children. And she has to work so much . . . and her oldest daughter went off with the first man she met. A stranger who did not love her—but who promised her the world."

"Then the daughter came back with a baby in her arms and the poor old woman has six people to support and she scrubs floors all day," River suggested.

"Go on," Natal encouraged him.

"I think she has a job in a shop during the day. And rich people come and treat her very badly and tourists take apart all the clothing on the shelves and throw it all over everywhere," River said. "And then, to support everyone, she has to have another job at night— that's when she has to scrub all the floors."

Natal nodded. "That's it—of course. She's put up with wretched people all day and they are rude and careless with her. Then she has to scrub floors. And then, when she goes home, the children are all hungry—and squabbling. Terrible. We should feel sorry for her."

"Poor, poor woman," River said.

Natal turned to him, lacing her fingers through his. "People can behave so badly to one another." She paused. "Would that they had taken pictures or videos of Reed Amato when the house was ablaze and the firemen and police came."

"I'd have liked to see his face."

"Me too." Her smile faded slightly. "I will just be glad when some time has passed—when we don't have to be afraid."

"I'm sorry."

"But it couldn't be any other way—you couldn't watch them kill a man."

"No."

They were silent for a time.

"One day, you'll meet Beluga," River murmured, stroking Natal's hair. "He's a kind man, one of the best friends I have."

"I would like to meet him."

"And my friend Theo. He's a scrounger, but he's always cheerful."

"I'd love to meet Theo too," Natal assured him. "In the meantime, where are we going?"

River dug through his backpack and produced his map.

Natal studied it over his shoulder. "There are so many places that I haven't visited in my own country. At some point, we must go to Punta Negra—the beach is amazing. It's where the surfers go. Do you surf?"

He laughed. "Um—no. But that doesn't mean I'm not ready to try."

She snuggled against him. "Yes, the beach at Punta Negra. We must go there." She broke away and looked up at him. "But we are on the train headed to Natal. What made you pick Natal? Because it's north?"

"Because it's your name. A place called Natal has to be beautiful."

"Perhaps I was named for Natal."

"You don't know?"

She shrugged. "Perhaps it was a name in our family history. I don't know."

Then she rested her head on his shoulder.

As the hour grew later, River realized they hadn't slept much.

"You tired?" he asked her softly.

"Mm," she murmured.

"Me too."

"I like you beside me."

"Do I make a good pillow?"

"I'm sure you will."

With a slight grin, he leaned against the side of the train; she eased herself against him.

No one else came to sit in the seats opposite them, so they were able to stretch out their legs.

It wasn't the most comfortable bed in the world—but at that moment it was the most wonderful, because they could doze together, because she rested against him, because he felt her warmth and listened to the rhythmic sound of her breath.

By the time he awakened, most of the people on the train seemed to be sleeping.

Using his pack, he created a pillow for Natal and he slid carefully from his seat, stepping over her legs. In the aisle he stretched and went in search of the facilities. They were at the rear of the car. He headed down the aisle quickly and was glad to find the restroom unoccupied.

The train switched tracks just as he was exiting. It jolted wildly to one side, pitching him against a man standing there.

The passenger began to curse at him wildly and furiously in Portuguese.

River didn't really have a prayer of following, but it didn't matter—he seemed to know exactly what the man was going on about.

Cursing seemed to translate well into any language.

"Hey—sorry! I'm sorry, okay?"

The man stared at him, then launched into another tirade, gesturing wildly.

River switched to Portuguese. "*Desculpe tê-lo incomodado—desculpe!*" he said, apologizing for having troubled the man.

That didn't help either—not a bit.

It didn't matter that River had tried to use the man's native tongue. The fellow reeked of sour wine.

River shook his head, at a loss, ready to walk past him. But the drunk just wasn't going to allow that to happen. The man flung an arm back and caught River with a sound right hook to the jaw.

Stunned, River stared at him.

There had been a time in his life when he'd spent too many days going house to house, well aware that insurgents could be around every corner, behind every door.

A man died if he didn't react to an attack with instant reflexes.

In the back of his mind, the sound came again.

The sound of bombs whistling in the air, the sound of the explosions ...

And he reacted.

He turned on the drunk, his fingers winding around his neck, his fury giving him an almost inhuman power.

"I—said—I—was—sorry!" River emphasized.

The man sputtered incoherently as he struggled against River's grip, fighting for breath. His face was starting to turn purple before River came to.

The veteran blinked and shook his head, releasing the man. He realized that if he'd held his position just a few seconds longer, the drunk would be dead.

The drunk had sobered up; he stared at River with wide, terrified eyes.

"Just leave me be," River said.

The drunk didn't move.

Before River could turn and head back for his seat, one of the conductors came hurrying down the aisle.

He was pointing—and he was angry.

River closed his eyes, hating how quickly he'd

launched into military mode. But he hadn't hurt the man, not really—he'd be fine as soon as he caught his breath. His own jaw throbbed viciously. As the angry conductor stormed toward him, River found himself praying that the man spoke some English so that he could try to explain.

To his amazement, the conductor wasn't angry with him—he was furious with the drunk. With River looking on, the conductor pulled at the other man's shirt and ranted on. Then he turned to look at River.

"You're hurt badly?"

"No, no—just sore."

"You want to file some kind of charges?" the conductor asked.

"Charges?" River repeated. "Um, no, no." He realized then that the conductor had seen the man strike River—he hadn't seen River respond in an explosive manner. That was because, he realized, he'd pushed the drunk into the well by the train car's exit, out of sight. "No—no charges," he said. "He's drunk."

"Drunk too often. Get yourself a towel, sir, and some cold water. Hold it against your face. This idiot is lucky—he will drink too much and get himself killed one day, but it will not be on my train."

River nodded blankly, wondering what—if anything—Natal had seen. He slipped back into the toilet and soaked some rough paper towels in cold water.

When he came out, the conductor was waiting.

"You have your ticket, sir?" he asked.

River reached into his pocket. He produced two tickets.

"You only need one," the conductor said.

"The other is for the lady—up in the front?"

The conductor frowned, looking back down the aisle. He looked at River.

"She's there—she must be sleeping with her head down," River said.

The conductor shrugged and punched holes in both tickets. He looked at River. "You are certain, sir, that you're all right?"

"Absolutely."

"And you'll file no charges?"

The last thing he wanted was any exchange with the police.

"No—no charges."

"He will be off at the next stop!" the conductor promised.

The drunk remained in the well, eyes closed. River told the conductor, "It's up to you."

He hurried back to his own seat, dismayed to see that the conductor had been right; Natal wasn't there.

His heart sank. She had seen him—and she was afraid of his violence. She knew that he had stabbed a man and knocked out two of Amato's goons. And now this . . .

Perhaps she had fled to another car.

But, then, as he neared the seat, she sprang up from her hiding spot.

She kept her voice low. "What happened?" she

demanded, eyeing River in alarm. "Is everything all right? Your face!"

He told her about the drunk outside the bathroom, omitting the fact that he'd nearly strangled the man.

She shook her head in disgust. "Some people! They cannot handle the Carnaval season. They cannot handle themselves at all. He should be arrested."

"It's all right—the conductor was furious with him."

"Your face," she repeated. "Come here."

She took the towels from him and pressed the sheets to his face, gently covering the bruising flesh, and then laying the sheets along his jawline and holding them there. He looked into her eyes as she cared for him.

"What? Why are you smiling? You're hurt," she chided.

"I don't feel a thing."

She actually blushed, looking down on him.

Then she kissed him, gently—and swiftly. They were, after all, on the train.

But as she held the paper towels to his face and laid her head back on his shoulder, she whispered to him, "Tomorrow . . . well, I will see that it doesn't hurt at all."

"How will you do that?"

"Distract you. I will distract you so thoroughly that . . . well, you will feel nothing." She leaned closer for a moment, whispering against his ear, "Except for me."

He ran his fingers over her hair and eased back into the seat, smiling. His jaw did smart, but the wet towels felt good. And his mind was on the days to come, and that took away from any pain he might feel.

The seat was hard beneath him; the train jostled ridiculously.

But as it did so, he felt her beside him, and the train could have spun in circles for all he cared.

For a while, he stayed awake. As the train made one quick stop, he noticed a road sign.

Natal. 80km.

They would hold the course that far, explore through the day, and decide exactly where they wanted to be. Maybe they'd start off by heading to Punta Negra and try surfing, as Natal had suggested.

He twisted and planted a light kiss on the top of her head. She made a little noise and snuggled closer against him.

He started to fall asleep and struggled against it— he had grown afraid of sleep.

Sleep brought dreams. And the dreams were never good.

But his exhaustion, the movement of the train, were too much to resist. Eventually he slept.

And as he had feared, he began to dream.

The dreams always came with noise first—that whistling sound, the sound of the bombs coming.

Then there would be the explosion as they hit the earth. A softer sound would follow—that of the earth falling back like rain upon the area the bombs had hit.

Then there would be screaming—the cries of those who had been hurt. A commander's voice would call out, urging the men to take cover, to regroup, to find the wounded.

That night, he was down on the ground. He'd headed out from the safety of a wall to drag in a fellow soldier who'd been hit with shrapnel. It was hard going over the rough terrain, pulling a big man with his gear. But River got him behind the wall and was inching out again when there was another explosion.

The wind shifted; black powder and earth and dust were whirling in the air as if they were all part of some man-made storm.

He saw someone—someone coming through the haze. He could still hear men screaming and shouting, but in the midst of it he heard something else.

Laughter. Innocent laughter. The kind of sweet and innocent laughter that belonged to a child, from a little girl's lips.

And there was the child. He could just make her out through the powder-mist clouding the earth and sky.

She was with a woman. They didn't know; they didn't know they were walking right into a war zone. He tried to reach out—tried to find his voice and call out to them. But he was choking; powder was in his lungs.

Then he felt as if another bomb went off, as if he was pitched forward.

He woke as his head butted into the seat across from him.

The train, he realized, had stopped.

"We're somewhere," he said, "I'm not sure that it's Natal yet. Rough stop. Are you all right?"

He was speaking to no one. Natal wasn't at his side.

He halfway stood, looking for her. *She's gone to the restroom,* he thought, *or perhaps to the café car.*

A few people were gathering their things to disembark. A woman walked by as he searched for Natal—when she passed him, he could see outside. Maybe Natal had stepped down to the platform already to check out their circumstances. Maybe . . .

Natal wasn't on the platform.

But the men in blue were.

Three of them now. He saw the man in the blue suit who wore the blue hat, the man in the blue suit with the bald head, and now, another one too. This one had a tuft of blond hair and wore a black shirt beneath his jacket.

They were talking to someone, he saw. He strained his eyes to see more clearly.

It was the drunk. It was the wretched drunk he'd encountered outside the restroom. And he was pointing to the car where he and River had engaged in their confrontation.

River swore softly beneath his breath and grabbed his backpack. Natal's things were gone.

Had she left him again? he wondered bleakly. Had she actually seen the fight and been afraid of what she must surely see now as his penchant for violence?

No. He remembered her eyes, her face . . . the way she had looked at him.

You will always find me, she had told him.

And he would; he believed that with his whole heart.

For the moment, though, he knew he had to get the hell away.

Maybe Natal had seen them and warned him—but he hadn't heard her. Maybe she had moved quickly, knowing full well that he could escape easier on his own and that they wouldn't be after her. That had to be it; he was certain that she cared as much for him as he did for her. And she did have faith in him.

The men in the suits were coming toward the train. River walked quickly, heading to the car behind the one he was in.

People barely noticed him. Some were dozing. Some were reading papers and a few were playing electronic games on their phones or squinting and staring out the windows to see where they were.

Looking out to the platform when he reached the next car, River saw that one of the men had already boarded.

River kept hurrying through.

In the next car he came across the sleepers. First—the cheap sleepers. He thought about finding an empty bunk and sliding into it.

No.

They would think to look there. Only idiots would refrain from checking the obvious and he was certain that these men, whoever they were, weren't idiots.

They were here—somehow, they had followed him here. How, he didn't know. He'd used cash for the train tickets. He hadn't seen them when he'd been at the station. He knew he hadn't been followed.

They were determined and thorough, he thought. They'd questioned cashiers at stations around the city. They had described him.

That was the only explanation.

The train lurched back into motion. The men were all aboard.

He hurried to the rear of the sleeper car and entered the next; it was filled with compartments—real compartments, with doors that closed.

River opened one; a woman saw him and screamed.

He closed the door quickly.

Even if one were open, River thought, the men would surely check each compartment, just as they'd check every bunk in the coach class.

River kept moving. He had to pull hard to open the next door; it led into a container car. Boxes were piled high here; he had to maneuver to make his way through them. Seeing a clearer area at the end, he hurtled over one box to reach it and then ran the remaining length of the car.

He came to another car. There were more boxes.

And crates.

Crates filled with chickens.

He didn't mean to—he accidentally knocked over a crate.

The chickens squawked in agitation; the sound of their distress was loud.

River kept running, hoping he'd created a few obstacles for the men in blue suits.

He had—but turning back he saw that, although they had been forced to slow down, they were still coming.

And as he moved on, he heard one of the doors sliding open when he had barely made his way through the next door.

They were right behind him; they were almost upon him.

He began to run again, leaping over a box in his way, pressing past a sleeping conductor in the last of the cars.

Then, he was at the end of the train.

Night was turning to day—the first of the morning's sun was just starting to appear on the horizon.

River could see the track—and the forests that seemed to surround it now on either side. The train had left the last stop far behind and was chugging on toward the next. But . . .

This was country. To each side of the track was an embankment—not roads, not cars, not hard pavement.

It was ground . . . soft ground, rich with grass.

The train had picked up speed; it was moving fast.

River looked back. He could see the men.

The men in blue suits.

The first—the one with the hat—was in the lead.

But the others were close behind him.

Natal was in his life now. Life meant everything. Life meant . . . Natal.

And he had to find her again—as he always would.

As long as he wasn't caught by the men in the blue suits.

There was no choice.

River stepped over the last car's guardrail and held on for a moment, trying to judge the impact of his leap.

Then he catapulted himself from the train, aiming for the grassy embankment to the side of the rails.

He hit the earth hard, the wind knocked out of him. He didn't know if he had broken anything or not; for one second, his entire body hurt. The next second, he could feel nothing.

He didn't move a muscle at first; he didn't have to. Gravity took care of that for him. He was rolling . . . rolling and rolling until a tree stopped him, and the pain began in earnest.

CHAPTER 18

River didn't know how long he lay in the ravine off the railroad tracks. It might have been minutes; it might have been hours.

He thought he might have blacked out—he remembered searing pain that seemed to shoot through his entire body.

But then he opened his eyes and when he did, the sky was blue, the sun was shining overhead, and he could hear birds chirping.

Something about the sound of the birds seemed absurd.

For a moment he lay perfectly still; he didn't forget for a minute that he had jumped from the train because the men in blue were just about to reach him.

And he remembered that Natal had been gone.

You will find me again, she had told him once. *You will always find me.*

Everything then seemed to be a dull ache—everything in his body, and his mind.

She hadn't left him—not really left him. He refused to believe it for a minute, no matter what doubts he might put in his head. She was gone because she knew that she was in no danger and that he could run much faster on his own.

He could blink, he could roll his head. He stretched one arm out in front of him and then the other. He was sure he had massive bruises on his shoulders but it didn't seem that he had broken any bones.

He was more afraid of trying to get up—but he knew that he had to do so.

He rolled first, slowly. He groaned with the effort—everything hurt. But his body obeyed his commands. He grasped a low-hanging branch to help himself to his feet, afraid that he would find that a leg was broken or that he'd torn a major muscle.

He could stand. He breathed a sigh of relief. There was a hard-hitting pain in his left shoulder, but he figured he'd hit his left side first coming off the train—he was lucky his collarbone wasn't broken in a zillion places and that bones weren't sticking out of his body.

He hurt, he was bruised—he was filthy. But he was in one piece and he was able to walk.

Then, he panicked. His backpack wasn't on his back.

He looked around hurriedly and couldn't find it. He had to have the pack—his gun was in it, a seond knife, and all his cash. It would be far too ironic to have saved the money by stabbing a man who had attacked him for it and then to have lost it to the men coming after him for justice or revenge.

A slow, agonizing walk back up the little stretch from the ravine to the tracks proved rewarding; he found his pack. He clutched it and sat down for a minute and closed his eyes—just to be thankful. Then he opened them again.

All he could see was the railroad tracks—and trees and brush forever. The going would be painful, he knew, but he had to get somewhere. His mouth was parched; he was covered with scratches and bruises, and he didn't even want to take off his shirt and jacket or pants to find out just how badly. His clothing, he realized, was ripped to shreds.

He needed to find a lake or a river. He needed water.

He probably needed medical attention too, but that was too risky. If he could just get to a pharmacy, he'd be okay.

And then, he could find his way back to Natal.

It was easy enough to judge his position once he had his map out. If he headed southeast, he'd come to something like a town or a village because he'd be heading toward the water, a harbor, and probably in there somewhere, a beach. With any luck, there would be a river, a lake, or some kind of fresh water along the way. Or, he could follow the train tracks.

But that seemed too obvious. If someone came looking for him, they'd assume he'd follow the tracks.

And they'd assume he'd be heading north again—the direction the train had been going.

He wouldn't be going north. He'd be heading back to Rio—and the one place he was certain he'd find Natal, the Christ the Redeemer statue. He didn't know which one of them would make it back to Rio first—he just knew that they would both go there.

Leaning against a tree, he studied the terrain again. There seemed to be something of a foot trail that appeared to lead south almost parallel with the tracks and yet obscured by the trees. He started that way.

He only made it about twenty minutes before he had to rest. He hadn't broken any bones but he had messed up an ankle.

River found a tree trunk to rest against. Listening to the birds chirping and the leaves rustling in the breeze. And there was something else.

Water. The trickle of water.

He had to be somewhere close to a stream.

He listened intently then made it back to his feet, crying out softly when he first put weight on his left foot. The ankle seemed to scream in protest.

He found a heavy branch to use as he hobbled in the direction the sound of the water came from.

He reached the stream and looked up to the sky, thanking God for small favors. It rushed over rocks that appeared to be smooth as glass—fresh water. The grassy bank by it was slippery; he fell as he tried to ease himself down to shimmy toward the water. Before he knew it, he'd slid all the way down.

But he hadn't hurt himself again.

Once there, he removed his boots and socks.

His left ankle was painfully swollen. Badly twisted, he judged.

He needed to stay off it.

There was no way to do so.

He tested the water and it was good and sweet and seemed incredibly pure. The stream was beautiful, rolling over the rocks, surrounded by trees . . . pristine.

Natal would love it here, he thought.

"And we will come back here—together," he said out loud.

Then he laughed softly. His voice sounded so odd—so out of time and place.

His thirst quenched, he rolled up his torn and dirtied pants and cooled his feet and ankles in the stream. He sat back, allowing time for the water to make him feel that he'd done a little something to improve his lot. Then he realized that his face was probably filthy and grass-stained, and he twisted around to wash it the best he could; the water felt wonderful.

At last, he got to his feet. He figured he'd follow the stream—at the least he'd have fresh water all day.

He found another sturdy—if crooked—branch that he could use as a cane; it helped. It helped a great deal.

He made his way along for another half hour.

He prayed that the men in blue suits would not come then. He wouldn't be capable of running.

As the sun rose overhead, he began to tire. He'd found water—the true necessity—but with his ankle twisted, every movement was arduous.

He thought again that if the men in blue came back, he was in serious trouble. But there was no sign of them.

There was no sign of anyone at all.

Toward the afternoon, he felt as if the world before him was beginning to grow wavy. He was hungry— it had been some time since he had really eaten— and his head was throbbing. By now, more than his ankle hurt—everything in his body seemed to be burning.

He sat down by the stream again, drinking, wetting his face. His legs dangling into the water from a little rock ledge, he leaned back, closing his eyes.

He thought he dreamed again at first—not about wars and bombs and dying men, but laughter.

The laughter of a child.

He opened his eyes. The sun was beginning to set. Looking up, at first he saw just rays of colorful light, and he had to blink against them.

For a moment, in the glare, he saw a woman. The light dazzled around her.

Angel, he thought. *I'm dead at last.*

She was there in the light, and the child was at her side, and they beamed down at him with mischief in their eyes.

A cloud moved in the sky or the sun shifted. The glare was gone. The sound of the laughter was real.

He struggled up to an elbow. His head still hurt— the world was still blurred. But down the stream, there were children playing. They were real. A boy of about seven was hopping over worn stones in the stream.

The little girl seemed to be about five—she was laughing and following her brother.

Their laughter. It was so beautiful.

He heard a man's voice; he wasn't sure of the Portuguese, but he could hear the tone. The man was chastising his son—he shouldn't be encouraging his sister to do something that she might not be old enough to do.

Then he saw the man, who was coming around a slight bend in the stream. He had a bag over his shoulder and River realized he'd been out collecting something. The man had on a worn denim work shirt and jeans; he appeared to be in his forties with a weather-worn face.

The little boy called out suddenly. He'd seen River.

River tried to stumble to his feet. He fell.

As the man rushed over to him, he couldn't help but feel fear. He couldn't run; he couldn't do any of the evasive tactics he had learned.

He was trapped and cornered.

The children reached him first. They called out in friendly voices, curious, he thought, to see a stranger lying there in the stream.

He tried to speak; no words came.

The man reached him and hunkered down by him, looking concerned. He fired off a rapid question in his native language.

River tried to say something; he tried to form words in either English of Portuguese. He finally managed English. "I'm okay—I'm resting. I'm an American—just taking a walk," he said lamely.

The man shook his head, telling River something. He helped him to his feet.

River hadn't been ready to stand. He nearly fell. The man caught him. River tried to thank him and tell him that he was all right.

The little boy suddenly spoke to him. "He says you're not all right. You come with us."

"You speak English?" River said, relieved.

"They teach it in school and my uncle married an American girl," he said, grinning and showing a mouthful of teeth. "I've been to San Diego!" he said proudly.

"That's great," River said. "Thank you. Please— tell your father that I'm all right, really. I wanted to see more of the country so I decided to walk, er, rather than take the train. And I fell." It was almost the truth.

The man said something rapidly. The boy responded. The little girl just looked up at River with wide eyes. He had to smile. She stirred something in his heart. Something beautiful—and something painful too.

The little boy looked at River. "My father says that no good Christian could let you go on as you are. You come with us. We have a little farm just on the other side of the stream. Papa will help you—and my mama will take care of you. And you must eat."

"Oh, no, no, thank you. That is so kind. But I could not impose upon you that way."

The child spoke to the man again. The man looked at River as if he were crazy.

The man spoke; the child grinned and told River,

"You will hurt him greatly if you don't let us help you. He'll be really offended."

He could barely stand, River knew. He was going to fall again. He was starving—and if the men in blue suits did stumble upon him now, well, he might as well be dead.

He had little choice.

He looked at the man. "*Obrigado,*" he whispered.

The man nodded. "Guillermo," he told him awkwardly, trying to introduce himself. "*O meu nome é Guillermo. Este é Juanito,*" he said, patting his son on the head. "*Esta é Anna,*" he said, pulling his daughter gently to him.

The boy rolled his eyes. "I'm almost eight," he told River. "I am Juanito to them because my grandfather is Juan too. But, *por favor,* when you talk to me, Juan will be just fine."

River gave his own name, and Juan started to laugh.

Guillermo wanted to know what was so funny. His son explained that River's name translated to Rio. Guillermo laughed too. River shrugged; Guillermo patted him on the back and offered him his arm to lean on.

River looked at the ground worriedly. His backpack was there.

"*Juanito, por favor,*" Guillermo said, and Juanito, struggling only a little, picked up the pack with everything River had in the world.

"*Obrigado,*" he told Juan.

He realized as he went with the family and they made their laborious way around the bend that he was lucky—he wouldn't have made it on his own.

When they rounded the little bend, River saw cows grazing in a pasture and in the distance, a little farmhouse.

There seemed to be nothing else there—not as far as the eye could see.

No men in blue suits.

He allowed himself to be helped along. Guillermo was a strong man and took a lot of the weight off his injured ankle. It was slow going.

"Vera! Vera!" he called as they neared the house.

A woman, wiping her hands on an apron, hurried from the front porch as they approached. She looked at her husband curiously but quickly came to River's other side to help him along. Guillermo, Juan, and even little Anna started to talk to the woman, explaining that they had found River and what River had told them.

River tried to pick out words. He realized that they were all agreeing to help him.

He was hurt; he was in their country. They must tend to him and help him—God and Christ and their own hearts made it so.

As they entered the house, River began to notice several things. He saw that the family was very poor. The dress that little Anna was wearing was nearly threadbare; her shoes were too big for her. They had been a boy's shoes—her brother's shoes, he thought.

The house was built of wood and there was a

wooden barn out back. River wondered if the family had built the structures by themselves. Perhaps other members of the family had come to help them.

While they had little, it was all clean and neat. The porch floor was freshly swept; a double swing made of raw wood offered a place to sit and look out over the land and down to the stream.

Guillermo and Vera brought him through a screen door to a small living room and got him seated on a couch—an old worn leather chesterfield. Vera dragged over a footstool and began to unlace his shoes.

"Please—*por favor*!" he said, leaning to do the task himself.

She shook her head, chiding him. He looked up at her. Her face was as weatherworn as her husband's, thin, and yet beautiful. There was warmth and tenderness in her eyes. She was drawn and haggard, too old for her years—and yet beautiful.

She took off his boots and looked at his ankle. She wagged a finger at him.

"My mother says that you are to behave," Juan told him, grinning. "This is good—she is yelling at you, not me."

River smiled. He thanked Vera in English and in Portuguese.

She gave him a smile in return and hurried on into the kitchen. Guillermo followed her; Anna and Juan sat there staring at him.

"So, you are just walking about Brazil?" Juan asked him.

"I love Brazil," he told Juan. "I came . . . to see the

country." For a moment, he couldn't remember exactly why he had come. "Right now, I'm heading back to Rio de Janeiro."

"Rio!" Juan said, his eyes bright. "How I would love to go! And go for Carnaval. My father says that Rio is filled with the wicked. It's dangerous. We are better here."

"All places have good people and bad people, Juan."

"You are going for Carnaval? You'll miss it if you don't go back soon."

"I don't care about Carnaval—though it is exciting. There are many performers."

"And many drunks, my father says."

River shrugged. "Well, that may be true."

"If you don't care about Carnaval, then why do you go?"

River smiled. "I'm going to look for a friend."

"You can find friends all over the world," Juan told him gravely.

River laughed softly. "A special friend. We were traveling together, but we became separated. I know that I will find her in Rio."

"Ah." Juan grinned at that.

Anna apparently demanded to know what was going on and Juan told her, acting it out by hugging her tightly before letting her go with a dismissive shake of his head.

"You are in lo-ve!" he said teasingly.

River grinned and shrugged again.

Guillermo came back into the room carrying a large, deep basin. Vera followed with towels and a jar of something. The basin went down before him and he was shown how to soak his ankle. He did so, thanking them again.

Vera set to work cleaning his forehead; he hadn't realized it but he had a gash there. She said something to her son; Juan ran off to the kitchen and came back with a large glass of something white—milk, he thought.

"Mama said you drink this and then she'll bring you food. You look like a starved rat—I don't think she means to be offensive," Juan told him.

"I don't believe your mother could offend me," River said.

Guillermo said something to the children and Juan sighed. He told River, "They say that Anna and I must go feed the chickens and do our chores." He wrinkled his nose. "And I must do my homework. But I'll be back to help when you don't understand Mama or Papa—and when they don't understand you."

He and Anna ran off—looking at him until they reached the door. He was, he thought, definitely an oddity to them. He broke up their usual existence.

In a few minutes, Guillermo began to speak to him, gesturing. River understood that Guillermo was off to do his work.

He thanked the man again.

When Vera finished tending to his wounds and ankle, she hurried back into the kitchen. She returned quickly with a steaming bowl of food. It was some kind of meat in a sweet and spicy sauce over rice.

It was delicious. He started to swallow it down, gulping.

She set a hand on his leg and shook her head.

His manners, he realized, were disgusting. But, as she pantomimed being sick, he understood that she didn't care about that. He was just eating too quickly.

He nodded. "*Obrigado.*"

"*Nao é nada,*" she said, smiling.

When he was done, she took the bowl from him and disappeared back into the kitchen.

He didn't know what herbs or substances Vera had put in the basin water but whatever it was, he thought it was magical. Or maybe it was just that the water was hot. He leaned his head back; he probably dozed a few minutes because when he looked up, Vera was before him with a bundle of clothing in her hands and the water had grown cold.

She set the clothing down and took the basin away. Then she pressed the clothes into his hand and pointed.

They wanted him to bathe, he realized. And he smiled because he didn't blame them; he was a wreck and their little home was spotless.

He started to get up on his own; she reprimanded him and offered him an arm. She led him around a little wall to a compact bathroom and started to enter with him. He flushed and shook his head, showing her that he could balance.

"It's better—so much better. You're an angel," he told her.

She didn't understand his words, but she did understand his gratitude—and his embarrassment. She waved a hand in the air but smiled.

She left him and he closed the door.

The water from the old shower head was only lukewarm but stepping beneath the spray was wonderful. He closed his eyes and let the water rush over him.

He thought about Tio Amato—and about this man Guillermo and his family. The world could be so different—and so much the same. People, no matter what their language, *were* the same. Everywhere, there was amazing goodness to be found in people.

And everywhere, there were monsters—the evil and greedy, like Amato.

He longed to stay under the rush of the water forever but he was afraid that they might get only so much warm water. He hurried out and dried himself with a large towel and balanced his way into the rough-denim fabric of the jeans he had been given along with a cotton work shirt. Guillermo's clothing was a little big and baggy but he was grateful to be wearing it.

His own clothing was gone. Vera, he thought, had slipped in while the shower was running and taken it.

When he came out, he heard her humming in the kitchen. She was setting the table for the family dinner.

"May I help?" River asked.

She seemed to understand. But she turned, shaking her head, and indicated that he must sit—his ankle was still bad.

As he sat, Juan and Anna came in. Vera spoke to Juan and he began to put glasses on the table.

Anna was given the napkins to distribute.

A moment later Guillermo came in. River watched as he set his hands on his wife's hips and kissed the top of her head. She turned with a smile.

They seemed so happy together. They had so little—but they were in tune with what mattered, he thought.

He looked away, oddly embarrassed to watch the emotional intimacy.

"You look good clean!" Juan told him.

"Thanks. Will you tell your parents for me how very grateful I am for all their help, please? And tell them that I have money—I can pay for my food."

"Oh, I won't tell my father that!" Juan said. "It would offend him. He has made you a guest. Guests don't pay."

"That's nice, but—"

He didn't finish. Guillermo spoke to his son, demanding to know what River was saying.

Juan replied quickly. Guillermo looked at him and grinned.

"What did you tell him?" River asked.

"I told him that you were in lo-ve," Juan said, again extending the last word and rolling his eyes.

River flushed.

Guillermo spoke again. Juan listened to his father and turned to River.

"He says that the road is not far—and that Jorge Maestro goes by every day, bringing produce down to Rio. You may probably ride with him."

River nodded. "Great!"

Vera put the food on the table, pointing out what she served. There was a big bowl of *sopa,* soup, and *salsicha,* sausage, and *salada,* salad. She brought bread to the table as well, and he thought he clearly understood her when she told him to eat up.

The dinner table—even with him there—seemed to be a lively and loving place. Conversation flowed across the table with Juan pausing now and then to tell him what was going on. Naturally, he told River, shuddering slightly, his parents wanted to know about his schoolwork. And they wanted to know if all his and Anna's chores had been done correctly.

Anna, he said, dismissively, just wanted to know if there was *sorvete*—ice cream.

They made such a beautiful picture . . .

There was *sorvete*. When it was served and eaten, and Vera and the family had begun to clean up, River asked Juan to bring him his backpack.

Juan did so.

"What are you doing? What do you need?" the boy asked.

"If they won't let me pay them, maybe I can leave you something," he said.

He pulled out his sketchpad and pencils and set them on the table. He didn't look at the family; he'd watched them all through dinner.

He drew the kitchen and the kitchen table. He drew them all smiling, Juan with a spoonful of soup, Anna leaning upon the table, and Guillermo and Vera smiling as they looked at one another and listened to their children. He hoped that he'd drawn the warmth of the kitchen—and all the love and goodness that seemed to thrive there.

He handed it to Guillermo. Vera came to look over her husband's shoulder. Little Anna tugged at her mother's skirt and Juan nudged between his parents.

Guillermo looked at River a long moment and then inclined his head and spoke.

"He says that he is humbled and you are a very good artist," Juan said.

Vera spoke.

Juan grinned. "And my mother says thank you— you didn't draw in all of her lines."

"Tell them I drew what I saw," River said.

The picture was done; there was no television and there were no computers. The children helped Vera with the dishes and then Juan suggested that he read one of the children's books that their uncle had sent them from America so that the children could learn English. Juan was good, if he did say so himself, he told River, but Anna needed help.

And so River read to Anna. She sat on the couch by him, almost curled into his arms. He loved that she was there, and yet . . .

Something seemed to tease at him, to plague him. To hurt somewhere so deeply buried in his heart he couldn't begin to understand.

It was a story about a stray cat. The cat was starving and the farmer took him in. There was an evil fox that was coming after the farmer's chickens. The cat, though small, caught the fox in the barn and battled the fox. When the battle was over and the fox ran away, the cat was so wounded that he was afraid he wouldn't live. But it didn't matter; the farmer had been kind.

The farmer nursed the cat back to health and the story ended happily.

Anna worked on pointing to pictures and identifying the creatures in English. "Fox, cat, chicken, farmer."

"Like Papa," Juan said, pointing to Guillermo, who sat in a chair reading the paper.

"Kind, like your father," River agreed.

Juan looked at him gravely. "You really think you will find your friend?" He laughed softly. "Your love?"

River nodded. "I will find her."

Guillermo looked up. Juan translated.

Guillermo turned to watch his wife, who was mending a sock beneath a lamp.

He spoke softly.

Juan made a face for River. River asked him, "What did he say?"

"He said that you will find her. He knows. He would look for Mama everywhere—and not stop until he found her. *Yucky.*"

"No, very beautiful," River told him.

The children were then sent off to bed. Vera produced a pillow and a blanket for River. The house became silent as everyone went to sleep for the night.

Sleep came easily for River; he'd been so worn and beaten and tired. Now his ankle felt better, and his belly was full, but he was still exhausted from the effort of moving through the day.

He feared sleep; hated sleep. He should have thanked Guillermo and his family and left—and slept somewhere along the way.

Sleep meant dreams.

They came so often now. More and more . . .

And he did dream. The dream seemed to pick up where the last dream had left off.

Earth, dirt, and powder filled the air. There was that mist—the dark mist made of the destroyed earth. But lying with his ears ringing and half blinded from the sting in his eyes, he could still see them.

The woman . . .

He couldn't quite see her face.

And the child. The beautiful child . . . golden, laughing, so sweet as she moved. They came toward him as if there weren't bombs everywhere, as if men weren't screaming.

As if they weren't dying.

He didn't know why he awoke; he just did. And when he did and looked up, he saw a face—a child's face.

For a moment he lay there frozen, just staring at her.

Then little Anna grinned and said, "Fox, chicken, cat—farmer!"

"Very good," he told her.

"Very good!" she agreed, and ran off to tell her parents that she was awake.

He could smell something good coming from the kitchen; it was very early, he thought, but this was a farm. And children had to go to school.

He rose quickly. He was still sore, but nothing like he'd been before. He tested his ankle and it seemed much better as well. His sketchpad was still at the side of his backpack and he reached over to put it back in.

His service revolver fell out as he did so. He moved to slide it back in as well, but noted then that he wasn't alone in the room.

Guillermo was there. He had come to call him to breakfast.

He saw the gun.

And now he looked at River with suspicion in his eyes.

River thrust the gun into the backpack. He met Guillermo's eyes. "I would never hurt your family—I would never hurt anyone on purpose who wasn't . . . hurting someone else."

He didn't know if the man understood him or his tone—or if he remained horrified.

Vera came out to the living room. She looked oddly at them both.

The children came scampering out.

"What's going on?" Juan demanded. "Breakfast is ready. Come, River, we'll have breakfast."

River slowly shook his head. "I have to go," he said.

He didn't understand Guillermo's sentences, but he

knew that the man agreed with him. *Yes, this man has to go.*

Anna cried out with a little, *"Nâo!"*

"Breakfast! You must have breakfast first," Juan said.

His father said something and Juan's shoulders slumped in dejection. "He says that you will miss your ride."

"It's true," River said. "And I—I have to find my love, you know?"

The children ran to him. Guillermo looked as if he would reach out to stop them but he didn't. He waited; he watched.

The children hugged him; River hugged them in return. He looked at Guillermo and Vera. "I can never say thank you enough. *Obrigado, obrigado.*"

The two nodded. Vera stood very close to her husband. She couldn't understand yet what had changed.

She just knew that it had.

River reached for his pack. He was afraid to dig into it—Guillermo might think that he was going for his gun.

But he had a few bills stuck in a side pocket. He managed to slip them out and turned to the big leather sofa. Pretending to plump the pillow, he slipped the bills beneath it.

Vera, he hoped, would find the money.

She was a mother. She wouldn't cast it away as an offense or ill-gotten gains.

She would use it for her children.

"Thank you," River said one last time.

Guillermo pointed to the southwest. River nodded; he would go that way to hitch a ride back into the city.

He left the house. He heard them speaking for a few minutes as he walked away. The children were going to miss him. Vera was still confused. But someone said something that lightened the mood.

He left, listening to the haunting sound of a child's laughter on the air.

CHAPTER 19

Though Guillermo had been afraid of him when he left—or, at the very least, wary of him—River didn't believe that the farmer intended to call the police on him. And if the men in the blue suits came stumbling upon the lone farmhouse there, Guillermo would most probably be too cautious to say that he'd seen anyone.

River believed that the men were heading north still—in the direction he'd been heading until his turn-around.

As he walked to the road, grateful for his time at the farmhouse, since he felt so much better and could move again, he started pondering Natal's where-abouts again. His heart beat too quickly when he allowed himself to wonder if she'd been picked up by the men in blue suits. He didn't think so—she had made her escape before he had seen them. He could imagine that she had gotten up—taking her bag with her precious computer with her—and headed to the car ahead of theirs that had a little café. She had seen the men then; she had been too smart to come back.

No, she had eluded them.

And she would have known that he had to elude them as well.

His plan was the right one. Head back to the statue. The outstretched arms of the Christ the Redeemer statue seemed to be perfect for the city. Despite Tio Amato, River loved Rio—and he knew that Natal did too. The Christ the Redeemer statue encompassed all that was good and joyous and loving about Rio de Janeiro. People wanted to like their neighbors—they even wanted to like strangers. They were giving, and they opened their arms to the world.

Yes, the statue. They both loved it so.

His ankle was barely tender—Vera had wrought wonders. Or maybe it had been the hours in which he had stayed off it. He didn't know. All he knew was that he could walk. He didn't, however, want to walk forever.

He wondered too if he should look for the farmer Guillermo had suggested. To play it safe, he decided that he'd be careful about which ride he'd accept. Not that he believed a man like Guillermo would ever willingly cause harm to another. But because he might be questioned, and if the men in blue suits did turn out to be criminal henchmen at the beck and call of Tio Amato, Guillermo might have to tell him that River had been there—and what he had advised River to do.

He was hovering between the tree line and the embankment along the narrow two-lane road that ran among the scattered farms in the area when he saw that a van was coming. There were several young people in it.

It was old and beat-up. From the antenna, he could see that the van sported a Brazilian flag—and the American flag.

He hurried up the embankment and stepped out onto the road and lifted a hand.

The van pulled to the side of the road. A young man was driving. He had light hair and bright blue eyes.

"Where are you going?" the man asked, and then quickly asked the same question in very bad Portuguese.

But a blond girl leaned over to the driver's seat. "American?" she asked River.

"Yes, I am," he said. "I'm heading to Rio."

"We're not going that far," the girl said. "But we can take you partway."

"That would be great."

"Open the sliding door and pop on in. Marty and Alicia are in the back; I'm Susan and this is Blake."

He said hello to all of them. The couple in the back were young too. They appeared to be in their early twenties. Alicia had raven-dark hair and an accent when she spoke.

"Brazilian?" he asked her.

"Mutt," she said dryly. "We're on a special study program from NYU. My parents are in the U.S. but my mother was born in Brasília. My father is half Cuban and half American, and I spent most of my time growing up in New Jersey."

"Nice," he told her. He turned to Marty.

Marty laughed and lifted his hands. "Nothing exotic about me. Jewish boy from the Bronx." River shook his hand.

"Atlanta," Susan said, lifting a hand and waving from the front.

"Detroit," Blake offered. "And you?"

River was glad that he was preoccupied by angling out of his backpack because, for the life of him, he suddenly couldn't remember where he was really from.

"All over," he said.

"Ah, army brat?" Marty asked.

"Something like that," River agreed. "What kind of special study?"

"We're social science majors," Alicia replied. "We're going into some of the rainforests and meeting with indigenous tribes."

"That sounds fascinating."

"Oh, it will be. We're here for three months; we'll get to see so much. I'm sorry we won't be able to take you all the way, but we're right around Espírito Santo now. We can get you down as far as Campos. We're about ten hours away—and then you'll only have a few more."

"That's very kind of you."

"Not so kind," Blake said. "I've been driving for hours and we're all taking turns. You feel like driving? I mean, you have a license? You drive, right?"

"Yes—of course," River said. He was a good driver, but he was still surprised. If they had a rental agreement, the slightest accident—even with a chicken truck—could be real trouble for him.

But Blake, driving to the embankment so they could exchange places, grinned at him. "You look concerned. Don't be. It's not a rental. We picked it up from Alicia's uncle in Natal. Altogether, man, from there, it's about a twenty-five-hour drive. If you're up and awake and in for it, you can take her for the next few hours!"

"Sure, of course. I can put in for gas too," River told him.

"Now, you're the best hitchhiker I've ever picked up," Blake said.

For a while, when he started driving, his new foursome of friends chatted about themselves and their studies. They considered themselves incredibly lucky that Alicia had relatives in the country—it made it cheaper for them. Alicia talked about Brasília—how modern and new and big everything was—and Blake argued that São Paolo and Rio were his favorite cities because they weren't new and big and modern.

They talked about the amazing wonders of the country. Alicia hadn't been to Santarém, their destination, a city of about a quarter of a million people where the Amazon and Tapajós rivers met. From there, guides would take them out into the rainforest.

River listened to them talk. And, to his amazement, while he hadn't been to the places they were talking about, he was able to converse easily.

He'd done a lot of reading on the country.

"You've been here awhile?" Alicia asked.

"Yes, awhile. I should have gotten further," he told her.

"Yeah, well, you find something you like and you stay in one place easily," Marty said.

"Oh, please, we stay in places because of people," Susan put in.

"Or," Blake teased, "we go places because of people."

"So that's it," Marty said, leaning forward. "There's a girl in Rio."

"There is a girl in Rio," River admitted. He was surprised that he was smiling—maybe a little foolishly. But it was nice, he realized, to be with these young people.

They reminded him that he was still fairly young. And that it was natural to want to be with someone you cared about. And it was actually fun to have them tease him about Natal. He described her in glowing terms.

"She's stunning. She has huge blue eyes and her lashes are rich and dark and her hair . . . it's glorious. When they say raven's wing—that is the color of Natal's hair. Her cheeks are high; she has a perfect nose. She's about five-seven, slim—but beautifully shaped, mind you. Honestly, it's not just the way she looks—it's the way she moves. It's that mischief in her eyes, or the sorrow and the anger in them when she's seen an injustice. She writes—she writes about the world around her and what she sees and thinks. She's . . . amazing," River told them.

Susan gave Blake a swat on the shoulder. "You should talk about me like that."

"I do," Blake protested.

"Wow. I know why you're going to Rio," Marty told him dryly.

"Hey, you," Alicia protested. She slapped his arm.

"Okay, okay—wait," Marty said. "My girl is . . . well, beautiful."

"Very good. Go on," Alicia said.

"She's got dark hair and a pretty face."

"Never mind. Don't go on—that's terrible," Alicia said. "Blake—what do you have to say about Susan?"

"Oh, well, she's beautiful, of course," Blake said.

"Standard start—let's see what else you've got," Marty said dryly.

"Well, she's blond. And energetic and athletic and—"

"Stop! Athletic?" Susan said.

"That's not good?" Blake asked.

"Hopeless," Susan said.

"Yes, the two of you just keep quiet," Alicia advised.

"I'm just saying," Marty protested. "Come on, Alicia. I mean, I don't have to go to Rio—I have you right here. Hey, River—way to make us look bad."

"Sorry!" River said. "I just—"

"Don't make it worse," Blake teased.

"You two are making it worse—you just don't sound the same," Susan said, sighing. She remained in the front seat next to River and spoke to him sincerely. "I'm so happy for you—and for your gorgeous beloved. Are you two going to celebrate Carnaval there?"

"At this point, I guess we will," River said.

If Natal managed to get there.

She *would* be there; she had avoided the men in the blue suits—she would be ahead of him. She would go every day to the statue.

Until he found her.

Or she found him.

You will always find me, she had said.

He smiled.

"Look at him, Alicia—just when he thinks about her," Susan said.

Marty groaned from the back. "Okay, he's poetic."

They laughed and teased awhile longer. Then, River realized, the foursome began to drift off. That was okay; he liked driving in silence as well.

He kept his eye on the gas tank and the road signs, knowing he would have to stop. When he did, he put his backpack over his shoulder and went in to the store. He pumped gas and when he headed back to the driver's seat, he saw that only Marty remained in the van.

"Bathroom break," Marty said. "You know girls. Well, and Blake too. No kidneys on that boy. I guess it will be easier for him, though, when we're in the rainforest."

"I'm sure it will be," River said.

He stood by the van, waiting and watching.

He was going to have to stop being so nervous; he was heading back to Rio. If there weren't more of the blue-suited men there, the ones he knew about would figure out that he had headed back to the city.

He and Natal would stay. Once he was with Natal again, they would make a new plan. Perhaps they would head to the rainforests too. A guide could take them and they could see the wonders of the Amazon River and meet indigenous people. In fact, it was something he was certain he had once dreamed of doing.

"We're back," Susan said, opening the front passenger-seat door. "And I bought you a soda—they had them in bottles in there and I thought you might like one."

"Thank you," River said. "What do I owe you?"

"Don't be silly—you bought gas and you're doing the driving," Susan said. Behind her, Blake and Alicia jumped back into the second row of seats.

"You could have left that pack, man, I would have watched it," Marty said.

River was afraid that Marty had noticed his hesitation, but he quickly thought of an answer. "I needed money out of it—you know. To pay for the gas."

He revved the van back into gear and headed out to the highway. He'd been foolish. No men in blue suits had appeared at the station.

They couldn't possibly know where he was.

He allowed himself to relax. Driving felt good. He didn't remember the last time he had driven. You needed a credit card to rent a car—and he just didn't use credit cards. It went against being a free spirit hiking his way through the country.

The group in the van, awake now, sang.

They accused one another of making up lyrics.

They were entertaining.

Then they began to drift off to sleep again.

He drove with silence around him then, other than the chug of the van.

Two hours later he felt Alicia's touch on his shoulder. "We're reaching the turnoff," she said. "Would you like to come with us? We're staying with an aunt for a few days."

"Oh, I would, but I really can't," River said.

She smiled. "That's right. You have a girl to get to in Rio."

He nodded and found a good place to pull off the road. When he did so, Alicia hopped out of the back door of the van and came around. No one else stirred.

"Don't worry, guys—I'll do the driving now!" she said.

She took the keys back from River. "When they wanted to stop for you, I told them no," she said. "You know—you see all those movies about kids in the country and picking up a hitchhiker and the hitch-hiker being a slasher and all, but . . . you've been great. You drove and got us here and you were fun and . . ." She paused, stood on her toes, and gave him a kiss on the cheek. "I hope you find your girl quickly. She's very lucky."

"Thank you—thank you for the ride, and thank you for your words," he said.

She hopped into the van and turned the engine back on. "Happiness to you, River. All the happiness in the world."

He waved and the van headed off.

Once again, he found himself watching from the side of the road before venturing out. He looked for trucks—he was pretty darned sure that the men in their designer blue suits were not driving a farmer's truck.

He saw a rusted old hulk coming down the road and he stepped out. The driver stopped for him. River wished him good day in Portuguese. He said, "Rio?"

The farmer shrugged and said something, telling River he could hop into the bed.

There were sheep in the bed. They didn't smell at all well and they *baa*ed loudly in protest of his joining them.

He didn't care. He dreamed about coming closer and closer to Rio.

After some time, the driver stopped and indicated that he was turning off. River thanked him, patted the most obnoxious *baa*-er in the group, and hopped out. The truck drove off.

He wasn't far now at all. There was a lot of traffic on the road. He caught another truck—this one with chicken crates. The chickens, at least, were penned.

He watched the sky. It had grown dark. He wouldn't find Natal that day.

But he could dream of seeing her the next day. And if he didn't . . .

He'd wait. He'd wait forever.

He had to hop out and hitchhike a fourth time to reach the outskirts of Rio de Janeiro. When he popped out of the last truck—goats that time—he was ready to do some walking. And he was hungry. They hadn't stopped to eat all day—and he hadn't had breakfast with Guillermo and his family.

The day had been easy, he reminded himself. He'd driven most of it. He'd been concealed by animals the rest.

He had to remember to be careful now that he was in the city.

He found a café he hadn't been to before and bought himself a sandwich and coffee. He tried not to wolf his food down—people were watching.

With his hunger appeased, he began to wonder what he would do while waiting for daylight.

Maybe he would head to Beluga's place.

Maybe the men in blue suits would look for him there.

But it might also be interesting to find out if Beluga had heard anything.

Actually, on the one hand, he wouldn't have to wait. He went to the counter and asked about a newspaper. They had them.

They were in Portuguese, of course. But River picked one up and paid for it and returned to his table. He didn't speak the language anywhere as well as he should have by then, but his reading skills were decent.

He quickly found what he was looking for—as he flipped the paper to read the bottom half of the first page, he came across a picture of Reed Amato.

There he was—in his Armani suit and white panama hat, his eyes narrowed and glittering with rage. A photographer had snapped a picture of him in the backseat of a patrol car. A man who should have been handsome—but who ruined his looks with his expression.

River tried to understand what the article said. He could definitely garner that Reed Amato had been arrested. A "large quantity" of drugs had been confiscated from his house—despite the fire that had destroyed half of it. Two other men, Aldo Mariachi and Miquel Hernandez, originally from Colombia, had been arrested with him. The men were being detained pending arraignment and trial. An anonymous tip had alerted the police to a murder that might have been committed: they should search the river near the bridge by his house for possible remains. Police were investigating.

"Yes." River said the word aloud and then quickly looked around. He'd drawn the attention of one pretty girl and an old man. Both looked at him. The girl smiled; the old man snorted.

"*Desculpe,*" he murmured.

The girl nodded; the old man snorted again.

River left the paper and rose and wandered toward

the city. He doubted that anyone could find him that night.

Tomorrow was Fat Tuesday. The last day of Carnaval. The city thronged with people—celebrations were wild. With each step closer into the northernmost neighborhood, the crowds were denser, the entertainment more frenetic.

He dared to hop on a crowded bus.

He didn't want to celebrate—not tonight. Tomorrow, when Natal was in his arms, he'd do his celebrating. For the moment, it was enough to bask in the pleasure of Reed Amato's downfall.

He had no fear going from bus to bus until he had come to the area where he could walk to Beluga's. He wasn't sure what he would do once he reached the hostel. If he saw Beluga outside, he might call to him. If he didn't . . .

He realized that he hoped he'd catch a glimpse of Convict. He just wanted to see that the dog was all right.

His ankle didn't hurt at all, he realized as he walked. He was on the mend, Amato was in jail, he was back in Rio, and tomorrow he'd find Natal. All seemed good.

He came to the roadside that led to Beluga's property. He waited there, peering through the darkness to see if Beluga was out on one of his chairs, smoking one of his Cuban cigars.

At first, he saw no one. Then Beluga was there. He was talking to a backpacking American boy, showing him where he could sleep in the overflow space in the barn.

At Beluga's side was Convict.

Every few steps, Beluga stopped to pat the dog on the head.

They were both happy. Convict looked well fed, and quite content to be with Beluga.

The backpacker went on into the barn, and Beluga and Convict headed over to the few chairs in front. Beluga sat and pulled a cigar from his pocket and lit it.

River started to move toward the house.

Then he froze. There was a car coming down the road and it was turning into Beluga's drive.

Beluga's deep baritone carried across space. "Who's this now, Convict, eh?" he muttered. "People who stay in hostels don't usually arrive in limousines!"

River ducked low, watching.

He froze as he did so. The limo, a dark sedan, parked in the drive; a man got out.

A man in a blue suit.

He spoke in low tones—tones so low that River couldn't hear him. But he did hear Beluga's reply.

"No, no—the man you speak of is gone. Long gone! He headed off to explore. That's why he's here—to see Brazil. He comes and he goes. As he chooses."

The man in the blue suit—the first man he'd seen, the one who had witnessed him leave the bathroom after he'd stabbed his attacker—was joined by a second man. It was the man with the bald head. He said something quietly.

"How do I know if he'll come back?" Beluga bellowed. "Maybe he will—maybe he won't. Maybe he will come in a month. He goes where he pleases; he comes when he pleases. That's all that I can tell you."

But the men in the suits continued to talk; Beluga listened gravely.

Were they telling Beluga that River was a murderer? No, the man he'd stabbed hadn't died. At least, River hadn't read that the man in the hospital had died.

He saw Beluga nod, then shrug, then listen again.

Maria came out onto the porch, drying her hands on a dish towel. She frowned and hurried over to where Beluga stood.

Beluga spoke quickly in Portuguese to her; Maria's frown deepened.

She looked at the men and spoke quickly in Portuguese—River couldn't tell what the men could understand. Did they speak the native language? He could only follow a bit of her long string of words himself, but he got the gist of it and it made him smile. She was telling the men that River was a good person; he was kind to everyone around him. They should leave him alone; he had chosen his life of adventure. And when he chose, he would be back and not before.

"He is not here—feel free to search. I'm telling you that he's not here," Beluga said in English, his tone harsh.

The man with the hat spoke again; he seemed to be in earnest.

And Beluga listened. He kept shaking his head.

Good for you, my friend, River thought. Beluga would not give him away.

The men headed back for the car. River decided that it wasn't at all safe to head in to try to speak with his friend—not that night.

And he'd seen that Convict was doing fine.

As the men got back into the car, River saw that Beluga set an arm around Maria's shoulders. The act made him smile. They weren't in love, but they did love one another. Like sister and brother. It wasn't what he had with Natal. But it was good. They had each other and that was something everyone in the world needed—friends who cared.

River blinked and turned his attention to the men in the blue suits. He quickly ducked down and moved into the trees across the street from Beluga's hostel. He kept low and watched as the men drove down the drive.

At the foot of it, they parked.

They were going to wait there, River thought. They were going to wait there all night.

Good for them; he wouldn't be there.

Sticking to trees and thick underbrush, River started back toward the city. He walked a long while before he saw a truck and hitched a ride.

This time, there was a group heading into the city to party in the back of the truck—a long flatbed.

There was plenty of room for River. The truck was, in fact, the perfect conveyance. The partiers offered him a swig of rum; he accepted and played the role of being part of them. Half were in full costumes; half simply wore Carnaval masks.

Someone offered him a mask. It had been cheaply executed out of something like papier-mâché but it was a fun mask—that of a demon of some kind. River realized that it was a perfect disguise for the night.

He laughed, accepted the mask, and said, *"Obrigado,"* over and over again. The partiers waved away his thanks. This was Carnaval—it was time to have fun.

When they reached the street where they were headed to party some more, River jumped out with them. He quickly got his bearings. He danced in the streets with some crazy-happy men for a few minutes and watched a samba dancer with them. They all laughed together over the antics of a stiltwalker.

Fireworks exploded over the city.

River eased away from the group and headed into another crowd.

He made his way to the club where he had found Natal dancing. It had been a few nights ago; it felt like forever. When he looked in and searched through the patrons, he didn't see Natal. That didn't bother him; it made him smile. She was waiting for him. She wouldn't expect him at the club; she would expect him at the Statue of Christ the Redeemer.

He walked out of the club. For a few moments, he stood there, in his mask, unnoticed by the busy crowds sweeping around him, all laughing and chattering in a variety of languages. He smelled the food on the street—so many vendors were out. He heard music everywhere; the sidewalk beneath his feet seemed to tremble with it.

Rio was alive that night; he felt that life.

And the city itself seemed alive with anticipation— tomorrow was the day.

Just as it was the day for him.

He looked around again at where he was and judged his distance from the cog train station; he would take the first train up in the morning. When he drew close to the station, he looked for one of the smaller inns. He probably couldn't get a room; the city was bursting at the seams.

At a small, out-of-the-way pensione with peeling paint and a broken window, he decided to take a chance.

River saw a broken, blinking red light. He had to stare at it for a minute to realize that it offered up the information that there was a vacancy. A shower would be good that night, if he was to greet Natal in the morning.

Inside he found a fat man in a dirty white shirt at the register. He was unabashedly drinking from an open bottle of whiskey.

"*Fala inglês?*" he asked.

"Yes, yes, I speak the English," the man said. He didn't even notice River's grotesque mask. Well, it was Carnaval. Everyone was wearing a mask. "You want a room?"

"You have one?"

"Little one. No elevator. Fourth floor," the man told him.

"There's a shower?"

"*Sim.*"

"I'll take it."

"Cash only."

"That will work."

The price of the room was way higher than it should have been. River didn't care. He paid the man and made his way up the creaking stairs. He checked out his bare-bones room first—it had a bed and a chair. It appeared, at least, to be clean.

With his backpack in hand he found the door to the hallway bathroom. There was no one there—whatever other guests shared the floor, they were out partying still.

He allowed himself the luxury of a long shower. He realized he still bore the scratches and bruises from his leap from the train.

That didn't matter. His ankle didn't hurt—and he could barely feel the scratches.

He donned clean clothing. His ripped things were back at Guillermo's house. He realized that he'd been wearing the man's oversize clothes all day.

He hoped that Guillermo didn't miss his own clothing or that at least River had left behind more than enough money to pay for it.

After he showered, he felt better. He set his mask on top of the outfit he had taken from Guillermo's house. Tomorrow, he would just leave the pile in the room.

He headed to bed; he wanted to try to sleep. He

warned himself that Natal might not have made it back yet.

But she would have made it back; she would have just taken the train south again.

The drapes on his window were thin. He could see that fireworks were still painting the sky when he lay down. The noise thrummed in his ears.

He didn't care.

He slept.

And that night, for the first time in as long as he could remember, anticipating his reunion, he didn't dream at all.

CHAPTER 20

The city of Rio de Janeiro was in full swing.

Usually, mornings were a quiet time. Rio was a late-night place—a haven for night owls.

But this was it—the last day of "sinning" and feasting on *carne,* or meat, had come to an end; tomorrow the period of Lent would begin, and while the world was changing and there were different beliefs worldwide, Rio remained a city where the population was heavily Catholic. Tomorrow, many would begin to abstain. They would give up meat—and perhaps alcohol or smoking or some other enjoyed vice—for Lent.

That would be tomorrow. This morning . . .

The city was already awake; there was a lot of partying to be done on the final day.

From his window he saw that street entertainers

were out; a troop of comic "dolls" was performing for those sitting at a coffee shop; a giant "bird" on stilts was walking down the street. A lone violinist played on a sidewalk, and a dancer was entertaining children where they sat about a block away, waiting for a parade.

He thought he'd be the true early bird; he had underestimated the ability of many to get in their last flings.

He smiled as he watched. Somewhere out there, of course, would be those taking advantage of those just in love with the day—with life. Pickpockets would abound. There would be trouble. People would drink too much and pick fights. Bad things would happen.

He hadn't dreamed during the night, nor, did he think, he daydreamed then. But he heard the sound of explosions again; in his mind's eye, he could see the world collapsing. He could see hatred in the eyes of those he fought when the combat became hand to hand.

But he could also see both the fear and the compassion in the eyes of those who had pulled American soldiers to safe havens when they'd been outnumbered.

He could see the eyes of the children who were allowed to play with the American soldiers. He had killed people he didn't know—because it was war. And he knew that men had killed men throughout history over doctrines they didn't fully understand.

But, even in war, the goodness in people could win

out. He smiled at himself, an inner voice mocking him. *What? Are you a philosopher now?*

No. He had to believe. And it was easy to believe when he thought he would find Natal again today.

He was quickly out of the poor place he had found for his night's lodging. It was too early for the first cog train to head up to the Christ the Redeemer Statue—he would love a good cup of coffee.

He wandered toward the cog train station, looking for a convenient café as he went. He saw one just down a side street and slipped in. There was a back courtyard to the place—a little quieter, as drums and music had already begun to pound from other venues.

He found himself a wrought-iron table and chair with an umbrella overhead and took a seat. When the waiter came, he ordered coffee and a "Continental Breakfast"—written in English on the menu for all the tourists who thronged to the city.

He hadn't thought to ask if the café sold newspapers; he noticed that a woman sitting at the next table from him was reading one; it was a Brazilian paper written in English.

She must have felt him watching her—or her paper. She looked up. She was a middle-aged woman with a nicely sculpted face and light hair and eyes—and a nice smile.

"Good morning," she said. "You're American?"

He nodded. "Yes. Good morning."

"Ex-serviceman?" she asked.

"Pardon?"

"Ex-military?"

"Uh—yes. How did you know?"

"A handsome young man looking a little scruffy," she said, smiling. "How rude. Forgive me. I've just seen it before. Men need time to shake out—well, men and women these days. My daughter served in the military. She joined the National Guard and wound up in Afghanistan driving a truck. She came home, thank God. She's in Peru right now—climbing mountains. I guess I'm talking too much; forgive me."

"Not at all," he told her. "Where is home for you?"

The older woman smiled. "Nebraska—Lincoln, Nebraska. It's still home and I love it, but I love to travel too. My daughter will meet my husband and me here next week, when Carnaval is over. She likes things a little quieter."

"She certainly has the right," River said.

"Me—I love the costumes and dancing and the spectacular floats."

"Me too," River said.

He added, "I didn't mean to stare at you. I'm sorry. I was just thinking I should get a paper."

"Oh, you can have mine—I just wanted to finish this article. It will just take me a minute. . . ." She flashed him another smile. "My husband and I are spending about three months a year down here. We've become involved with the schools and the severe drug problem they're having in some areas. I hope that what I'm reading is going to prove to be a very good thing for us—especially Brazilian children. They've arrested one of the city's richest men—Reed Amato—and I'm praying that they really get the bastard. But . . ."

River's heart sped into overtime. They'd caught him. "But?"

"Well, his lawyers have finagled something. He will go to trial—and I do think they'll get him, and that it will be so publicized and world pressure will be so heavy that he will have to go away and do serious time. But . . ."

It was an effort not to shout. River didn't want to terrify the woman. "But?" he pressed.

"They have him out on bail for now. He isn't due to appear in court again for almost a month."

River stood. He didn't care about his coffee anymore; he had to be on the first cog train up to the statue. Natal might not be there yet, but he'd wait. He'd wait there until he found her—because he had to find her and they had to get out of Rio together. He didn't know where she had gone, but he was absolutely certain that she would come back to the one place they talked about so much, loved so much.

"Thanks for telling me," he said, trying to appear interested—but casually so. "Let's hope they lock him away—for Rio."

"For Rio, for Brazil—for the betterment of man."

"Amen," River muttered.

He left money on the table and started out.

"Sir, you're welcome to the paper!" the woman called.

River barely heard her. He hurried to the station.

The windows had opened; he bought his ticket. That done, he bought water and sandwiches, since he didn't know how long he'd be waiting. Within a few minutes he was on the platform, considering his situation.

There was no question; Amato would now be after him.

It didn't really make any sense, though.

Hadn't Amato already been after him? Hadn't he sent the men in the blue suits?

Or were they police? Did he have to worry about police—*and* Amato's revenge?

There was only one thing for him to do—find Natal and get out of the city. He loved Rio, but . . . Brazil was such a big country. And he and Natal needed so little. She just wanted to write—and be with him. If they could get to one of the cities by the rainforest, she'd be in seventh heaven. She could write wonderful articles on the way the forests were being torn down; she could write on the native people. They'd be far from the crowds of Rio, where no one would look for them and they could idle the days away until Amato was in jail for good and his reign in Rio was over.

People thronged into the station. He searched through the crowds for a glimpse of Natal.

He didn't see her.

It was possible to take a complicated system of buses and vans or a taxi and a van to reach the statue. Then, as always, there would be a lot of uphill walking.

Natal had no reason to take a number of modes of

transportation. She would come the way they had come—she would love the view from the cog train.

It came time to board the train and for a few moments, he looked around at the throngs of tourists. His heart sank. So many people. So many people in a city of millions—nearly doubled now with Carnaval at its peak.

You will always find me.

He would find her—or she would find him.

He'd had a seat on the train but stood to accommodate an older woman. She thanked him and sat. Around him, people talked about their parties, about the shows they would go to that evening. A Japanese family talked excitedly and looked out the windows. He heard French being spoken, and he was certain that a group behind him was speaking Russian or another language from an Eastern European country.

They stopped for the view, and it was indeed breathtaking.

But it was nothing without Natal.

Eventually they reached the station and he disembarked, looking up at the Christ the Redeemer statue.

It was dazzling in the sunlight. It seemed to cast a benign and welcoming watch over the city below.

He was jostled and realized that he'd stopped abruptly.

He didn't see Natal—but then, it was almost impossible to see anyone. He thought about the times they had come before as he began to circle the base. He was watchful, for Natal—and the men in the blue suits. This was, after all, Rio. Returning here was risky.

But he'd risk anything for her.

At one point River thought that he caught a glimpse of her and he hurried around the corner again, tapping her arm when he reached her. But the young woman who turned around wasn't Natal; it was a pretty Chinese girl with long dark hair. He apologized and turned away.

There were so many places she might be, and they could miss each other time and time again.

She would have had to come by train or bus— private cars had to have permission from the parks' department, and the parks' department had to have permission from the Church for those who wished to drive up the mountain themselves.

What about the men in the blue suits? If they were police, they'd have easy access, he thought. *Authorities could usually get through to other authorities.*

A tour guide was speaking in English, mentioning that over two million visitors a year came to the statue.

They came . . . and there were several ways up to the base.

River began to walk, heading back to the cog train platform, and then to the bus parking lot. He realized that he was gauging the area surrounding the statue as well; if she didn't come today, she would come tomorrow. He looked back to check the crowd—no Natal, and no men in blue suits.

"Pardon!"

River had stumbled into a man in an army uniform. The soldier was young, a private first class.

"Sorry," River said. "Hey, it's busy up here."

"Yeah, my last fling. I head out in two days."

"Afghanistan?" River asked.

"Yeah." The soldier squinted at him. "You've been there?"

River nodded. "Yeah. Two tours. But I've been out—medical discharge."

"Ah, man, you doing all right?"

"Yeah, I'm fine. Just . . . hanging around Brazil."

The soldier smiled. "Beautiful, huh. And the women?" Looking at River, he smiled. "Is that why you're still hanging around down here?"

River smiled. "Yes. I've found a woman,"

"Good for you, man. Maybe I'll have the same luck."

Luck?

Something uneasy began to stir in River. But the soldier was smiling at him; River looked back at him and saw himself a few years before. Still so young. Still able to sleep without the sound of exploding bombs echoing in his ears.

But it wasn't the memory of serving that tore at him. He had done his duty. He had fought, and he had remained alive. And when he had been wounded, they'd tended to him and. . . .

The memory stopped there.

He waved to the soldier and moved on. He was looking for Natal.

And this time, he was waiting until she arrived.

At the rear of the statue, at the roadway below the retaining wall for the base, the forest of the mountain gained hold again. He made his way down the stairs to that level and then looked over the encompassing wall.

It was impossible to wait until there was no one around.

River made a leap over the wall.

In areas, the ground pitched almost straight down. He'd avoid those.

But there was an area that had nice spacing between the trees; he could see the one entrance to the statue, and he was in a good position to see up to the base. Natal could come and he might not see her right away.

But he would see her.

He sat in the trees, ate one of his little sandwiches, and decided to hop the wall again. Once again, he headed up and circled the base.

Then he walked down the long pathway of steps toward the front of the statue, and then back up them.

He circled the base. He looked at the sky. It was growing late.

Even up the mountain, he could hear the celebrations in the city. It wasn't dark yet but fireworks and explosions were rocking the sky.

On an impulse, he went into the chapel located at the base of the statue beneath the black granite pedestal. Many people had come in. A priest was speaking softly to a young woman who held a baby. The priest blessed the baby.

River slipped into a pew and went down on his knees. He couldn't really remember ever praying.

That night, he prayed.

Let me find her. Let me find what I seek. Let us find truth . . .

Some time later, River opened his eyes to find the middle-aged priest watching him with kind eyes.

River walked over to him.

"Father," River said. He realized he'd spoken in English, but before he could switch to Portuguese, the priest replied.

"My son. You would like a blessing."

"I'm not—sure. I'm not Catholic, I don't, I'm not . . ."

His words stumbled from his lips.

"While it may be true that the Catholic citizens of Rio de Janeiro were the ones who raised the funds for Christ the Redeemer, you don't need to be Catholic to enjoy the chapel, my son. All are welcome."

"Thank you." The priest wasn't Portuguese. He spoke with a different accent beneath his English. Priests, he remembered, went all over the world.

The man might be Irish or Scottish.

"Whether you believe or not, God is here," the priest said. He gave River a blessing.

River smiled. "And best wishes and good luck?" he asked.

"Peace," the priest told him. "That is the greatest gift. Inner peace."

"And love? What about love?"

"When we're at peace, we learn to love ourselves. Then we give love to all those around us, and find love in return. God go with you, son."

"And you, Father," River said, and he turned,

quickly leaving the chapel. The man had been kind, very kind. What a man of God should be.

And yet . . .

That very kindness had made River uneasy.

It had grown late while he'd been in the chapel. The sun had begun to fall—a glorious golden globe to the west. There was nothing like a sunset—or a sunrise—here. Up in the clouds, the sun created beams of light in the most glorious colors.

People would be forced down from the statue when the park closed. He wasn't sure about the hours; they might start asking the people to leave soon.

And it might take some time.

For many tourists, it was an amazing trek to get to the statue—some tried taking taxis to the vans in the parking lot far below to the zillion steps to get to the statue.

Some liked to take the escalators.

Once there, some of them liked to lie on the ground while their friends tried to get them into pictures that placed them beside the statue, which was so much larger. There was plenty of space for that, but . . .

River preferred the trees. The area where no one else went, from which he could watch the main path.

At any other place here where he might find a place to rest for the night, he just might be seen.

He wondered if others had hidden out at the statue before, anxious to enjoy its mysticism and beauty on their own.

It didn't really matter, he thought, amused. It was Natal's place. It was his place.

But they were both happy to share.

He picked his time and leapt over the wall again. He was glad that he'd gotten food. He found himself a safe place to bed down among the trees and listened to people as they left, and to the sounds of the city, rising all the way up the mountain.

Then he realized he and Natal would not spend the last night of the year's Carnaval celebrations together. He wasn't depressed. He wasn't worried. He should have realized that she would wait until tomorrow.

Tomorrow, the city would be quieter. People would be sleeping.

Many of them would be nursing hangovers.

Tomorrow, she would come.

He lay awake a long time, studying his map of Brazil with the penlight he kept in his backpack. He took in the enormity of the country and figured different ways of going to the cities on the Amazon—and into the rainforests.

Eventually, he slept.

He thought about the soft-spoken priest in the chapel with his lilting accent.

Peace.

That was the greatest gift. Loving oneself, then giving love, receiving love . . .

He wasn't sure he loved himself. He was sure that he loved Natal. When she was with him, he was at peace. The encounter with the man of God, though, had been a nice one. River dozed off at last, thinking about the priest, about his words. They let him sleep well.

When he woke, the sun was just beginning to rise. He wondered if any of the park employees had arrived at the statue yet.

Standing, he watched the sun again. It was beautiful. There was a soft layer of clouds; the rising sun played upon them as if they were cotton in the air. Rays of pink and violet and gold shot through, while a streak of magenta stretched across the horizon.

River headed to the wall, leapt up to get a hold, and crawled over it. Then he ran up the steps and circled around to the front.

For a moment, he looked down at the city of Rio. Then he turned. The sun dazzled down upon her. She appeared almost as an angel, cast in a golden ray of brilliant light.

"Natal!" he cried, taking a step toward her.

The light shifted as he did so—and Natal was gone.

But he wasn't alone.

No.

He was staring at one of the men in the blue suits. The man with the blue hat. The man he had seen the night he'd been forced to stab another. Who had seemed to lead those other men who had been following him as well.

And the man was staring directly at him.

River looked around swiftly; Natal had been there. He had seen her. He knew that she was there.

He didn't draw his gun at first; there were other people coming up to the statue now. Not so many yet—but there were other people.

"Where is she?" he shouted to the man.

"River, please, don't run. I need to speak with you."

His heart skipped a beat. How did this guy know his name? Angrily, he shook his head. "You will not speak to me until I know where she is. I demand to know where she is."

"River, if you'll just calm down—"

He wasn't about to calm down. He drew his service revolver from his backpack and pointed it at the man in the blue suit.

The man lifted his hands. River saw him shake his head—and then he realized that the two of them weren't alone. The other two suits had arrived.

One was by the wall; the other was angled at the edge of the statue's base. He thought that they'd been about to draw their weapons and aim them at him.

But the first man had stopped them.

"River, my name is Ted. Ted Henley."

"I don't care what your name is. Where is she?"

"No one wants to hurt you, River."

"And I really don't give a damn about me. Where is she?"

"River, I don't know where she is because I don't know who 'she' is—I don't know what you're talking about."

River shook his head. "Don't pull this crap on me. I know she was there; I just saw her. Believe me, I hate hurting people—I hated using this gun. But I will shoot if you don't let her go. She has no part in this; she never hurt anyone."

"River, put the gun down. Sometimes, no matter our best efforts, innocent people wind up being hurt."

The innocent wind up being hurt . . .

"River, listen to me. All we need to do is talk."

The man's voice suddenly took on a faraway quality, almost like an echo to River's ears. His head began to throb. All they had to do was give him Natal. She was everything to him.

He blinked, hard, then opened his eyes again and looked toward the statue.

She was there, in the sunlight.

Yes, Natal was there. Beautiful, her dark hair curling around her shoulders, her big blue eyes on him. She was there, so lovely, loving, and kind and . . .

And then she wasn't.

She faded as if she were a wisp of cloud in the heights; there—and not there.

The men in the blue suits remained.

River stood still as the dead, a terrible, long-forgotten agony creeping into his soul.

It had to be some kind of trick they had played with lights or projection.

How could you play tricks with the sun? Where could a projector be?

"River, no one is here to hurt you!" one of the other men called out, the bald one.

River shook his head, becoming keenly aware of his finger on the trigger of his gun.

"I don't know why the hell you've been after me, following me, trailing me—but it ends now!"

"We just need to talk," the man, Henley, said.

"No talking. I want her."

"Her who?" Henley demanded again.

"Natal! Where is she?" River shouted. "Where is Natal? What have you done with her?"

The two suits who faced him looked over to the third—the blond man—who remained hovering at the edge of the statue's base.

"Bring one of the friends, please," the man who had called himself Henley said.

River stood still. "No tricks!" he cried.

He had a gun, yes, he had a gun. He was trained to kill; he knew how to shoot.

But they weren't pulling weapons on him. He was sure that they had them, that they were armed; but the man Henley, facing him, in his direct line of vision, wasn't pulling a weapon. And he wasn't allowing the others to pull weapons either.

To his amazement, the blond man in the blue suit moved, allowing a man to pass by him. It was Beluga.

Beluga—who came to stand next to the men in blue.

Dismay rippled through River. Beluga had betrayed him. Yet, he'd seen the men at Beluga's house, and Beluga had sent them away. He had stood with Maria and Convict—and he had sent the men away.

But now it seemed that, despite everything, Beluga had betrayed him.

"Beluga. How could you?" River asked quietly.

It looked as if there were tears in Beluga's eyes.

"You have to listen to them, River," Beluga said. "Talk to them. They need to take you home; they need to get you to your doctor—to your family."

"My—family?" River said. "I don't have a family."

"Yes, River, you do."

River faltered and then gripped his gun more tightly; his own mind was playing tricks on him. Sounds came to him again—the sounds of the bombs whistling, the earth exploding . . .

The laughter of a child.

His head was suddenly pounding.

Why did the horrid sounds of war combine with that of a child's laughter?

He stood facing his friend. A friend who had apparently betrayed him to these men, and yet, these men didn't seem to want to hurt him.

Still, Natal had been there. Then they had appeared. And she was no longer there.

"River, please, I beg you, listen," Beluga said.

"I can't listen to them, Beluga. Can't you see? They're after me; they've been after me. I can't believe that you could have betrayed me to them."

"I would never betray you, River. I love you." Tears were falling down his cheeks.

"No, Beluga, no," River said. "Natal—"

"There is no Natal, River."

The world fell silent as it closed in on River. It made no sense. He'd seen her. He'd *kissed* her—

"There is!" he protested.

"No."

"I drew you a picture of her!"

"You drew me a picture of—"

"Of what?" River demanded.

"Your wife." The word was so soft. Beluga paused and stared at him with his face contorted in compassion. "Your wife, River. Your wife."

"My wife?"

"Your dead wife, River. Your wife—Natal."

The entire sky seemed to burst; the world began to crumble. Pain wracked him as if he were being torn limb from limb. River fell to his knees, the gun gripped tightly in his hands. He knew. He suddenly knew. They were telling the truth.

And truth was absolutely unbearable.

"River."

He thought he could hear her—Natal. He thought he heard his name spoken in the soft sweet timbre of her voice.

He looked up, and there she was. And yet, she wasn't. She was a shimmer of light in the trees and yet he could see her so clearly, hear her voice.

"River, don't you remember?" she whispered to him. "We always dreamed about this. Adventure— backpacks in the jungle, in the wild, and blowing our money on a few nights at Carnaval, dancing into the night. It was our dream. But then Harbor was born so soon and it didn't matter, our daughter was so beautiful and so sweet. River, my precious River."

She was there, that shimmer of light, and yet so strong in his memory that he could have sworn that he actually felt her touch.

"River, remember, because to forget what is painful steals the mind."

But I want to forget; I can live when I forget.

She seemed to hear his silent words, this woman he loved, this . . . illusion.

She continued to speak softly, and still, she was so real; the sound of her voice in his ears was what it had been always, rich and sweet and true.

Memories flooded his mind. River joining the military so that they could have a better life when he returned. Reading letters that Natal had written. Skyping with his daughter, who would laugh when she saw him over the computer screen. How happy she would be, and how much he loved that laughter. The battle in which he was injured and resulted in his being sent home . . .

The battle. He had lived it over and over in his dreams. The explosion of the bombs, the screams of the people, adults and little children, soldiers and civilians . . . He remembered trying to reach one of his buddies . . . the man's legs had been blown off by a mine . . . he remembered . . . pain. His flesh burning, his ears ringing so loudly . . .

But now, there was Natal's touch, fingers so gentle as she brushed his cheek.

"You survived—but Harbor and I did not."

Her words were soft, like the breeze. They were filled with love—the love that he could never forget, never live without.

He reached out for her . . .

So damned real before the eyes of his mind.

But he knew that she wasn't there. He lowered his head, wishing he could cry and scream and deny what had been there all along.

"River, man, please . . ."

He looked up. Theo was there now too. He held on to Beluga's shoulder.

"River, drop the gun, my friend. Please, I beg you. Drop the gun, no one wants to hurt you, and you—you will never hurt me. You are not one to hurt others, my friend." Theo tried to smile. "You are the good guy."

Maybe that wasn't true. River suddenly wanted to kill. He wanted to believe that he was at an arcade—that he could shoot them all like ducks on a track; if they were just gone—then their words would be the lie and not his dream.

"River," Beluga said, "please, other people are coming. Right now . . . it's just us. And these men."

"These men . . . they've been following me," he said to Theo and Beluga, still at such a loss.

"They're here to help. I didn't believe them at first," Beluga said. "I called . . . I called your home. They are who they say they are."

"Fine," River said, turning to look at the man who had called himself Henley. "Who are you—who the hell are you?" River asked.

"I told you—I'm Henley," the man said. "That's Clayton by the base of the statue over there, and Maxwell by me. I'm a private investigator. River, you have a mother and a father who love you very much. You have a sister who is heartbroken."

River winced. He felt as if he were ripped in two again.

Yes, he had a mother and a father. And they loved

him. And his little sister was sweet and beautiful and wisecracking, but . . .

They didn't know his pain. They couldn't live his pain. They couldn't understand that his soul was broken.

"River!" Theo said. "We love you, man. Beluga and me . . . you've been such a friend. You've kept my ugly mug from being trampled, you . . . we love you. Please, man, drop the gun. You don't want to hurt people, but you can, and we all know it. Me and Beluga, no—never. But if you see these others as enemies . . . You gotta drop that gun completely. You must live, man, we need you."

River almost smiled at that. It was good to be needed. And good to be loved.

He looked at Beluga and Theo, standing arm in arm, both of them with tears running down their faces.

He forced a smile. "How's Convict?"

"He's good; he loves you too. He wants you to get well and come back to Brazil," Beluga said.

They looked so funny—giant Beluga, scrawny little Theo. They were holding on to one another like mismatched twins cast adrift on a lifeboat.

River dropped the gun.

He could see it all now—see it as it had really happened. He hadn't seen Natal that first morning; he had seen Maria in the room, picking up.

He hadn't seen an article written by Natal—he had seen an article written by another woman—but Natal had loved to write, and so River had seen her face as that of the author.

Natal hadn't been at the Laundromat—he had been there by himself. He had played with the children at the arcade by himself.

He'd been alone at the beach . . . except when he'd crawled on the boat and danced with those partying on it. Of course he had danced with others . . .

Because Natal had not really been there.

He had been alone at his picnics, in the jungle, at the deserted house . . .

He pressed his thumbs to his skull.

What had been real?

Anything? Was he capable at all of discerning reality from his fantasies?

Yes. They had forced him.

The man who had attacked him at the restroom had been real; his attacking Reed Amato's house had been real—but he hadn't been there because of Natal. He had gone . . . because he'd known the man had been a murderer.

He thought about walking through the farmland, going to the club—dancing in the street.

He had gone to the park and he had plunged into the lake and slept, tired from swimming beneath the stars and the fireworks . . .

Dreaming of Natal.

Dreaming; just dreaming.

He cast his head back and screamed; it was a cry to the heavens, long and loud and piercing, filled with agony and anguish.

Natal.

He closed his eyes, and he saw her in memory then.

His wife. His beautiful wife. The woman he had loved through high school, married when they'd barely graduated. So young—and yet so in love. And the love had stayed through trials and tribulations, through the birth of their daughter, through every decision they had made.

When he'd gone into the military . . . and been deployed.

Yes. They dreamed of Brazil. Then, when they talked, they had planned their trip. And before . . . while they'd lain awake at night in the little apartment they could afford when they'd first married, when the baby had been born, they'd talked about Rio and São Paolo and all the other wonders of the country they both longed to see . . .

Like Natal. Of course, they had longed to see Natal because Natal was her name.

God, yes, they had dreamed of Brazil.

Together.

Then he had come home in bandages, a limb shattered, his head bashed. But he had come home to the hospital . . . only not before the man had broken into his house. A man who killed for pleasure—a man the police had been seeking, but never caught. And while River had lain in that hospital bed, he'd broken into his house. A monster who had killed the people he loved most in the world, and left them lying in streams of blood.

River had served; he had met the guns and the bombs. It had been Natal and his precious little girl who had died.

The irony . . .

He had healed.

They had died.

And so, he had come here the minute after he had buried Natal and their beautiful child. He had run away from the truth. Sanity had, at times, tried to slip through to him. Mercifully, it had not often touched him. But there had been moments. Moments when he had heard sounds that didn't exist. The laughter. The haunting laughter of a child. It had been his child. Killed along with Natal.

He sat there, shaking, too broken to sob.

Beluga came to him to draw him to his feet. "You need help, my friend. You need help. And your mother and your father—they want to see that you get that help. That you can be healed."

Theo came too, followed by the men in the blue suits.

"You'll heal, you'll heal," Theo promised.

"We'll get you home," Henley added, and the other men in blue nodded.

They weren't police.

The police had never been after him.

Tio Amato had never been after him.

The men in the blue suits had him.

He wasn't going to a Brazilian jail.

Worse.

He was doomed to the prison of reality.

EPILOGUE

"You brought him back to us—I can't tell you how grateful I am," Elizabeth Roulet told Ted Henley.

She stood with her daughter, April, outside the room at the Phoenix Rising Therapeutic Spa—a very fancy name for the facility to which they had brought River. His room had been prepared from the time Henley had called to say that he'd found River.

Elizabeth thought that she had finished crying. The last year had been so brutal that she wasn't sure she could take anymore without imploding. First, there had been the news that River had been wounded—but at least he was coming home.

Then, while Natal and Harbor had been planning a party for River's return, the man had broken in.

The man the FBI finally had in custody—too late for Natal and Harbor.

She couldn't bear to think about what had happened. She couldn't bear to remember the policeman's face when he'd come to deliver the news, the news she'd denied at first. Not her lovely daughter-in-law, and certainly not Harbor. Harbor was so young; she was pure energy and smiles. She made every day beautiful.

She would never forget her grandchild. And she would never forget the way her son had collapsed when he'd heard the news.

"He never stopped being brilliant at evasion," Henley commented dryly, watching River through the window to his room. "He was impossible to find at first because he never used credit cards. I had to go on hearsay from other backpackers. Thank God you knew to look in Brazil."

Of course she'd known. She'd listened to River and Natal talk about it time and again. They'd had their lives so well planned out. River liked the idea of the military—he'd receive training while he was enlisted, then go to school afterward, while Natal got her journalism degree. And, River had often said, looking at Elizabeth teasingly, Grammy would watch Harbor. Of course, she would watch Harbor. Her granddaughter was beautiful and sweet with the best laugh in the world.

Had been, she reminded herself.

Elizabeth looked now at her son. He seemed all right; he was lying back, hands folded behind his head, watching television and smiling now and then. When she had feared that she'd lost him . . . she'd almost booked a room here for herself. But she'd had April to think about; April, who was just eighteen now and not yet in college.

Her husband's voice brought her back to the present. "Think he'll make it? Think he'll get better?"

Henley shuffled his feet a little uncomfortably. "I—I went to find him, Robert. I'm not qualified to really judge anyone."

"Yes, but you followed him. You watched his movements."

Henley spoke carefully. "I know that he was going about with the use of his full faculties—except that he often believed that Natal was with him. To him, there was no real past except for the war. His Natal in Brazil was a beautiful stranger. She filled a void, perhaps. And maybe the concept of her helped him; I almost had him one night when a Brazilian drug lord's man went after him—for the money in his pack, I imagine. River held his own and sent the man to the hospital—and on to jail. What he did at the drug lord's house, I'm not sure."

"He killed someone?" Robert asked painfully. "War taught him just to—kill? Or was it because of what happened to Natal—our Natal, the real Natal?"

The PI shook his head. "No, he didn't kill anyone. He did manage something no one else had; you have to think of it this way. Oddly enough, he did a lot of good."

Dr. Freeman, the psychiatrist working on River's case, appeared down the hall.

"Can we see him yet?" April called anxiously. It was the first time she'd spoken since seeing her brother again. Mostly she'd only stared at him, shaking a little.

The psychiatrist walked toward them. "Yes, just greet him and be loving and honest. Don't bring up the past—unless he does. And even then, keep your answers honest and caring. Don't make him feel badly in any way for having left. Remember, nothing he has done was done to hurt you in any way."

"Is there hope?" Robert asked again. "Did the head injury cause this?"

"We believe that all of his physical injuries have healed," Dr. Freeman replied. "What has to happen now is a healing of the mind." He looked at April. "You can go in now."

The family didn't need to be told twice. April raced in ahead of her parents. River rose when the door opened.

"Short-stuff!" he cried. She rushed into his open arms.

"River," Robert said, his voice tremulous.

Soon the four of them were mashed together in one big hug.

Laughing and trying not to cry, Elizabeth broke away first. April hopped up on the side of River's bed.

"How's the food?" she asked.

"Dreadful. Can you bring me stuff?"

"Of course," Elizabeth murmured.

"And how do you feel?" Robert asked.

"Good. I've slept a lot. They give you stuff for that," he said, laughing. "But, hey, sleep is good, right?"

"Yeah," April agreed. "They never let me sleep enough."

"Yeah, but you're starting college, right?"

She shrugged. "Well, I gotta graduate first."

"You can sleep late all summer," Elizabeth said, touching River's hair. She knew that she shouldn't cling to him, but it was hard not to touch him, to make sure he was real and there and no longer lost. "How's this place besides the food?"

"It's cool. I've got the TV with all the cable channels. I have a table there for drawing—and my sketchpad and my pencils . . . I've got what I need."

"Well, when you need anything else, you let us know," Robert said gruffly.

"I will, Dad, thanks."

Elizabeth felt herself breathe a little easier. He was talking with April, answering his father.

Smiling.

They were there for a while, talking all about the little things, like April's friends he hadn't seen in a while, about Igloo, the family cat, a fat white Persian. They talked, and they were together, and it was good.

At last, Dr. Freeman walked in.

"Time for today, family. You can come again tomorrow."

Elizabeth swallowed and nodded. They went through another round of hugs. She had a difficult time letting her son go and went back to hug and kiss him three times before Robert took her hand.

They had to leave slowly. They'd been warned.

Henley had waited for them to come out. Elizabeth was grateful for his presence. She and Robert had determined that they'd sell everything they owned, if needed, to hire someone to head up the search for River. They were lucky to have found Henley.

"So Rio—a city of millions. You found him mainly through other backpackers?" Robert asked.

Henley nodded. "His was an unusual case. He'd cleaned out his bank accounts, as you know. And I couldn't trace his movement by plane because he got himself on a boat going over. When I tried Rio, though, I immediately believed that you had to be right—I found a story in a student journal about an American drifter wearing army fatigues. The girl who wrote it had been there studying post-traumatic stress disorder and at some point, River had talked to her. Even when I knew I was on the right track, it was tough to find River. He always did all right financially because he apparently had a knack at the track. And you have to remember, he's had some of the best survival training to be found anywhere. He knows how to blend in with the environment, slip around anything—and over any wall. I'm sure that's all a result of his military training. When I did see him at first, I figured I had to try to learn something about why he had come and what he was feeling and thinking. His behavior could be odd—I realized I couldn't just walk up and say, 'Hey, let's go home. Your family is worried sick.' I don't believe he remembered when I first saw him that he had a family."

That hurt. And yet Elizabeth knew that no hurt had ever been intended for her or Robert or April. And again she thought about what River's disappearance had done to her. What had happened to Natal and Harbor had been brutal on them all—but not totally devastating, as it had been to River.

"I'm sorry; that's the way it is," Henley said. "I needed a way to reach him with someone who could talk to him—who knew him in Brazil. I don't think I could have gotten him without vio—without someone getting hurt—if it hadn't been for a few friends he made down there."

"We'll need to write them—and thank them," Elizabeth said.

April nodded. Once again, she was looking through the hallway window at her brother.

Dr. Freeman cleared his throat, "What River is suffering from is PTSD—but not just because of the war. What happened to his family . . . well, it's no wonder, really. The human heart, like the human body, is fragile. It can only take so much."

"But he will get better," April said fervently.

Elizabeth put her arms around her daughter and held her as they all looked through the window to River's room.

He looks good, Elizabeth told herself. He was sitting at the table they had given him, sketchpad in hand.

He looked up, smiling. Elizabeth thought that he was smiling at them. She waved.

But he didn't seem to see her.

It was all right. He looked like he was happy. He reached out a hand across the table; it looked as if he caught something, but there was nothing there.

His smile, though, was beautiful. Soft and tender.

"You found me," Natal said softly. "You will always find me."

River's smile deepened as he looked at his wife. "Or you will always find me."

He heard a laugh. A sweet, delighted laugh. The kind of laugh that was like music in his ears.

Harbor sat on her mother's lap. River reached over and squeezed her little fingers.

"Now, what's so funny? You just love to laugh, don't you. I'll draw you a picture. What shall I draw? A bunny rabbit?"

"Bunny!" Harbor echoed.

"Now," Natal said, trying very hard to sound stern. "You two may play with your art—which is wonderful—but, not too late. It's nearly bedtime. And, of course, I will be making pancakes in the morning, so that is worth going to bed on time, right?"

"Yes, Mommy!" Harbor said, and giggled. She and River knew, of course, that Natal would make them pancakes in the morning, no matter how long they drew! But, it was getting late, and they were both sleepy anyway. They gave each other their secret look, and then River looked back at Natal.

Natal smiled, and something inside River caused

a little trembling sensation that raced through the length of him and he had to try hard then to tear his gaze away from her to look at his pad.

"We will always find each other," Natal said.

"Always," River agreed.

Later that night, with Harbor curled beside him and Natal dozing in the big chair by the window, River watched television. The news came on.

They were showing Brazil. He saw the majestic mountains surrounding Rio—with the Christ the Redeemer statue's open and outstretched arms.

He glanced at his sleeping family and turned the volume up slightly.

"This is a special report from Brazil," an anchor announced. The screen switched to a shot of Rio, and the newscaster's voice continued as different scenes of the city—and Reed Amato—were shown.

"The trial of Brazilian drug lord Reed Amato has begun. Amato is no longer out on bail. He has been taken into custody, pending a new arraignment. Prosecutors have informed the press that further charges will be added in the morning as Amato will also be charged for murder in the case of Frederico Damani, whose decomposing body was found in a river near Amato's house. Physical evidence directly links Amato to the case, according to prosecutors. The city of Rio anxiously awaits the trial as it will be telecast daily; we understand that many in South America, the Caribbean, and North America will be equally interested.

Amato is also suspected of owning acres of land dedicated to the production of illegal drugs that have flooded the continents. While Mr. Amato made many donations to the city of Rio, it's alleged that he also threatened his workers, bribed many officials, and created an atmosphere of absolute fear that demanded complete loyalty while he engaged in his criminal pursuits."

River let out a breath. They'd really gotten him. Reed Amato would spend the rest of his life behind bars.

"And now over to Maria Coppella, on the streets of Rio, for a very different story," the anchor announced.

The scene switched.

"Thank you, Tom." A woman stood on the street, outside one of the downtown buildings of Rio. "While we're talking about Brazil, we can turn to some happier news. A local Brazilian man, Thiago Norway—known as just Theo around the city and the track—has hit a big payday. Mr. Thiago Norway is the sole winner of a lottery ticket that came in with a ten-million-dollar payoff. We are pleased to offer our congratulations to Mr. Norway."

River stared at the television.

Could this be true?

Yes—there was Theo near the reporter in a square before a large skyscraper. All kinds of people were surrounding him, laughing, shaking his hand, and congratulating him.

River strained to see, sitting up higher.

"Yes," he said softly.

Among the people surrounding Theo was Beluga. While others kept trying to reach Theo and pat him on the shoulder, Theo grabbed Beluga and gave him a huge kiss on the cheek. Beluga moved away, laughing— and wiping his cheek.

Convict was there, at Beluga's side, barking with excitement.

"Way to go, Theo," River said softly, watching his friends.

"Mr. Norway," the reporter asked, "what will you do with all that money?"

Theo grinned and bent down suddenly. River saw that he had found a barely smoked cigarette. He looked at it as if it were the true prize.

"What will I do?" he asked. "Share—share with friends. What good is money, eh? Except for what it can buy? Maybe a new school—we have a few areas that could use one. And maybe I will travel. I have friends, you know? I will travel—see old friends and make new ones."

River grinned. He could almost believe that Theo could see him through the TV.

"There you have it," the pretty anchor said.

River lay back down. He felt good.

Really good.

Harbor huddled against him. Natal rose, grinning with the news of Theo, and came to his side. She bent down and kissed his forehead. "Good things for good people," she said.

River reached up to touch her hair.

"My girls," River murmured, snuggling them both to his side.

He was going to be all right.